AMBASSADOR 2: RAISING HELL

PATTY JANSEN

CAPRICORNICA PUBLICATIONS

GET FREE EBOOKS

Visit pattyjansen.com
or scan the QR code below with your phone to sign up for Patty's
mailing list. You get four series starter ebooks for free!

DID YOU KNOW?

Ambassador 2 is also available in audio. Visit https://pattyjansen.com to find out more.

1

THE WORDS "just a small party" were probably the misnomer of the decade, and I had known this the moment they were out of my mouth. Thayu smiled at me and shook her head, as if she wanted to say, *Is anything you do ever small?*

I just smiled back.

It *was* our sort-of-wedding, after all. Of course Coldi don't marry but take out contracts, and of course we'd already had a ceremony in Auckland with my relatives and a celebrant. That wasn't officially a wedding either, because Thayu didn't hold any legally recognised citizenship on Earth, but we held a party for my family anyway. Then we'd had a slightly larger party at the Exchange in Athens for all our colleagues. And now we were having one in Barresh.

Just a small party, I insisted, and that was when Thayu laughed.

I looked around at all the people.

Naturally, we'd invited Thayu's brother Nicha, who lived with us anyway, and sat at the far end of the table.

Of course we had to invite Thayu and Nicha's father, Asha Domiri, never mind that he happened to be in command of the air force of Asto, the largest and most populous *gamra* world. Of course he brought some personnel and his customary guard as per protocol. They ensconced themselves in the hall and in my apartment's communication room, watched, in turn, by my staff in regular command of these rooms.

His presence in my apartment, being a non-local military leader, required me to invite local dignitaries, just to make sure I wasn't discussing inappropriate subjects, such as invasions of third party entities. I didn't really want them there, but I managed to get away with inviting two of the least obnoxious councillors. Neither of them were bad, as long as you didn't count the Barresh Council's propensity to be somewhat combative about the suggestion that they had a hand in the establishment of subversive groups that had recently threatened the peace, which, um, was a legitimate accusation, because the Barresh Council was not the most vigilant of governing bodies. These gentlemen loved their relaxed ways and long lunches.

Those round-waisted men were safely tucked away on the couch, and I'd entrusted Yaris, a local member of my valued staff, with the task of keeping them there. For some reason both of them had brought their daughters. Well actually I knew the reason, because native Barresh society was still pretty patriarchal and their fathers probably hoped that their daughters would meet some influential men here on the island that held the *gamra* headquarters that was normally off-limits to them. Those very men I was trying to keep their fathers away from.

Except the councillors probably hadn't expected that two of the three most influential guests were women, which the girls' fathers were trying to keep their daughters away from in turn, lest the girls get *ideas* into their minds, but it seemed it was already too late for that.

I could see the girls ogling Margarethe Ollund, who was one of those women becoming more graceful with age. She was immaculately attired in a rich ochre dress—don't ask me the type; I know nothing about women's clothes—but it contrasted with her pale freckled shoulders and neck, which held nothing more than a string of pearls. Her hair, now more grey than blond, was swept up in some sort of bun, with a few curls escaping on both sides of her ears.

Being dressed in a colour other than *gamra* blue and gold, she stood out in a very elegant, heart-stopping way. She was regal. She was stunning. And as new president of Nations of Earth, she would be powerful. Of course people watched her.

She had been allocated the spot next to me at the main table, not in the least because I was the only local person in the room she could talk to.

I'd known her for a long time of course, since she used to come to my father's house when we lived on Taurus and both he and she were in the administration. Never mind I'd been fifteen then.

I'd contacted her again as soon as I heard her name come up in the election campaign for the presidency of Nations of Earth. Out of all things, Danziger had hired me to assist him with the off-Earth part of his campaign, but my heart had been with Margarethe. She'd be a terrific replacement for Sirkonen.

She'd been elected last month, and had expressed gratitude for my indirect support without which, she assured me, the balance of off-Earth votes would never have swung the pendulum in her favour. Sore subject. Maybe Danziger had expected to win with me on staff, as if my appointment would heal all bruised toes that he'd stomped on.

Margarethe would take office in February. So when Thayu and I held a party for my family in Auckland, which happened to be around Christmas time, I contacted her by way of congratulating her and asked if she would like to visit my headquarters at *gamra* in Barresh, and she said yes.

So there she was, sitting at our table in her splendid gown.

Even though she was not yet here in her official capacity, *gamra* protocol afforded her four guards, who were in the hall, and I'd employed two translators so she could freely communicate with all the people who'd invited themselves and whom I hadn't been able to refuse entry.

Gamra Chief Delegate Joyelin Akhtari was one of those people. I suspected she had imposed her invitation upon us because she was curious about Margarethe, seeing Danziger had made such a mess. My relationship with her wasn't bad, but it wasn't warm either. She was aloof and kept things close. Moreover, on a very basic primordial level, I didn't trust her. She had played *games* with me when Danziger was being an arsehole last year. Secondly, she was Aghyrian, and Aghyrian technology had been used in the murder of President Sirkonen, which had necessitated the election. A different group had been convicted of the murder, but personally, I was convinced that Sirkonen's death had suited the Aghyrians well enough.

Chief Delegate Akhtari had brought an assistant who sat next to her, who appeared to be recording notes, something I didn't like but couldn't prevent; I'd have my own set of notes from the listening equipment in the room's back cupboard—something I only turned off on very private occasions. There were also Delegate Akhtari's usual guards—four Aghyrian soldiers half a metre taller than me with weightlifters' shoulders—in the hall with all the other security personnel.

The Delegate herself sat opposite us, looking more like a hawk with advanced age, asking Margarethe questions which had more thorns than an African Acacia. Questions which, when the other guests allowed me to listen, Margarethe deflected with a skill I judged adequate, but I dearly wished that this conversation wasn't taking place here and now, where I could not give it the attention it deserved. Who knew how many future conflicts were being seeded between these two hyper-powerful women over the dinner table?

Margarethe was the de-facto leader of the second-most populous single inhabited world—which wasn't even a member of *gamra*—and it seemed that both parties were finally waking up to this reality. If Earth decided to swing a bat, it had the capacity to put some major runs on the board very quickly.

Delegate Akhtari had more years of experience than Margarethe had been alive. With her silver curtain of gossamer hair, she looked like an ancient fairy queen, but the similarities stopped there. Underneath the regal appearance was more than a hundred years' worth of hard-nosed political experience, and who knew what else.

Over the past few months, I had used some of my off-time to read up on the Aghyrians, and I had to admit I didn't like what I saw. About two hundred years ago, they'd started using aggressive breeding programs to get their numbers back from the brink of extinction. They had recombined much of their scattered genetic variability thought lost after the Aghyrians had been almost wiped out by that meteorite that had struck Asto. Most importantly, they had money and a lot of it.

And there was another one of them in my living room, that damn Trader representative, Marin Federza, who had wriggled himself into a seat next to Delegate Akhtari and seemed to be trying to get her attention. I wondered what he wanted to talk about. And I had no idea how *he* had managed to get into this private party. Then again, I'd left the invitations to Eirani, who was bustling about with dishes and trays, voluminous hips wriggling and looking very happy indeed. She had a big heart and as a local, welcomed everyone. I would have to talk to her about that. Again. Not that it made much of a difference. And I hated talking to Eirani like that, because she was very valuable to me. But she tended to let every man and his dog into the apartment.

Ezhya Palayi, Chief Coordinator of Asto, was someone I had wanted to invite. I had considered him somewhat of a friend after the crisis following Sirkonen's murder, for which Asto had initially been blamed. He sat at the other head of the table and was talking to Melissa Hayworth, the outspoken and rather belligerent Flash Newspoint journalist who had—to my horror—come with Margarethe. At the moment, she seemed to make all the right gestures and look in the right directions. You did not look a superior in the eye. We didn't adhere to that custom in Barresh, but if faced with someone of that calibre, it seemed prudent to adhere to their customs. Many people on Earth decried the custom as demeaning, but at least Melissa understood it. Her Coldi stepfather must have told her, and for once, she wasn't making a fuss. She probably recognised a journalistic opportunity. I would have to talk to her about how far that information could travel, but for the time being, that side of the table was safe. Unlike that where Delegate Akhtari was still drilling into Margarethe and the latter was acting or pretending innocence.

As Eirani came to serve me, she gave me a broad smile.

"Busy enough now?" I asked. She always complained that the apartment was too quiet.

"Oh, Delegate, don't you tease me. The kitchen staff has been working for days. Do try the fish. The new cook has made it."

She held the platter under my nose and I helped myself to little portions of as many different dishes as I thought polite to eat. Eirani had been very pleased with herself that she'd managed to snag this new cook, who was said to be somewhat of a local sensation.

I didn't feel very hungry, stressed out as I was over this explosive combination of people in the close quarters of my living room. I wanted to speak to Ezhya, since he paid for most of my stipend and I hadn't spoken to him since Margarethe's election.

I drank and ate with automatic gestures. I smiled at Thayu, I made polite conversations, I watched everyone.

In the middle of this gathered assortment of dignitaries, as the golden light of Ceren's two suns slanted in through the window, Nicha rose and called for silence. It was the one occasion where he could tell all these dignitaries what to do, and he played the role well. Nicha often moved in my shadow, but today as celebrant, he had his spot in the sun.

He gestured for Thayu and me to stand at the end of the table closest to the balcony doors, so that the sunlight lit us both. He told us to face each other.

I had attended contract ceremonies a few times, a few in Athens and a couple here. Normally, this was done on the steps of the new couple's house. Often it was a mere formality because love was hardly ever a consideration.

"I am glad to welcome everyone here on this joyous occasion. Gather around, friends, so that we can accompany this couple as far as we can to the task that will be theirs."

They were formulaic words, in the formal dialect of Coldi as spoken in the *gamra* assembly. In our case, *the task that will be theirs* would have to refer to something other than having children because Thayu was Coldi and Coldi people rarely bred with any other of the human species.

"We are glad to see them happy with their choice of each other. My sister has been very happy. I also see that our esteemed Delegate has returned home in a somewhat less hirsute condition than when he left."

There was laughter in the room, most people being familiar with my constant struggles to find shaving gear—because most *gamra* men didn't need to shave—and being bemused by my admittedly somewhat radical solution. In Auckland, I'd had my face laser-treated. I'd been sore and red for a week, and I had to go back twice, and would probably have to go back a few more times, but I was now blissfully beardless. Frankly, I didn't understand why more men didn't consider this procedure.

"We will proceed with the ceremony. You will be familiar with my dear sister Thayu of the Domiri clan." He nodded briefly to his father.

Asha Domiri's face remained emotionless although he acknowledged the address with a raised finger.

"My sister is a good match, because she is much smarter than me, she is stronger than me and she can beat me in any arm-wrestling match."

There was some laughter at this.

"Cory Wilson is a good match, because he can talk anyone under the table, he has no idea when he's outclassed, goes in and wins anyway and because . . ." Nicha's dark eyes met mine. ". . . because he's the best *zhayma* I've ever had, who is only feeling his way around with our native Coldi concept and playing off my cues. He's doing it very well, and I would proudly say that he is the non-Coldi who is closest to understanding us."

Come on, Nich' don't make me cry.

He grinned at me.

"These two people have come together and arranged a contract for their mutual companionship to be ratified in the presence of all those in this room. In presence of all these people, they will now be bonded to each other."

We faced each other. While looking into each other's eyes, Thayu took off her right earring with the blood red stone of the Domiri clan, and I took off mine. Then I slipped the hook to my earring through the piercing in her ear, and she did the same with me. She wore a black dress that left her soft-skinned shoulders uncovered. Close up, she smelled of perfume. My hands were trembling.

I whispered, "I love you."

She whispered, "I love you so much." In Indrahui, with all its correct fiddly noun inflections, and because it was the only language we both knew that no one here spoke, except my personal guards who were, surprisingly, with the others in the hallway.

And in a moment, amidst more dignitaries than anyone would be able to drum up for an official function, her eyes were swimming with tears.

"Thayu, please don't."

I could feel my eyes pricking as well.

All my failed love affairs, my heartbreak, and my fear that I'd lost her last year flashed through me.

Crying in public would never do, so I hugged her, feeling her warmth through the dress she wore.

She sort-of pushed me away, half-heartedly, because half the people in the room would consider any kind of intimacy inappropriate behaviour, and I could almost feel her burning with the need to be alone with me.

All around us, there was cheering, and toasts, and laughter, and for a moment all politics and jockeying seemed to be forgotten. Even Marin Federza cheered. Asha clapped slowly. My eyes met his.

Thayu stepped back, having wrestled control of her feelings.

"I'm yours," she completed the formal part of the ceremony, replacing all the clauses that specified duration of the contract with, "to the end of time."

I repeated, "To the end of time."

There were cheers and gasps because Coldi rarely had open-ended contracts, but they would just have to get used to it. It had taken me a lot of negotiation with the man I'd had to buy out of a contract with her, nasty stuff I'd rather forget, but now I was hers and she was mine.

After the ceremony, after the readings by friends and official offerings of presents, the kitchen staff trooped in for the less formal part of the day, taking plates, pushing the tables to the side and serving drinks. Most guests got up and mingled. It got dark outside.

I wished I could retire with Thayu, but I had to make sure I didn't offend any of the guests by ignoring them. I made some polite conversation with Asha Domiri.

He was tall for a Coldi, taller than both his children, and in full uniform. Because Asto military usually went in civilian clothing when mingling with other people, one rarely saw Asto military uniforms. People on Earth would make fun of the fact that most of Asto's armed forces uniforms involved some shade of pink, but I've never met anyone who could carry off wearing pink in such a threatening fashion.

"Nice day," he said.

In the few times I'd met him, he never made small talk, and those words seemed to hurt him while coming out of his mouth.

"It is my pleasure to have you here." I used far more formal pronouns with him than I did with Ezhya, and I was never quite sure if he cared if I looked him in the eye or not. Unlike Ezhya, he'd never given me official permission to do so. I just did it, constantly wary that it might spark anger.

"My daughter will be useful to you."

"Thank you." Cringing all the way. It was a formulaic statement from him, but it showed just how little Coldi valued emotional content of relationships, at least on the surface. "I hope I will be useful to you."

"It will be interesting." A small frown. "Do you really intend to make the contract open-ended?"

"I do." The words *I love her* would be wasted on him.

"You are a curious fellow."

And that was pretty much it. He announced that he had some business to attend to and was going to excuse himself shortly and went in search of his daughter. I watched them talk to each other, Asha stiff and formal, Thayu more demure than when she spoke to most people. It disturbed me that she looked so much like him, much more than Nicha, with the same perfect eyebrows, and the same intense eyes. He had a small nose like Thayu and similarly expressive lips. Thayu wore her hair in a bun today, but her father had it, as per army regulation, tied back from his face in a ponytail and slicked down with so much gel that it probably would never come out again.

Their exchange was brief. He touched her shoulder, a statement of her subservience, and slipped out of the room, leaving me with a chill in my heart. The man was my father-in-law, and to me he was like a big black bag with unknown content sitting on my doorstep. I could poke it, and sometimes I would get a reaction. I could stick my hand in, with the likelihood of having it bitten off. It was too big for me to move it or look inside and I would have to learn to live with this looming *thing* in my life, never knowing when it was going to open and spill all over me, or over everyone else.

When I dated Eva, her father, Polish ambassador to Nations of Earth, expressed many political opinions opposite to mine. He called me a fool and we had many debates, sometimes late into the night, and not always friendly. Yet, I liked him more and understood him better than this man. A lot better.

When he was gone from the room, tension I hadn't known I had fell off me. I would have to make a much more serious effort to establish where I stood with him.

I looked around the room to see if any fires needed to be put out, or if maybe I could snatch a moment with Ezhya. He hadn't told me when he planned to return to Asto, but he never stayed long. He was no longer talking to Melissa and no longer sat at the end of the table, since the tables had been removed.

I searched the room for him and found him on the other side, behind the couches with the surly Barresh councillors and their daughters, talking to—of all people—Marin Federza.

Talk about political spot fires.

The two were in an intense conversation. Federza was much taller in a gangly sort of way. He wore his silken honey-coloured hair in a loose ponytail tied back with a jewelled clip. His cobalt blue *gamra* shirt was of the latest style, with three-quarter sleeves that had a little slit and gold button at the elbow. Over his shoulders he wore the ornamental Trader cloak, fastened with more gold buttons. His loose pants were matching cobalt blue with very thin gold thread woven through and forming paisley-like patterns.

In contrast, Ezhya looked like a wall of muscle who could pick Federza up by his pretty belt and throw him out the window. His build was sturdy and stocky, like most Coldi. The silver temperature-retaining suit was a necessity for him to stop his body going into adaptation but it looked like a uniform, and the red sash over his shoulder was reminiscent of old-style European royalty. The fact that he'd left his weapons with his guards didn't take anything away from his imposing appearance.

They stood close, and Ezhya spoke in a low voice. Whereas Ezhya's face was emotionless, Federza's eyes were wide. He spread his hands in an *I have no idea* kind of way. Ezhya grabbed the front of his pretty shirt and said something I could not mistake for anything other than a very angry remark. He let go of Federza's shirt just as quickly and Federza reeled a few steps back, before retorting with another angry remark.

What the hell?

2

"DELEGATE, can you come with me for a bit, if you please," someone said at my shoulder.

Heart still thudding from watching that curious exchange, I turned around and looked into the serious moss-green eyes of Telaris, one of my Indrahui guards. Back at the scene of the disagreement, the two had separated. Federza, his face disturbed, rubbed his arms. Ezhya was making his way to the other side of the room.

Throughout the room, a number of guards had returned to duty, mingling oh so casually with the guests. One of the Aghyrian guards spoke softly to Delegate Akhtari. She gave him the clearest *What the hell?* look I'd ever seen from her, before guarding her expression again.

I did not miss those cues. Something had twigged an alarm. Ezhya did not lose his temper easily.

I went with Telaris into the hall where I found that Asha hadn't yet left my apartment. He stood with his guards in the hall, discussing something. He raised his eyebrows at me as I went past following Telaris into the communication hub.

On occasions like these, when important people came together, guards often had meetings where they discussed protocol and tools of the trade. A few of them were still sitting at the hub bench and on chairs they had dragged into the room. When I came in, many rose, and there were bows and nods and respectful mumblings. "Delegate."

"*Mashara* will vacate the room."

A bunch of them rose and, with respectful nods, made for the door, following their fellows into the living room.

I sat at the bench, still warm from where the guards had been sitting. From my position, I could see Asha Domiri's military guards in the hall, in deep and serious discussion.

Evi, my other Indrahui guard, had remained at the hub controls. This morning, to the great hilarity of some of the staff, Evi had been subjected to Eirani's hair styling skills. He still wore his hair in many tiny braids which wove intricately over his head and ended in small silver beads just above his armour's neckline. His hair normally covered a tattoo in his neck of something vicious and fanged. He'd gotten this in his youth with the rebel gangs of Indrahui. I thought it suited him, but he preferred to cover it up. It now showed in faintly fluorescent dye.

"Right, what's going on?"

"Delegate, we just received this." His hands went over the hub controls.

A projection of text sprang into the air, made to look like a formal, hand-written document, such as written out by calligraphers for official *gamra* correspondence or voting documents. It said,

Many years ago, our forebears the Aghyrian people founded the greatest civilisation there ever was. They laid foundations for technology still in use today. Most of them died in the meteorite strike on Asto. The world recovered, the Coldi people emerged, expanded quickly, and took our place. But we Aghyrians are not extinct. For many generations, we have been hounded, vilified and kept away from our rightful home. The world of Asto is legally ours and this document details our official claim to it.

I scrolled through a long list of points written in legal language. There was no name on the document, only an ID.

Shit.

I stared at Evi, then Telaris, then my staffer Devlin who sat on the other side of the bench.

The voices of people in the hall reached me as if coming through a sheet of glass.

An Aghyrian claim on Asto.

We'd known this was coming.

I'd been talking to the Aghyrian contingent in Barresh, their head-quarters.

The claim was rightfully theirs to make, until *gamra* changed the citizenship laws, which were geared towards giving a voice to native minorities being repressed by native or non-native majorities. In practice, the law had led to some of the most violent and longest-running conflicts in all the settled worlds.

We were in the process of changing the laws so that it would be much harder for a small minority to make huge claims over a majority, especially if both would satisfy the definition of *native,* which was the case with Asto.

But we *hadn't* changed the laws yet. It was a tedious process.

We'd judged that there was no point in making a claim for Asto, because Asto was too hot for anyone except Coldi to live.

This document was going to require the full legal response: the court, the lawyers, a formal hearing, and all the bells and whistles.

The Aghyrian faction in the compound in Barresh had given me assurance that they had little interest in lodging a claim.

Why this, why?

This, of course, was why Ezhya had torn into Marin Federza.

Damn it.

I pushed myself from my seat.

Thayu was just coming into the hall, eyes wide.

"What's going on?" She looked so pretty and unusually *feminine* in that dress that it pained me to yank her back to work. I'd seen such a change in her since making our relationship official.

I told her in a few sentences what had happened, and her expression changed from one of wonder to horror.

"But Marin Federza said to you that the Aghyrians had little interest in doing this." She'd sat next to me during our talks. "Does this mean that he lied to us?"

I had visions of the first time I'd met the man, downstairs in the *gamra* clothing store, which he loved to visit. His words had been full of barbs and double meanings which, at the time I'd been unqualified to identify.

"I don't know. I don't think he'd lie. He's smarter than that. He just got rattled by Ezhya. I think I'll go and talk to him, too." I nodded towards the living room, where the tone of talk had become more excited.

She glanced at the bedroom, where she kept her work clothes—armour and clothing that would allow her to run better than the dress she was wearing—and I gave her a *leave it* sign. I didn't want to spoil her rare day off.

In the living room, I found Marin Federza in Delegate Akhtari's company.

They sat on the couch in deep discussion and her secretary was making copious notes. I gave Thayu a signal to turn up the listening equipment. She made her way to the cupboards where the dining table normally stood, and I went to join the pair. They stopped talking.

Delegate Akhtari met my eyes. I shifted a few cups aside on the low table that stood in front of them, and sat down, facing them. Neither of them looked guilty or self-assured. In fact, Federza still had that bewildered look on his face that Delegate Akhtari might be far better at hiding.

Marin Federza rose from his seat. "You'll have to excuse me."

"Actually, I wanted to talk to you."

He froze, guarding his expression better. He was a Trader after all, although it had probably been a long time since his business had seen any commercial action.

"I have to return to my people. I cannot comment on this situation until I've had advice. My official position is that I have no official position."

All defensive pronouns. Oh, how delicious.

"Can I make an appointment to see you then?"

"Yes, yes, sure. I'll get in touch as soon as I know more." He took out his comm. The little box in the corner of the screen said *10456 messages* and in the few seconds I saw it, the count had jumped by a hundred.

He entered a reminder to contact me. His hands were sweaty.

He nodded to me and his jaw worked with tension. "I will see you later, then. Have a nice day."

He left after a polite bow to Delegate Akhtari, leaving me to look at his well-clad back.

Crap. He'd go to his Aghyrian fellows in town and once he was at the fortress-like Aghyrian compound on the other side of Barresh's main island, the slippery bastard could hide there for as long as he wanted. The Aghyrian Council ruled in there, and we were mostly stabbing in the dark as to who exactly was on it and how they influenced Delegate Akhtari, despite her assurances that she had no ties to them. I'd mostly dealt with Federza, but I was certain that he was only a representative. Dealing with a group that had been secretive for that long wasn't easy at the best of times.

I folded my hands on my knees and met Delegate Akhtari's gaze squarely. "This is unexpected."

"It is," she said.

Meaning what? "I would very much like an explanation." I used the most respectful pronouns, reverting to the hyper-formal forms of Coldi that were standard with *gamra* protocol.

"The Delegate might *want* an explanation, but there isn't one." Her voice sounded harsh.

Um . . . excuse me? No explanation because she wasn't going to give one? "I was under the impression that we had an agreement that the Aghyrian faction would not claim any part of Asto or their judicial process until we sorted out the legalities. Or was I mistaken?"

Hell, some of my anger had to show through.

"You were not."

Meaning?

"This claim has nothing to do with us. It's as much a mystery to me as it is to you. And, I should add, to Trader Delegate Federza."

"Then where does the claim come from? Are there other Aghyrians?" Any influential ones I didn't know about? There were only very few left of the original inhabitants of Asto. Most of them were in Barresh. There were some in Miran, but those tended to side with the Mirani view of politics and preferred to stay loyal to their place of birth rather than join the push for a united Aghyrian faction. There were still some at Hedron who did the same thing for the same reasons. Knowing about these people, who they were and what they wanted, was part of my new job, damn it. Had I really missed something?

"The group in Barresh may be the most important Aghyrian and certainly the most powerful group, but we're not the only ones. This claim originates on Asto. We're suspecting that it comes from a section of the *zeyshi* rebels."

"*Zeyshi?*" Those were the rebels who lived along the fringes of Asto's big cities. My voice must have lost all pretence of formality by now. Seriously, what the hell was going on?

"There are some Aghyrians amongst the *zeyshi.*"

"There are?" I wanted to scream, *How can that be? It's too hot for them on Asto!*

"Aghyrian children are born to all sections of Coldi society, but the only place where they can survive on Asto is in the underground warrens of the *zeyshi.*"

True, and, damn it, something I hadn't thought about. I had forgotten about the Aghyrians born on Asto, because there were never many and they belonged to the most deprived part of Asto's society in the Outer Circle. And yes, most of those children died soon after birth. The only news anyone off-world ever heard of *zeyshi* was that they caused trouble.

"How many of them are there?" I felt weak.

"Not many." But I sensed the implications. Aghyrians were very cunning. They used to go mad and kill themselves, or each other, in the time before the group in Barresh led by the legendary Daya Ezmi worked out how to neutralise their bodies' ability to absorb and store energy. Those practices were standard everywhere. Aghyrians lived full lives. They lived longer than any of us. They were manipulative. They accumulated knowledge, money and power. The *zeyshi* rebels, without the safeguard of the Coldi loyalty networks, would be a rich breeding ground for their ideas.

I felt chilled just thinking about it.

"And this group has made the claim? Do you know any of these people? Can you do anything about this?"

"No, to all your questions. As for the claim, once *gamra* has received the correspondence, the plenary assembly will have to deal with it, unless the claim is retracted by the claimants themselves."

And the next assembly session was not until next solar. "Will the Aghyrian faction or *gamra* contact these people?"

"Likely. You will have to wait for Delegate Federza to establish exactly what is going on. I don't know what they hope to achieve. To me, it seems that they are a small band of rogues. I certainly don't agree with this course of action." And that was about as direct an *I* as I was going to get from her. "I assure everyone here that I will spare no effort in trying to get to the bottom of this. You will have to excuse me while I go and do just that."

She rose, too, collected her security at the door and left. I caught one of the Barresh councillors frowning at her back.

She *seemed* to be angry, but I had already learned that with her, appearance and reality weren't always the same thing. Likewise, she *said* she didn't know anything about this group or their claim, but . . . Damn, I wished I could trust her.

One thing I knew was that whenever there was some instability at Asto, the *zeyshi* outlaws who lived on the fringes of the large cities tried to capitalise on it. They weren't part of the vast networks or associations of the mainstream Coldi, and made a point of being different and at times loud and obnoxious. But I hadn't been aware of such an instability on Asto.

I rose from the table. Melissa asked me if Thayu and I would mind posing for some more pictures. She didn't seem to have picked up on the fact that something was going on. I told her to find Thayu—whom I'd seen leaving the room after Delegate Akhtari and who, I hazarded a guess, was at the security station trying to squeeze the last bit of functionality out of my listening bugs to see if she could pick up anything that Delegate Akhtari might say to her staff while walking along the gallery.

I felt sorry to send Melissa on a wild goose chase, because she wasn't going to find Thayu if Thayu didn't want to be found.

I wandered through the room looking for Ezhya.

I couldn't see Margarethe, and that was probably a good thing with all this going on. She had a room in the apartment and might have retired. I knew her adaptation hadn't quite settled and she'd be feeling hot and tired, possibly a bit feverish.

The Barresh councillors were at the dining table getting stuck in the food, which was mostly local fare. They were laughing at jokes told by Yaris, for whom I'd have to instate a most useful employee award. Their daughters still sat on the couch, under their fathers' watchful eyes, looking very bored. Good. No scandals would come from that quarter tonight. Neither did they seem to have picked up on the fact that something was afoot, although Yaris met my eyes in a questioning way as I passed. I gestured *later*. I'd brief them tomorrow morning, when I had a better idea of what was going on.

Then I spotted Ezhya Palayi on the balcony, leaning on the railing. I could see his back from inside the room.

I went out, but the moment I stepped onto the balcony, I realised he wasn't alone.

". . . It was a good move," he was saying, goddamn it, in Isla, albeit thickly accented. Then he turned and met my eyes, shamelessly. "Good day, Delegate." In Isla, too.

I reminded myself to never, ever underestimate this man.

There were only two people he could have been talking to. He'd already spoken to Melissa—under duress probably, because Coldi in high positions did not waste much time speaking to people far down their pyramids of power.

The other person was Margarethe Ollund. She sat on our lover's bench, where Thayu and I often spent our evenings sipping a cool drink and looking out over the marshlands that surrounded the artificial *gamra* island.

"Nice evening, Cory." She smiled, probably unaware of any of what had just passed. "He was just showing me the impending eclipse."

I leaned against the railing, my mind wanting to scream out *you know he's just been listening in on us for the past few months and there is a crisis going on?*

But none of that affected her, and I tried to force my rattled mind back to chatter.

Ezhya looked at me, and the expression in his gold-flecked eyes told me that no, he'd probably taken up learning Isla on a whim a few days ago, being faced with the prospect of seeing me again, with some of my kinsfolk, and unable to understand our language. It was the sort of thing he'd do, the sort of thing he'd have the intelligence to do, and leaders on Asto were selected for their intelligence. It was, I figured belatedly, also not something he would do if he was under a lot of stress at home.

Well, that was something at least.

Calm down, Delegate.

I focused on the telescope. Yes, the eclipse. Astronomers in Barresh had talked about little else for the last few days. Eclipses occurred every twenty days, when the smaller sun Yaza went behind the bigger sun Beniz or the other way around, and the two suns merged into one big star, and then a smaller star. The entire period lasted most of a day, and the light grew dim, and, depending on which sun was blocked out, either yellow or bluish. If the eclipse happened to coincide with monsoonal cloud cover, it seemed like day never came. Temperatures dropped dramatically and some people always panicked.

It was rare, however, for a complete eclipse of Beniz, the stronger sun, to coincide with an alignment of the planets, so that Asto would be passing between us and the suns at the time of the eclipse, and there would be a very strong eclipse on Asto as well, one that would last longer than ours.

The screen of the telescope showed it all, the vivid pink spot that was Asto nearing the suns, both of which were very close together and about to vanish behind the horizon.

I sat down at the telescope, fiddling with the settings on the display and was about to say something, although I can't remember what, when the screen flashed.

"Did you see that?" Ezhya said.

"I did." I stopped the live feed, returned the cache and replayed. Just the stars, then a burst of light in the corner of the screen.

"Strange."

"I didn't see anything," Margarethe said.

Oh, right. I stuck my finger in my eye and removed one of the protective lenses I wore. Dang. Her dress wasn't ochre. It was reddish bronze. I replayed the segment, with the eye that still contained a lens closed. Saw nothing.

Right.

This was something high in the spectrum, a narrow frequency that Margarethe couldn't see, but Ezhya could, and I could with the aid of my lenses that shifted the spectrum of ultra-violet light into the visible.

Ezhya and I met each other's eyes. This smelled of Aghyrian technology.

All right. So, Federza had arrived back at the compound, and they were using their—illegal—Exchange bypass to warn his fellows elsewhere in the settled worlds? I had visions of people balling fists and whooping at screens.

I said nothing, but glanced at Margarethe, because it was precisely this sort of technology that had killed her predecessor, when the group called Amoro Renkati had used a one-way illegal Exchange device to move a piece of glass to kill President Sirkonen. That technology produced a red flash, which the Coldi had been unable to see.

"It's probably a flare in the receiver," I said. I didn't want to alarm Margarethe.

Ezhya nodded, but his gaze was far off. He put his hands together and squeezed until his knuckles were white.

With a sigh, Margarethe pushed herself off the seat. "I could sit here forever, but I'm quite tired. I might go to bed if you don't mind. It was a lovely occasion."

"I understand. Good night," I said.

Ezhya turned to her. "Don't forget what I said."

She smiled. "I won't."

And then she was gone.

Excuse me, but *what I said?*

Silence lingered.

I strolled across the balcony and leaned on the railing next to him.

Side-lit by the light that flooded from the living room, his face carried lines I hadn't noticed before.

He appeared flustered, with his nostrils flaring and having undone the neck fastening of his suit. I dearly wanted to ask if he had any problems at home, but leadership or political problems were not things we freely discussed, unless he raised the issues. At times he allowed me to forget that he was what people on Earth would call an absolute dictator with the power over billions, but there were subjects where I didn't go with him.

Eventually, he said, "Unfortunately, it seems that the thing we feared has come to pass."

I nodded and again we said nothing for a while. Frustration clawed at my inside. He usually spent very little time talking to anyone. Likely he'd leave very soon.

But then he said, "I might take you up on your offer for a room."

What? He had never stayed overnight at my apartment. Never. "You're most welcome. I'll let the staff know."

There would not just be Ezhya, but all seven of his guards as well.

"I'm sorry to impose myself on you, but my apartment is in use by the Asto delegation while their apartment is being renovated." After a short silence, he added, "I need to sort out a few people."

"I understand."

When he remained silent, I said, semi-casually, "So, a claim, huh? Delegate Akhtari insists that she has nothing to do with it."

"That's what Federza told me as well." He snorted. "I don't understand him and I don't believe him or like him."

I nodded. That made two. Slippery snake. I was still seething with how he'd been trying to rope me into joining his anti-Asto club.

Ezhya blew out a breath. "If the Aghyrians have any sense, they wouldn't upset the status quo. There is a lot of money involved in Aghyrian interests, and when they behave like this, they'll lose their supply contracts. We have other places to buy our construction materials than the Hedron Mines."

"They just about own the Trader Ledger on the island." *Gamra*'s main financial institution—Federza had a lot of involvement with them.

"Many threads are going where the blood cannot." Coldi loved their proverbs.

I said, "Misha Palayi, Chief Coordinator of Asto." If one person cited a proverb, the other was meant to reply with the person to which the proverb was credited.

I'd heard this proverb many times and still struggled to understand it. It seemed to say that loyalty network threads were stronger than blood ties.

I took a deep breath and asked, "Do you believe the claim might come from the *zeyshi?*"

"Ridiculous." He snorted. "The *zeyshi* are illiterate scum who couldn't put together any kind of basic correspondence to save themselves. One of them might have signed it, but this claim is a front for someone else. Remember, we're dealing with the cowards who gave Amoro Renkati technology, and then watched, without interference, how they killed your *president* and were punished for it. They managed to walk away from the mess without taking any of the blame. This has been the Aghyrian game in the grand scheme of things. Find someone to blame if things go wrong. Find the most obscure Aghyrians you can and get them to put their names on a document like this. Make it look authentic."

"You think it's bogus?"

"No, the ID on the document scans as belonging to a woman called Vanu Ezhidi, who is also known as Evala Sadet Arwan. Trouble-maker, *zeyshi*. She has a good list of notations against her name."

"That second name you mentioned is an Aghyrian name." They always had a three-part name. The first name would only be used amongst close family and friends, like Delegate Akhtari's name was Pahini Joyelin Akhtari, but even people at the same level of authority, like Ezhya, called her Joyelin.

"Yes, but that's not her legal name."

"Is she Aghyrian?"

"Of course she is. What you people need to stop doing is treating them with more awe than they deserve. They're people. They make mistakes. There are smart ones and dumb ones. They aren't any more special than the rest of us."

He'd said this many times before, but I disagreed with him. Telepathy and mindreading were not skills I associated with normal people, nor was a life span of a hundred and fifty years. It was true that the push for expansion had diluted the telepathy skills, but that didn't make the average Aghyrian any less manipulative.

"Anyway, the *zeyshi* haven't been much of a problem since I told Risha to sort them out." That would be Risha Palayi, one of his seconds. "I told Risha I didn't care whether or not they moved to Eighth Circle, as long as they sent their young people to get an educa-tion in anything other than fighting and blowing stuff up—and skim racing. A lot of them took it up and there have been very few raids. The ones remaining in the desert are not going to raid areas where family members live, right? That is *their* weakness, their families. If there were significant Aghyrian interest in that group, we'd know about it. This claim exists for the sole purpose of tying up resources in *gamra* with the discussion of irrelevant details with a group that is by itself irrelevant."

"Representing not-so-irrelevant interests."

"It's a stupid thing, some scheme by a big-headed small-time leader. Not worth the cost of transmission. If there was any issue within the *zeyshi,* Risha would have told me. Federza says he doesn't know about it. He fancies himself a lot, but I think he's high enough in the Aghyrian network to have access to these kinds of plans, if there were any, so for a change, I believe him."

Funny how being dangled by the front of your shirt by someone much stronger than you tended to bring out the truth. I agreed with his assessment. Federza had seemed most upset and wrong-footed by the news.

"What are we going to do about this claim?"

"Nothing. Now that it has gone out into the world I can't do anything or it will be seen as interfering."

True.

"Let the assembly discuss it," he said. "We'll sit back and observe. These people who have made the claim will have to send representatives. We'll poke the *zeyshi* about their record with Aghyrians, which isn't particularly good. We'll watch everyone's reactions to them. We'll bug the hell out of their accommodation. We'll learn a lot."

"I wish I could be so relaxed about this." As a very worst-case scenario, the Coldi might lose their right to live on Asto, and that would be a disaster of immense proportions. No one wanted that, right?

"A claim was going to be brought anyway. It's better that some fringe element claims, because their legal pockets are shallow and the case shoddy and their claim won't pass. When it's defeated, we're free of the fear of claims for at least twenty years. Let's deal with it. Talk to Federza. Make him nervous. Let me know if you need any lawyers. I'll send you however many you can handle. Investigators, too. Find out who is making this claim and take them seriously enough to gain some of their trust. In that light . . ." A slight hesitation. "I think we are getting to the stage where we could consider a visit."

"A visit?"

"To Asto."

"Who?" I frowned at him. "Me?"

"You. As special envoy to talk to these claimants. They're certainly not going to talk to me."

But. Asto. I stared at him. "Has the climate changed that much recently?"

"It's changing rapidly."

But certainly not that rapidly. If there was anything I had learned from talking to climate scientists over the past year, it was that twenty years was a blip in time. I heard something else in his words: with current average temperatures—which Asto didn't share freely—visits by non-Coldi had probably been possible for a number of years. Of course the administrators and quarantine officers had been keen to keep Asto isolated as long as they could. They liked their isolation.

He explained further, "With some help of technology and some planning, and my personal approval, it should be possible." His eyes met mine. The characteristic gold flecking of the black irises was especially strong in him.

Was he really saying, *We lied about this to everyone for years, but please come now because I need you to talk these people under the table for me?*

I didn't dare say anything for fear of saying something out of place. Ezhya and I might be quite friendly, but there were areas where you didn't go with him. Such as internal politics.

"I will . . . consider it, after the wedding."

"I invite you."

His eyes were pools of mystery. Often I thought I understood him, but at times like this, he was as alien to me as he could possibly be. Just *what* did he want me to do? Find these Aghyrians hiding with the *zeyshi* rebels in the hottest part of the desert plain and tell them to roll over and do tricks? From what I knew, *zeyshi* were possibly the toughest people in the universe, living in unbelievably harsh conditions. They hadn't been swayed by anyone for thousands of years. What made him think that I could make any difference?

And that was as much as I got out of him. He diverted the discussion to more enjoyable subjects and I couldn't figure out if that was because he was genuinely unconcerned or because something else was going on beneath the surface.

Damn. Well, *I* thought this was a serious matter, and I wanted to know what was going on, especially the origin of that flash, which he didn't seem to be overly concerned about. He hadn't seen that Aghyrian technology in use last year, but the thought that someone could pick up a ship, a person or a weapon from one world and unilaterally move it elsewhere still gave me the shivers. They could make an entire army vanish or send an influential person they disliked to a part of space from where he'd never be able to return.

When Ezhya said he was going to bed, I excused myself, went inside, crossed the party room as fast as I could without running, and went into the communication room. Evi and Telaris still sat there, now in discussion with Devlin and a couple of the contracted guards.

I gestured, and both of them came to the door.

"I need to ask you to do something, *mashara*."

They gave me solemn nods. Likely they would have anticipated my demand for their services. They certainly looked the part, having shed their relaxed party dress in favour of their security gear.

We walked a little down the corridor, towards the sleeping quarters, away from the talk of the party.

"Go and talk to the Barresh Exchange," I said. "There was a flash in the high end of the spectrum. Get them to send out immediate scouts to the Aghyrian compound to see what's going on."

The men nodded, without question, and set about doing it.

3

I INTENDED to go back to the living room but Thayu had followed me. I closed her in my arms. She nuzzled my cheek and stroked hair out of my face.

"What a damn thing to have happen on this day," I said in the hollow of her neck.

"Don't worry. It's out of your influence."

"No, it's every bit in my influence. Ezhya has just asked me to go and talk to the *zeyshi*."

She frowned deeply. "But they're on Asto."

"Yes. He wants me to come. He says it should be possible. I think it's been possible for a while, but he's just kept quiet about it. I don't know what to think, Thayu. On the one hand, he says *zeyshi* are nothing, on the other hand, he wants me to risk my life talking to them."

"Because he can't do it."

True. With his position, the difference in status was too big. "He told me he'd sent Risha to defuse a number of issues that *zeyshi* care about. That's what I don't understand. He *has* been working with them. Why hasn't he been aware of these people and their issues?"

"Risha will have sent others. Risha is Coldi and adheres strictly to the *sheya* instinct code. He's not going to get far with people who don't have the instinct. If he's really going to talk to *zeyshi*, he needs someone who doesn't have the instinct either."

I stared at her. "Are you saying that you think Risha lied to his superior?" And was she saying that Ezhya had made a mistake?

"I'm not sure, but no one can simply walk from the Inner Circle into the *zeyshi* settlements. Ezhya understands. He needs someone like you to talk to them. Risha *would* have used someone, or else he's lying."

"But what do they want and why would they get involved with an Aghyrian claim?"

"I don't know. Because they're *zeyshi,* they're not logical anyway." That was pretty much the standard Coldi response. Give up trying to understand these people because they can't be understood, and also: it's their own fault that they have to live out there in the desert. If only they behaved like us, we'd give them places in society.

"But Thayu, think of all the work we've put into trying to coordinate the parties in this potential conflict. We put out a call for opinions. The Aghyrians on Asto or the *zeyshi* never said anything. No one has ever come forward from the *zeyshi* and they've had every opportunity to do so. Ezhya thinks this claim is a front for something else."

"Like what?"

"That's a good question. Some internal politics in the Inner Circle?" I spread my hands. I had no idea how that would work.

"I don't know. He already told you more than he would have told anyone else. If he asks you to do this job, perhaps you should stop wondering why. It will be revealed in due course."

That was another infuriating thing: the Coldi's blind trust in those who ran society. I guessed it came with the *sheya* instinct, but I didn't *have* that instinct.

I let it rest and told her about the flash we'd seen.

She frowned. "Why now? They've been silent for so long. The Renkati complex was shut down and subjected to inspection. Their illegal exchange equipment was removed and taken apart. The whole organisation doesn't exist anymore. The issue was dealt with."

I shrugged and we looked at each other, knowing that whether or not this flash was artificial or a natural phenomenon, the deeper issues of that conflict had not been dealt with: the fact that *gamra* was split over the dominant role of Asto in dictating policies, and that Asto itself was a planet facing major upheaval of its climate, that had, by

Ezhya's admission, changed enough for the Aghyrians to make their claim. And processes to change *gamra* laws had been too slow to prevent that possibility. Which was probably why everyone had kept quiet over the declining daytime temperatures on Asto.

I wanted to say more, but there was an explosion of raised voices inside the communication room.

We went into its semi-darkness and found Thayu's father's military guards, the ones I wasn't too happy about giving free reign to my equipment anyway, cursing about a power surge and loss of some log data, and I was reminded uncomfortably of how fragile communications were. Quite soon, they were all laughing and things were back to normal. All the lines had come back on.

I eyed Devlin, who had been forced to relinquish his position as controller of the hub and stood near the door.

"What was that about?" I asked, my voice low.

"Frequency mismatch," he said. "It's been going on for some time, some days more often than others. It doesn't usually last very long."

"Oh?" I vaguely remembered them talking about this, but now, after having seen that flash, that information suddenly became relevant. "Any reason?"

"The Exchange says they're working on it."

Which wasn't really an answer.

We went back to the living room. The party was winding down, and people went to bed, either my guests Ezhya and Margarethe Ollund in my guest quarters, or in their own apartments elsewhere in the complex or the city.

Thayu's father turned up from wherever he had been. Nicha spoke briefly with him, but it seemed he had been on an unrelated visit and didn't have any more information. "These are matters for civilians," he'd told Nicha, and Nicha had not questioned further. I was of the opinion that he *had* to know more, but I was a civilian of non-existent ranking in Coldi society and everything in his behaviour showed that he didn't think I was worth his time.

Damn, why had he even approved of my buying out his daughter's contract? I was under the impression that it had been arranged as part of his obligation to the family of Taysha Palayi, who had wanted Thayu as mother for his child. Next thing, I blunder in, going into the sordid mess of horse-trading over a woman with a cunning man of Asto's Inner Circle—Ezhya's second, to boot—and he says not a peep.

Bah, this subject was giving me indigestion that spoiled what should have been a relaxed day.

I was in the hall, showing the local councillors out when Evi came up behind me.

"*Mashara* has had contact with local security," he said in a low voice. "They went to check the complex. It's locked up and empty. They performed heat scans on the building. There is no one inside, and no working equipment has been used. The Exchange logged the flash, but doesn't know its origin. They say it may have been a wayward satellite."

Miran, across the border, had put a fair number of those in orbit in the past. Many of them were no longer functional and one by one met their doom in the atmosphere.

That sounded a likely explanation—except for that frequency thing.

"Thank you, *mashara*."

He left, having allayed only one half of my unease. Knowing that Renkati had somehow reformed and re-started their experiments with illegal Exchange equipment would have given us something to focus on. Knowing they weren't likely to be responsible only left the question: who was?

I still didn't think that the flash had been harmless, but in my high-vaulted bedroom, with its large white-covered bed and with Thayu sitting on it and waiting for me as my official wife, I had other things to do. I did mumble an order to Eirani to wake everybody up at a decent time because I had planned some trips for Margarethe, and then I shut the door and turned to Thayu's arms.

I HAD no idea what time it was when I woke up to a frantic banging on the door.

"Muri!"

That was Eirani's voice.

It was pitch dark in the room, with only the merest glow of reflected moonlight coming in from the window.

I sat up and flicked the lever to the light.

Thayu lay on her stomach, her black hair mussed up. She mumbled something but didn't stir. Sometimes I was jealous of her ability to sleep like a log. I looked at her, filled with such love that it almost made me cry. That was *my* earring that lay against her skin in the hollow under her ear. I still couldn't believe it. I'd become convinced that my living on the edge between two worlds had permanently bumped me off the marriage market.

"Muri," the voice came again.

I jumped out of bed, across carelessly discarded clothes on the floor and opened the door a crack.

Eirani stood in the hallway, in a loose gown I assumed to be her nightgown. Behind her stood my trusted guards, Evi and Telaris, taller than her, with obsidian skin and bronze-coloured ringlets glistening from the rain. They regarded me with their moss-green eyes. Dead serious looks.

I added the facts, liking this less and less.

That they were wet meant they'd been outside. They wouldn't go outside at this time of the day unless necessary. They wouldn't come and wake me before dawn unless . . . something had happened.

"What is—" I asked at the same time Telaris began.

"Where is the lady?"

In Indrahui. *That* was significant.

I was going to ask *which lady,* but I realised. "Margarethe?"

"She is not in her room."

"Has she gone for a walk?" I knew what the twenty-eight hour days did to your system. It was her first time here, too.

"She would have worn a tracker."

That was true.

I ran into the communication room, where Devlin, the lone staffer on duty, sat staring at a projection. I'd been too busy to keep up with my staff duty roster, but he looked alert, so he must have slept.

He was studying communication, I saw to my satisfaction. I'd commended him to the civil authority for a placement. He'd get paid more if he had qualifications for Exchange work.

Now he looked up, wiped the projection and stared at me. "Muri?"

"Who left the house after the party finished?"

He checked the log. "No one who wasn't authorised to be here."

"Anyone who was authorised to stay here? Like Margarethe Ollund?"

A quick glance at the screen. "Yes, she did, indeed."

Ok, phew, calm down Delegate. She'd be time-lagged and have her sleep patterns all jumbled-up. She might have fancied a walk in the tropical night . . . and gotten lost, or accosted by undesirables, or . . .

Visions of last year were fast crowding my head. Shit. Calm down. Security at the island was pretty strict. Nothing would have happened if she just went for a walk.

"Wait, let me get changed."

They waited at the door while I went back into the bedroom and rummaged around between shamelessly-discarded clothing on the floor. I found my pants but where the hell was my shirt?

"What about her comm unit?"

"Not responding," said Evi from the corridor.

"Her guard?"

Yes, what about those four guards who were supposed to be watching her?

"Downstairs."

"All four of them?"

"Yes. About to be severely reprimanded."

"Never mind the reprimanding. Did anyone ask them when they lost sight of her?"

I was hopping on one leg trying to pull on my trousers. I found a shirt, yanked it on and went into the corridor, letting the door roll shut behind me. If Thayu still hadn't woken up, the rattle of the slats would do the job.

"*Mashara* hasn't spoken to them yet. There is a . . . situation."

Ah, I was getting through to the problem. Something else was happening that made the men reluctant to interfere.

I did up my waist band. "Let's go and see these guards then." Because that seemed to be what they wanted. I had an inkling about what that might be. *How about, mashara, just for once, you give it to me straight.* But that was not in their nature.

We plunged into the darkness of the hall, and down the staircase at the end.

Downstairs, in the staff quarters, was a spare room whose function

I had never figured out. It had only a door into the corridor, and not to adjoining rooms, as most rooms did. It also had only one window, high up near the ceiling. Frankly, the place looked like a prison cell, and failing to discern a purpose, I had used it to store items of the previous owner's furniture I had no use for, but I'd sold that furniture some time back. Currently, the room was empty except for some plain chairs and a few boxes of tools that belonged to the technicians who had been busy pulling all listening equipment from the walls and installing my own listening equipment, which I could be sure was not siphoned off to somewhere else.

There were voices coming from inside this store room. Light blazed through the slats of the door.

Before we entered, I could hear Melissa's voice ranting, in Coldi.

"How could you leave her? How could you not know where she is? You were being paid to look after her."

She stopped ranting when we entered, and turned to the door. Her face was red. Margarethe's four *gamra* appointed guards stood in the middle of the room, surrounded by various other people in uniforms, including three of the kitchen staff, the two translators and four of Asha Domiri's guards.

The four, all of them Coldi, glanced at me. Two of them looked down, subservient, which they didn't have to do for me. The other two continued to meet my eyes, intense.

Melissa was pleading to me in Isla. "Thank God, there you are. Cory, get these idiots to talk." She gestured at Margarethe's guards, and went on in Coldi. "Why won't you just tell me what you've seen and what happened? What sort of security is this?" And back to Isla, "They're hopeless, Cory. All they said was that the matter was off limits. As if we're talking about state secrets here. Someone very important has gone missing—"

Something clicked in my mind. "Wait. Did they say that? Off-limits? Did they use the word *zharu?*" The literal translation of *zharu* might mean off-limits, but what it really meant was that somebody of higher rank had put a gag order on the matter, and that, when you came to think about it, meant something different altogether.

"What does it matter what word they used? This sort of information should not be withheld—"

"It does matter." I already saw the answer in the guards' defiant eyes. *This is not a good time to push the boundaries of habits that have existed for hundreds of years.* "If they said *zharu,* it means that security has everything under control."

"But they won't tell me where she is."

"No, they won't. They are sworn to the person they're protecting, and whomever she, in this case, says they should obey."

"We're talking about our president—"

"Who is clearly doing something that she means to be off the record, private—"

"We don't know that. Hell, she doesn't even know about any of these customs. This is exactly what I meant the other day, Cory. How can they expect us to trust them, when they're exclusive, and secretive? We have a right to know what's going on. Otherwise the Nations of Earth will never trust *gamra.* Never, Cory, never."

We faced each other. Her chest heaved with deep breaths. Her eyes blazed from under her fringe. I hated fighting with anyone at the best of times, and the middle of the night was definitely not a good time.

"Melissa, things *are* under control." Why the hell had Margarethe brought her, of all the journalists she could have chosen?

"Prove it."

"OK." I turned to the guards and continued in Coldi. *"Mashara?* Tell the lady what the situation is with our president."

The men hesitated.

"They've been instructed not to say any more," Evi said behind me. *"Mashara* assures that the lady will return by morning."

Yes, it was as I thought. This smelled very much like—

The door opened and there stood one of the people I had expected to be here already: the formidable head of Ezhya's guard. She made a few movements with her hands, and her six colleagues slipped into the room from the corridor, and crowded around Melissa, a solid wall of silver and red.

Melissa's eyes widened. "Hey, what's going on? Cory, what are they doing?"

"Mashara asks you to leave." I understood that much of the guards' sign language. "You're making an undue disturbance."

"Heck disturbance, Cory. You can't just send me away. I have a right to know what is going on."

One of Ezhya's guards gently gripped her shoulder. Melissa tried to push his hand off. "Who says you can touch me?"

"Melissa—" I said, more insistent.

"No, Cory, don't 'Melissa' me. They have no right to touch me—"

"They do and they will. Listen to me, please, and listen carefully. You will never, ever be safer than with a pair of *gamra* guards. They will never reveal either your secrets or your whereabouts to anyone unless instructed by you. This is the mechanism we're watching here. They know where Margarethe is. They are telling us it is nothing to worry about."

"No, Cory, you're weak, letting everyone walk over you—hey, didn't you hear me? Let me go!"

The guards hustled Melissa out of the room. I cringed. There would be a lot of patching up about this later.

The door shut but I could still hear her voice. I breathed out deeply. "My apologies, *mashara*."

Was I truly weak, trying to play by the *gamra* culture? Hell, they better have a good explanation for what was going on, because to be honest I didn't like it any better than Melissa did.

I asked Ezhya's female guard, "I presume your boss has something to do with this? He's gone with her?"

I felt dread in the depth of my stomach. It wasn't just Melissa who wouldn't like this; most of Nations of Earth wouldn't like this. It was so typically something Ezhya would do. He could be such a boy when he got excited about something. I remembered the telescope. He'd said, "Don't forget what I said," which had puzzled me, but in hindsight shouldn't have. He'd been talking about an arranged meeting. I drew my conclusion.

"He's taken her up in his craft to view the stars."

"Yes. They were due back before dawn."

A little silence followed that announcement. I glanced at the small window at the top of the wall where light blue sky was showing, definitely dawn.

Were due before dawn.

Ezhya never reneged on a promise. I realised that this little trip was something he hadn't intended anyone to find out about. He did those sorts of things, too. The perks of being what, in Earth terms, would be called an absolute dictator.

And the guard said *had*. He *had* intended to be back by dawn. But . . . clearly, something had gone wrong.

"Mashara?" My heart was hammering. An attack by hostile forces? Ezhya's enemies? An accident, rare as they were?

The guard said, "The Exchange has gone down."

4

I SAID, "SHIT." And then again, "Shit." And a bit later, "Is there a record of him using the Exchange?" Goodness knew where Ezhya liked to take his private guests for stargazing. Back in the days of my first involvements with him, he'd taken me to view Asto from orbit, its mega-cities, its landscape crisscrossed with open aquifers. I'd come to treasure that trip and the wonders I'd seen: the pinkness of the desert, the livid green of the aquifer communities, the vile yellow and orange oceans, the crater with its purple mist and the crystal wastelands.

The guard said, "The Exchange is in a state of chaos. *Mashara* did not think it prudent to disturb them with questions."

Wise, probably. "Has *mashara* spoken to the Yetaris Damaru?" The Barresh Exchange was unusual within *gamra,* as the only Exchange to be in private hands, owned by a single commercial family.

"He was busy and not in a very good mood, but the Exchange has released a statement, which says that they are aware of problems and are working on it. They don't expect contact to be re-established before morning."

Holy shit. I met his moss green eyes. "Do they know about this, um, situation with Ezhya?"

"Not that *mashara* has established."

The implications chilled me. The top of the Asto society which

Ezhya occupied was a pretty precarious position. A Chief Coordinator juggled the demands of so many loyalty networks that to satisfy his connections and provide them with work and guidance was a constant, never-ending job. In the old days, Chief Coordinators used to barely leave the command room, and certainly never left the planet. These days, Ezhya had his feeders which kept him in constant contact with his seconds and various other networks. He was said to have three feeders. I hated having even one; I didn't like other people's thoughts in my mind, but the feeders gave him the freedom to keep up with all his networks wherever he was. It was not just that he controlled a lot of minutiae in daily life, or that people expected the Chief Coordinator to do this, but that the Coldi had a pathological need for someone in this position.

If Ezhya's political rivals knew that he could not get back to the position of leadership soon, they'd pounce on the top spot.

I lowered my voice. "No one must find out that he's missing." For as long as we could keep the news a secret.

"Certainly not, Delegate."

"We must go and see if we can discover where he is."

Calm down, Delegate.

If he'd gone to Asto, as he had with me, things might not be so bad. He'd quickly take control. Margarethe would be in a difficult position, but surely, with some care, she could be transferred to a space-enabled craft that could bring her back to us as soon as the Exchange came back online. Failing that, the Asto military had a station in orbit. No doubt she could stay there.

I went back into the bedroom to get changed again, because no Exchange meant I could not use the hub room, and going outside the apartment meant I had to dress appropriately and take the guards, and Thayu. All on what I had thought would be a relaxed morning in which I could catch up with Margarethe and her plans.

Margarethe. Damn, she was with him. Asto might see this as an opportunity for political upheaval, and Nations of Earth would make a big fuss in their own way, even if they only found out after the fact.

This needed to be solved, and fast.

Thayu was sitting up in bed when I entered, looking puzzled and only half-awake.

Yes, she had been drinking a bit more than usual yesterday, and she usually didn't drink at all.

I explained quickly what had happened and her reaction was as astonished as mine had been. "The Exchange never goes out. Not for long anyway."

"We're going to check it out. Get changed."

"Sure." She jumped out of bed, looking more alert now.

"Seen Nicha yet?"

"I'm coming," came Nicha's voice from the door that connected our bedrooms. He was all dressed and ready to go.

Lately we'd been doing things with three of us in a rather unusual association. Nicha was my *zhayma*. I couldn't really take a second *zhayma* unless she was part of a completely different loyalty network, and Thayu was of the same network—but that's how it seemed to have worked out: three *zhaymas*. Fortunately, despite its unusualness, the arrangement worked fine. Brother and sister were very good with each other.

Then I had to tell Nicha what had happened. He listened quietly, his face grave as if he'd been waiting for this news. Thayu finished getting dressed before I had finished combing my hair. Eirani came in to plait it, which I could do myself, but it wouldn't look much good. While she was doing this, I asked her about the status of Ezhya's guards, but I was informed that they had gone out. She didn't know where.

She said, "I do not understand, Delegate, why those guards have to be in here. Outside, yes, but what risk do they think we pose to their bosses? All we have in here is brooms and cooking utensils. They upset the kitchen staff—"

"Did you see them leave the apartment?"

"This morning, yes, while I was taking delivery of the laundry."

"How many of them?"

"I counted seven."

So it was just Ezhya and Margarethe who had gone.

That was at least something. If there were seven guards, those fighting machines would likely form a complete association with their own leader. One at the top, two below that and four at the bottom. Did this mean I needed to worry less about the guards now that they were unsure about where their boss was? Complete associations, three people, or seven, or fifteen, were more resilient to stress from outside.

Eirani fussed over the crumpled state of my jacket, which I'd left on a bench. I told her it didn't matter, I just wanted to get going, but she went to find another one, and I knew in my heart that it *did* matter at *gamra*, and I was no longer a junior Delegate and so I had to look the part. She came back with another jacket, and insisted on re-plaiting my hair because "I was still addled from the party and didn't do a very good job. I'm sorry, Delegate." I sat through her ministrations, teeth gnashing, but I knew she was right, and I just had to put up with it.

When we were just about to leave, the front door opened and Ezhya's guards marched in, in perfect formation: the tall woman in front, two men behind her and the other four behind that. They all wore full uniform: a silver temperature retaining suit with a maroon sash and belt. Each carried several weapons, mostly guns in arm brackets, but some had sticks or knives.

The woman leader halted.

Regarded us. She looked at Evi and Telaris who stood next to me like dark sentinels. Both were tall and well-trained, but they were not a blip on these guards.

Nicha and Thayu had taken up subservient positions. A person's bodyguards were considered a special small branch of the important person's association, and their ranking in society was only marginally below that of the person they protected.

"The Delegate is going out." Telaris was the first to speak into the uncomfortable silence.

"Need any assistance, *mashara?*" the tall woman said.

Given her ranking, that was the oddest imaginable request.

Telaris hesitated.

"We are going into town," I said, breaking protocol by butting into a conversation that would normally be conducted between guards.

Her eyes flashed to meet mine. "To the Exchange by any chance?"

Thayu inched closer to me. I was pretty sure she'd passed the Inner Circle exams, but she had never seemed comfortable around Ezhya's guards and right now her behaviour even suggested that she thought I needed protection from them.

"Yes, we are." Then I said in an impulse. "Is there anything you would like me to ask?"

"No."

An expression of distaste flickered over her face.

"Let's go then," I said, and we filed past them out the door. No one spoke.

From the apartment's front door, we went to the end of the gallery, down the stairs, through the atrium and out the arched entrance to our building.

Once we had enough room to walk next to each other, I met Thayu's and Nicha's eyes in a *What the hell was that about?* look. I said, "They seem . . . unstable."

Nicha nodded. "Not good. They're facing some pressure, somewhere."

Thayu said, in a low voice, "Do you think it was wise to leave them behind in our apartment?"

"What harm can they do? They can't communicate, they can't go back home. Ezhya's unit across the hall has been taken by the Asto delegation to *gamra* and I can't see why they'd want to go into town and create trouble there."

"You do realise that Natanu ranks higher than my father?"

I presumed Natanu was the tall and menacing woman.

"Yes." Well, I hadn't given it so much thought, but I guess I should have realised that. Thayu and Nicha's father was in the second layer, under Risha and Taysha, both of the Palayi clan. Risha was his immediate superior.

She continued, "With Ezhya absent, either my father or Natanu is going to want to test the other sooner or later. Ezhya is the pin that holds all those networks in place. If he's taken out and not immediately replaced . . ." She shrugged. "Something like this hasn't happened before, so it will be interesting, especially since we have a couple of people in high positions right here in our house."

"Where is your father?"

"He got up early this morning and left."

"To the orbiting ship?"

"Oh no. He would never leave your house without formal thanks."

Formal thanks? That man truly baffled the living daylights out of me.

"He's likely to come back to the apartment some time today and may run into Natanu and her association. There may be trouble. We may want to be home for when that happens."

Then again, we might not. What could I do as puny human when these Coldi powerhouses decided to have a fight? I seemed to remember someone telling me that rank fights never involved weapons, but I wouldn't want to swear on that.

Damn, was there anything that wasn't going to fall apart?

The walk from the apartment across the island to the station would have been a pleasant one had it not been for the tension.

The leafy avenues between the residential blocks were still quiet, while Delegates woke up and had breakfast, or maybe were still having their morning baths. Evidently, those who knew about the Exchange outage either viewed this as a minor hiccup, or the proverbial calm before the storm. What had Devlin said yesterday about misaligned communication?

What would happen if the Exchange remained off-line for a substantial period? I didn't even want to think about that.

By providence or design, a couple of shiny carriages waited at the train station, and Evi and Telaris commandeered one for our party. This had to be one of the much-lauded new carriages, made locally to a design from a Mirani company.

We climbed in and sat down on the soft seats with blue covers. The walls of the carriage were clad in patterned wood. The air inside even smelled of wood. Much was said about Miran and their lengthy slide into oblivion, but they did elegance very well.

Thayu sat next to me and dumped a bunch of electronics on the table between us and Nicha.

"Does any of that work?" I asked her.

"Without the Exchange, most of it doesn't. I'm hoping to get some local network codes so we can at least use it within the city."

The train set off and, outside, the view of the station was replaced by an expanse of water and reeds. Nicha stared out the window leaning his chin in his hand.

Thayu was fiddling with all her equipment, picking up this device and then that one. After much checking, she handed me a comm. "You can use that. They have the local backup running."

While I took the device from her, I bent over so my lips almost touched the skin on the back of her neck. "Any messages?"

"No. Just the official statement that there's an outage for off-planet communications and travel and that they're working on it."

The train whizzed low over the water. From my window, I could see the artificial island that was the airport, where Ezhya Palayi's craft wouldn't be. I worried that if he hadn't gone to Asto, he could have gotten caught somewhere in mid-space between transfers and anpar lines. In that case, we'd probably never see him again. That was too depressing a thought. No, I had to believe that he was someplace from which he and Margarethe could at least return.

Return, with what consequences, and in what state?

Would Melissa be right about Nations of Earth panic? Would faith in the Exchange be shaken? Would the Aghyrian section see this as an opportunity to push their alternative Exchange again?

Moreover, there was that all-pervasive Coldi custom they called *nethana.* The word translated as "without meaning". After settling on an agreement or completion of negotiations, Coldi upper-class people often went for a private dinner followed by a sex romp for fun, which was what *nethana* related to.

Ezhya loved his *nethana.* He would try it on her. Damn.

In my explanations to Margarethe about Coldi culture I hadn't covered the subject of *nethana* yet. That it was a sign of appreciation and respect, that it didn't mean anything, that it certainly wasn't lewd or inappropriate. That it was not impolite to refuse, but that it strengthened relationships immensely, often in unspoken ways.

Damn. Here was another potential for a major diplomatic situation. Given my experience with Coldi customs, I'd gone stargazing with Ezhya knowing his likely intention at the moment I accepted the invitation. I had more or less grown up knowing about the custom. I was fine with it, even with taking part.

Margarethe was an entirely different story. I should have seen this coming, especially with his cryptic remark to her, and told her all these things last night. However, this would have involved some blunt and sexual statements I wasn't comfortable making to an elegant woman who was only a professional acquaintance. But Coldi held doctorates in blunt and sexual.

Damn it, damn it.

The train was slowing. From my window, all I could see was water and islands, but the window on the other side of the cabin showed the lush green streets of the main island of Barresh, with its large houses of the local rich families, interspersed with some commercial buildings. There had never been any space on the islands to build railways, and as a consequence all the train lines went over water and skirted the islands. Now some low-cost housing was being built over the water, too. A number of poles and cranes stuck out of the mist.

I rose and waited at the door before it opened.

"Don't worry," Thayu said at my shoulder. These days she rarely even needed a feeder to know what I was thinking. "Exchange outages have happened before."

I met her eyes. "Have they?" Not while I'd been in Barresh. Come to think of it, I'd always been impressed with the reliability of the Exchange system, with its backups upon backups. Everything I knew about what could go wrong gave me the heebie-jeebies.

I interpreted her silence, while we waited for the door to open, to mean that she'd said this to calm me. I didn't think she was so calm about this either. I knew her better than that. The last time the Barresh Exchange had blinked was before the equipment had been upgraded, and that was a long time ago. Before I was born. A long time before I was born.

And then the unbidden thought came into my mind: would it have something to do with that flash I saw yesterday?

I had to push such thoughts away, focus on the immediate. No good panicking over what I couldn't change.

We went out of the carriage, onto the platform, up the stairs to a flat area that used to be the location of the airport, but where in the last few years a market had sprung up with purpose-built shops. It was an expensive place, and serious shoppers went to the proper markets on the other side of the island, but this one served tourists, and so the merchants were only just arriving for work, whereas the old markets would have been in operation since before dawn.

But the smells and the sounds were the same, and they were normal and soothing. Nicha bought a bag of roast fruit coated with nut meal that we shared between us by way of breakfast. Eirani would be grumpy that the guests and I had yet found another thing more important than her cooking.

While we walked through the streets, several people greeted me, recognisable as I was in blue.

Good morning, Delegate.

Nice day, Delegate.

Their tone was oddly relaxed and in contrast with how I felt. An Exchange outage wouldn't affect most people in town.

We went across the square, with its trees that had been planted recently and had begun to spread their canopies, to the Exchange building with its ancient foyer, sweeping stone staircase and coloured glass ceiling window.

Here, the relaxed air dissipated. The hall was full of people, all cramming to get up the stairs to the Exchange office on the first floor. Most of the people were merchants.

Someone up there was shouting in keihu, the local language. I didn't catch enough of it, but understood the gist: be calm; we're working on the problem. But that didn't faze my companions, who wedged a way in through the crowd.

People mumbled and grumbled, looked over their shoulders at my blue tunic and expressions changed.

"Delegate."

"Out of the way, *gamra* delegate coming through!"

Others pounced on me with questions.

"Any news about what's going on?"

"How long is this going to take?"

"I have my family arriving on the next shuttle from Kedras. Will things be back to normal soon?"

I waved the questions away. I couldn't answer them any better than they could. I continued up the stairs, shielded by Thayu and Nicha and my trusted guards.

On the first floor landing, a few Barresh guards in black stood at the door to the public office of the Exchange, keeping the queued-up merchants and business people in order.

When the door slid open to let a man out, I caught a glimpse of another queue in front of the public desk.

The guards waved people aside so that we could get through.

"I need to speak with Yetaris Damaru," I said. "It's a matter of utmost importance."

One of the guards nodded. "I'll let him know that you're here."

He told us to wait in the corridor inside, where I sat with Thayu and Nicha at a bench against the glass wall that closed off the Exchange room. Evi and Telaris remained standing.

The merchants in the queue before the public counter gave me and my entourage curious looks.

The air was cooled and dry, and felt cold on my sweaty skin.

The guard in black had gone into the large Exchange room and I could still see him through the glass, speaking to someone. Most of the employees who normally sat at workstations had gathered in the middle of the room, which was the space where a 3D holographic image of near-space anpar approaches was usually displayed. A short line to Asto in the same system, longer lines to space-based travel ports at the edge of the system. Longer lines still for the nearest settled world, Kedras. Sometimes, the operator would zoom out and display more anpar lines, if direct transfer from other places was required. But today, there was nothing. Oh, the projector worked; there were the small icons displaying various notations of time and date at the bottom of the central display, but nothing else.

The guard had gone to talk to one of the people in the group. It was Yetaris Damaru, of the family that had run the Barresh Exchange for hundreds of years. He rose from his seat and came with the guard into the corridor.

He gave our party a grim nod. *"Gamra* representation?" I doubted he knew me personally.

"Not officially. *Gamra* will send someone along later. I have a serious matter to discuss."

"You are aware that the Exchange is—"

"I am. It's related."

"Best come join us."

We followed him inside the room, where the absence of the electronic hum normally made by projectors made it eerily quiet.

Some people looked up when we joined the group, and most reformed the circle to include me and Thayu and Nicha, while Evi and Telaris remained at the back of the room.

I needed to ask no questions about the status of the Exchange. The emptiness of the projection area spoke for itself. The damn thing just wasn't working.

"Failure of the core?" I asked. The high-tech, highly-sensitive and hyper-powerful core was the very thing that made the Exchange work.

He sighed, which I took as a yes. "It's not at the end of its lifetime. All the functions test out fine so far. We can't get it up again, because we're getting no response from nearby nodes."

I'd had it once explained to me that if the Exchange network went out, individual nodes would have to establish traditional radio contact with nearby nodes and would have to do something they called wave resonance in order to jump to anpar lines, which they often called the anpar dimension. Only in anpar mode could they reach out to interstellar space and reconnect with the rest of the network. Because of this resonance requirement, nodes had to exist in clusters, and the Ceren-Asto cluster was one of the biggest. Ceren had two Exchange nodes, Asto had three, and there were a couple of satellite relay stations, precisely to avoid a situation like this.

"Surely Miran can cover for us temporarily and explain to the main node what has happened. What do they say?"

"Miran is out as well. They can't restart their core either."

Damn it. "And Athyl?" On Asto, they would be on half an hour delay for the time it took radio waves to travel there from Ceren.

He shook his head. "They're not up either. They're not in contact with anyone else. To be frank, Delegate, we have no idea what has happened. It looks like this whole section of the network is offline."

Shit.

"What is our functionality?" asked Thayu.

"At the moment, close to zero. We have a backup running for some peripherals, such as local communication, but the radio lines with Miran and Asto are running down the emergency charge pretty fast. I have all maintenance personnel working on securing those links. We need to get some dedicated transmitters going. Also, I've sent a team into the core to check it."

That chilled me. Exchange cores were pretty damn radioactive, and usually well shielded in giant basins of water of behind concrete and lead plates.

If something had damaged the cores of all those nodes . . .

Cores were made at Hedron, which was the settlement furthest away from virtually anywhere, an extremely old world far on the very end of the Sagittarius arm of the galaxy. Without the Exchange no one could get there to bring a replacement core. Without the Exchange, no one would get anywhere.

And that again made me think of Ezhya Palayi and where he was now, and Margarethe Ollund, and what would happen on Earth if she vanished.

Shadows of Sirkonen all over again. All the effort I'd put into repairing relations gone down the drain.

This was a disaster.

"Look, we have a, um, situation. I need to talk to you privately."

He raised his eyebrows, in a *can it get any worse?* way, but gestured me, Thayu and Nicha to the very edge of the Exchange room near the large window. The rush of air from the ventilation made his hair ruffle.

The window looked out over the courtyard and the gate that was the main entrance into the building, to the square beyond. Between the food stalls and trees, I could make out the shapes of a couple of aircraft on the offshore artificial island that was the city's airport. There was a passenger shuttle on the tarmac. *They* were all stuck here now.

"Yes?" he said. He looked tense. Like his forebears of the Damaru family, he was not as rotund a man as many keihu. Quite small of stature, too. His face was pale and he had bags under his eyes. I felt sorry for him that I had to bother him with yet another problem.

I spoke in a low voice. "The situation is this, and I wish for this to remain absolutely secret. Ezhya Palayi and President-elect Margarethe Ollund of Nations of Earth took a little tourist trip last night. They took his craft and they haven't come back."

He swore, loudly, and a number of the employees turned around.

"Excuse me," he said.

"No matter. The situation warrants the language. You understand that this is extremely sensitive."

He nodded. "What do you want me to do? I can't track them or bring them back."

"Well . . ." I didn't know what I had hoped. Maybe that he *could* work wonders, but obviously that wasn't going to happen. "Make sure that when anyone suggests that Ezhya is missing, you allay their fears if at all possible."

"That will only work for so long. They'll find out the truth."

"I am aware of that." Damn, the trouble we'd be in if this went on for longer than today. "Just stall giving an answer for as long as you can."

He nodded, his face grave with understanding.

"How long do you think we'll be out?"

A deep sigh. "We've had to cool down the core to send people in. Starting it up will take most of a day, and that is assuming they can fix whatever is wrong. At the moment, we're stabbing in the dark."

5

WE WENT home no wiser than we had come, and with an increasing feeling of dread. None of us said so, but we all knew: this was not going to be solved quickly. Not today, not tomorrow, maybe not even within a week.

In the hall of my apartment, I found the reason for Ezhya's guards' foray outside the apartment this morning: several boxes of odd electronic equipment that looked to have been bought at the second hand stalls at the markets.

Someone had been unpacking the supplies. Rolls of wire spilled onto the ground, and there was half of the casing of what looked like an old hub transmitter, as well as a couple of circuit boards and plugs and a screen.

The guards themselves were in the hub room, huddled around the rest of this strange collection of electronics.

Devlin stood outside the door, leaning against the doorframe, his arms crossed over his chest and a suspicious and flustered look on his face.

Telaris spoke briefly with him and turned to me. *"Mashara* apologises, Delegate. It seems they *invaded* the room while we were gone."

I glanced into the room at the knot of guards. Only six of them were there. The four men and two women spoke in low voices, in language peppered with jargon that was unintelligible to me.

A screen on the equipment lit their faces from below. Their dark eyes glittered with little blue dots of light from the screen. "What are they doing?"

Devlin said, "They wouldn't tell me that, Delegate. I was just studying here when they came in. I wasn't doing anything to bother them."

"They sent you from the room?"

"They didn't tell me, Muri, but they took up all the space and started making a lot of noise. I couldn't work anymore."

Telaris said, "I think *mashara* has taken steps to obtain information. It is likely for the good of all."

And *obtaining information* clearly required a heap of junk from the markets and upsetting my staff.

I don't know what Telaris thought, but I needed a better explanation than that.

I went into the room, where it smelled of Coldi bodies. "Excuse me, my staff would like to use this room."

A couple of the guards turned around, including the fearsome woman Natanu. She rose, left the group and faced me. The average Coldi person was a bit shorter than me, but she towered over me. There was not a skerrick of humour on her face.

"Apologies."

Her single word sounded like shorthand for, "Go away and mind your own business," or, "Do you want a fight? Be my guest."

I had to restrain myself from taking a step backwards. That would be seen as an admission of defeat. "My staff are upset that they can't use this room."

"None of us ever said that they couldn't."

"You intimidate them." Oh, that *you* was much too direct.

My heart was hammering against my ribs. Giving her a direct challenge was probably not a good idea. I wasn't sure whether to look her in the eye or not. Normally, Coldi didn't react to people from other races, but Nicha had felt a reaction to me.

Nicha had remained by the door, looking tense.

I had to risk it. I looked up. Her eyes were very dark, and her skin a darker tint than Thayu's or Nicha's. She had prominent cheekbones and deep-set, slanting eyes. Her earrings were both the same, which meant she wasn't contracted to a partner, and the stones were lime green. What clan was that again? Not one of the ones we commonly saw in Barresh. Damn, I'd seen the table with all the different clan names, but I couldn't remember this one.

As our eyes met, she stiffened briefly. I held my breath—but then her stance relaxed. Apparently I had satisfied the test.

"*Mashara* apologises to the Delegate." Her voice had lost some of its edge. "We are trying to ascertain the whereabouts of our leader."

"Any luck?"

"Nothing yet."

"I may not be able to help, but if I can do anything, I'm offering."

She bowed stiffly. "Thank you, Delegate."

She gestured me into the group of her colleagues, which opened up, and the guards all looked at me. Whenever Ezhya had come to visit, his guards had never met my eyes. That was part of the Coldi make-up, not to look anyone in the eye unless the ranking issue was settled. Coldi on Earth had un-learned the habit, but this was an area in which Earth humans could blunder in and make bad mistakes.

I sat down on the spot they vacated for me on the bench. All of them wore temperature-retaining suits with the distinctive red sash, as well as several patches with symbols that were mostly unfamiliar to me. Two were tall and imposing like Natanu, others were of a typical size. Some were pale, others darker-skinned. Some had prominent cheekbones, others the round faces I'd come to think of as typically Coldi. Every one of those faces was gaunt with stress.

On the floor in the middle of the group stood a hastily-rigged piece of equipment so old that it looked like it had survived the last war. That was the last war in Barresh, again fought before I was born, about two hundred *gamra* years, in fact. The other female guard sat in front of this bank of machinery, adjusting levels and wearing an old headpiece which she pushed half aside.

"We accessed the emergency beacon, Delegate. We have established radio contact with Asto."

"From here?"

"There is an antenna on the roof."

One of those many features of the apartment I'd never noticed. One day, I should take a plan of this building and study all the attributes.

"We are expecting the reply any time now."

Just then, the crackle came in, followed by a Coldi voice speaking slowly as if read from a prepared response.

"Receiving you. Not very clear but adequate. The Athyl Exchange cut out at 20.22 *gamra* time and we've been unable to establish a cause or to repair the link. It appears that the core is damaged. Our technical teams are investigating. We are still getting some communication through the local network. Our backup orders are still active and can last us until Ezhya gets back from Barresh. The situation is currently stable but we are on high alert. We continue to try to re-establish contact with the local Exchange network."

I met Natanu's eyes.

Hidden behind the news about the Exchange, the bit about backup orders was obviously the important part of this message. But I didn't know enough about that part of Ezhya's job to catch the meaning of the statement.

But these people assumed at Asto that their leader was with us. They thought that Ezhya was at the most sixteen days away, if the Exchange didn't come back before that time. Sixteen days without a leader was an eternity in Coldi understanding, but they judged the situation stable under those circumstances. What if they found out the truth, that I had no idea where Ezhya was?

The guards composed a reply, which would take another thirty-odd minutes to reach Athyl. Natanu then took the headpiece and replied on behalf of the group, asking about other people I didn't know and about the state of the Beratha Exchange and the military base.

We waited, and waited. Thayu scrunched up the fabric of her tunic. "I presume my father thinks he can keep control of the military," she said in a low voice.

And, damn it, that was another trouble spot. Presumably Asha stood on top of the military network. If that crumbled, things could get really ugly.

I asked in a low voice, "Who is this person she's talking to?"

"Mizisha, the Inner Circle's security chief."

Then the reply came,

"We confirm. The same time the Athyl Exchange cut out, as well as the Beratha Exchange. We have used military sling relay and confirmed that Kedras is out as well, or else they are not responding to our pings. They're not receiving us, or we're not receiving them, or . . . It's starting to look like the entire network might be down."

"Shit." It wasn't really appropriate language by a *gamra* delegate in public, but the word slipped from my lips before I could stop it.

Everyone stared at me.

Into the silence, I said, "Anyone else who wishes to swear is entitled to do so now."

~

"So—what?" Thayu said in a low voice after we left the room. "The Athyl Exchange is out, as well as Beratha, Miran and likely Kedras? A total system failure. Why?"

I shrugged, remembering with unease how I used to feel a certain amount of fear when going through the Exchange. Since when I was a student and first had the system explained to me, it had never ceased to amaze me how blasé people got over such an intricate, precise and deeply vulnerable system. "Whatever has caused it, this is unlikely to be fixed in a day." I said in a lower voice, "You know what worries me? If Ezhya had gone to Asto, he would have already let himself be heard. He'd have broadcast an official statement using the military's installations. So he has not gone to Asto, and he didn't stay in orbit around Ceren because otherwise he would have come back here."

"I agree. By not mentioning Ezhya, they assume that Ezhya is with us. They don't even want to draw attention to the fact that he's not in Athyl."

"What can we do?" I asked, and lowered my voice further. "I mean —what can we do that inflicts the least damage on Asto and on Ezhya's position?" There was no way that we could let the news out that he was missing from Barresh as well. "How long can we keep quiet before real trouble hits?"

Nicha said, "When the Exchange went down, they'll have felt his absence immediately, because his feeders would have fallen silent. It seems that he'd given some advance orders or some regular routines are still running. I don't know enough about that part of his position. Given the general outage, most people will understand the situation, but if it goes on for too long, there will be friction. The most rebellious ones will have already started asking questions."

And damn, there had already been signs of trouble with *zeyshi*, because they were always at the forefront of this sort of trouble.

I asked, "Would Ezhya's guards be able to help?" They'd have a high interest in keeping Ezhya's position safe, since without him, they'd lose theirs, too.

"Likely."

"Has your father come back yet?"

"No, but I know that he went to the shuttle, to communicate with the main ship."

"I'd like to speak with him." I wondered how much information I could get out of him, especially if he, as Thayu suggested, would have interest in claiming the top job.

Eirani came walking through the hall, wheeling the dinner trolley out of the living room. "There is food on the table, Delegate. I don't suppose anyone wants something to eat. No one ever does in this house. Everyone is always too busy."

I put a hand on her shoulder. "Oh, Eirani, we do want your wonderful food. You've done very well." I turned to Nicha. "Come on, let's get everyone up here. Let's have a proper breakfast. I'm hungry."

Nicha said, "Yeah, me, too."

"It smells wonderful," Thayu said to Eirani.

Since their public dislike of each other when Thayu first moved in, the two women seemed to have settled on an atmosphere of forced politeness.

I had barely taken a step in the direction of the living room when there was a commotion down the hall, raised voices.

". . . but I'm not going anywhere!" That was Melissa.

Someone replied, but I couldn't hear what was said.

I frowned at Nicha, but he shook his head.

"You start on breakfast," I said. "I'll go and see what's going on there." I rushed down the hall.

Melissa stood at the top of the stairs, thunder on her face. With her was the last of Ezhya's guards, the one who hadn't been in the hub room. Melissa's expression cleared when she saw me.

"Cory, what is this 'you are not allowed to leave'? Since when can't I leave this apartment? Since when do I have to listen to these thugs? How am I supposed to do my job like this?"

"*Mashara?*"

The guard turned around and immediately snapped into a subservient position, his arms down his sides, palms facing backwards. "Our excuses, Delegate. *Mashara* is much obliged."

For what? What the hell was going on? Why was he even displaying that behaviour to me? If I had a ranking in Coldi society, he would be my superior.

My heart was hammering. Damn, this little association of dangerous highly-strung and armed people was unravelling fast.

I calmed my voice as much as I could. "The lady is coming up to the dining room for breakfast. She is not leaving the apartment. Why don't any of you who don't need to be in the hub join us? Have any of you eaten anything since last night?" And that wasn't right either. I should extend this invitation to their leader, the tall woman Natanu.

His shoulders slumped, and he looked down. "Excuses, Delegate."

"Do go and have something to eat. Tell your associates that I will expect them."

"I'll communicate the order." He started off down the corridor.

Shit.

Melissa looked at me, her eyes wide. "What's up with him? He tried to stop me leaving the room!"

I was sure there was a bit more to it than that, but I let it rest. "Listen, I'm afraid they're all upset, so please try to be understanding. The Exchange is out and Ezhya is out of contact. They're rattled, unsure what to do."

"And that involves harassing me?"

"Well . . ." The way she had behaved last night had probably made her a focus point, someone they needed to watch. "They've been harassing me, too."

In a way, I felt sorry for her. I'd left an instruction with Eirani that she would be allowed out of the room but not out of the apartment, and evidently she had intended to do just that.

I took her to the office downstairs, sat down and let her rage. She called me names, and called the guards names, and even got stuck into Eirani, but none of those people heard any of it.

Getting no reaction from me, she grew tired of raging. "Why do you take it all with so much patience? How can you even do that?"

"I grew up in space. There were always *gamra* people around, from way back when I was eight."

"Where were you before that?"

"I lived in New Zealand, Bay of Islands. My father was a scientist with the wave-energy project. He ended up pretty high in the bureaucracy, and on a whim, after my mother died, applied for the job of director of Midway Space Station. He got the job. We lived at the Nations of Earth complex. I went to school there. My father married a Damarcian."

"You're probably one of the first people to have lived off-Earth for most of their lives."

"No, I'm not. It's just that those who leave don't tend to come back."

She nodded, in thought.

I said, "One thing I don't understand about your reaction to the current situation. Your stepfather is Coldi. He hasn't taught you about all the societal links and the pyramids of associations?"

She snorted. "My stepfather never took part in that stuff. He would never stop telling us how stupid he thought it was."

Something clicked for me. "He is from Hedron."

"He is."

Damn, that was a mistake on my part. The Hedron Coldi were descended from the *zeyshi,* a group who didn't have the pathological need for social order. Most of them looked down their nose at it.

"Melissa, you must understand this. Even if it's not important to you, the stability of Asto affects us all. It affects *gamra,* it affects my job, and your job, everything."

"Will you stop talking about *them* and their political problems? It's about us, about Margarethe. She is *missing,* too."

"She'll be fine. As soon as the Exchange is back up, they'll return and no one will care about this anymore, at least not on Earth." Considering Margarethe, I had other worries, but she wasn't technically *missing,* just out of communication.

"You're just saying that to shut me up. There will be hell at Nations of Earth when they hear about this."

"How are they going to hear it unless the Exchange comes back? By that time, Margarethe will be back, and things will continue as normal." Except, if this situation lasted too long, at Asto. "Margarethe will be fine."

"And how am I going to excuse this slip-up, Cory? We can't lie to

Nations of Earth. For heaven's sake, this will be worse than the Kershaw affair. Somehow I'm starting to believe that Danziger was right: this is just going from bad to worse, from one misunderstanding to a worse one."

Well, there was a kernel of truth in that. Should I have warned Margarethe not to go with him? Should I have told her about this Coldi habit of *nethana* about which she might have found out already? Did I trust Ezhya's understanding of our society? He *had* dealt with Nations of Earth on several occasions. He had received advice. Had any of it contained the information: "These people do not consider intimacy between business partners appropriate"?

Damn. It was no good thinking about it. If it was to happen, it would have happened already.

She asked, "So what are we going to do?"

"Until the Exchange is back, we do nothing. After that, I don't suspect we'll have to do anything at all."

"How long is that going to take? Days? Weeks? Who knows what's going to happen at Nations of Earth in that time?"

"Not that long." Oh hell, I hoped not.

"What do I do all that time? Sit here and stare at the walls?"

"You might go into the assembly and see what is being discussed there. There are meetings every day. The public gallery is open."

Melissa snorted and turned to the window.

What a mess.

I turned to the door, where Nicha waited as if he wanted to speak with me.

"Anything new?"

"We're waiting for you in the dining room. My father is back."

"Sure."

Let's deal with another ticking time-bomb in my apartment.

6

———

MELISSA WAS too angry to want breakfast, so I left her in her room, making a mental note to ask Eirani to bring her something to eat later.

In the living room, most of the guests in my apartment sat around a big table where the usual wide choice of dishes was spread out.

When I first moved into the apartment, when it still belonged to Renkati, I had wondered what need I'd have for that huge table. Today, we had two tables of similar size put together.

Asha Domiri and his guards had taken up seats on the far end, then there was an empty seat and then the first of Ezhya's guards. The woman Natanu sat in the middle of that group, which stretched around the other side of the table. No one spoke.

Right. We had a problem here.

I crossed the room and boldly sat in the empty seat between the two groups. Nicha and Thayu settled opposite me.

I asked, "Anyone else coming?"

Eirani shook her head. "I don't know, Delegate. I asked everyone, but some people don't seem to be here. The lady is still angry, I think. I don't know what I did wro—"

"Don't worry about it, Eirani. It's not about you."

"But she got angry when I told her—"

"I know. Don't worry about it. Please, Eirani. You may want to bring her some food later."

"Certainly, Delegate."

Six seats were still empty. Apart from Melissa, I presumed these were for Margarethe's guards, but I hadn't seen them since early this morning and didn't even know if they were still in the house.

Eirani went around the table pouring tea.

A few conversations began in different corners. Asha asked his son about the weather—which, by the way, had behaved remarkably well, with the notable absence of the heavy afternoon storms that were typical of Barresh. Natanu asked Thayu about trains into town. I observed that conversation, noting Natanu's proud posture and Thayu's slumped shoulders and the way she kept her gaze below Natanu's chin.

It was all very polite and reserved, three groups, with just the top tier of each of the Coldi associations taking part in the discussion. The others—lower-ranking guards in both groups—were silent and avoided eye contact with other people. Asha's guards kept glancing across the table, as if Ezhya's guards could pounce on them any minute. None of them ate much.

I had intended to have an open discussion about the situation and what we might do, but that had been a silly *Earth* thought. A discussion would never work in this atmosphere of distrust.

Asha was the first to get up from the table, and his guards followed him out of the room like little ducklings. He didn't say where they were going. Ezhya's guards went back to the hub room after asking me if that was all right.

When they were gone, I heaved a big sigh and leaned my elbows on the table.

"This is not going to be easy," Nicha said.

"No. Do you think they'll come to blows?"

"If we do nothing, likely."

Thayu said, "I suggest that you go across the gallery to Ezhya's old apartment and tell the Asto representatives to make room for one of these groups. We can't have them both here and expect nothing to happen."

Nicha said, "But where are Delegate Ayanu's loyalties? She isn't part of Asha's network." And she wouldn't have any relationship to the guards either.

"If there is going to be trouble, she's just going to have to move out to the temporary accommodation." Like the Asto delegation would be impressed with that. They were arrogant and entitled at the best of times. "Whatever we do, we need to do something."

Thayu and Nicha both nodded, but said nothing. Thayu blew steam off her tea.

"Are you two affected by all this? I mean—your loyalty networks?"

Nicha shook his head. "We're bound to you."

In the beginning, I'd been uncomfortable with him talking like that, but that was simply the way Coldi people saw things: where they belonged in a network at any one time.

Thayu said, "I have two networks on Asto, but neither are related to the people here."

I thought for a bit. "The fact that we're outsiders, does that make us more acceptable as keepers of the peace?"

Thayu said, "To stop rivalry between Ezhya's guards and our father? That's not going to go away until Ezhya returns."

Nicha shrugged. "Short of Ezhya returning, the only other thing that's going to keep this sort of rivalry at bay is to have the command key back in the Inner Circle."

I'd heard of this mysterious command key. It was supposed to be a sequence of orders programmed into the main command hub in the Chief Coordinator's quarters in Athyl's Inner Circle. Apparently the sequence was unique to the current leader, biologically-keyed to work only at his say-so.

"You say 'have it back.' Where is this command key?"

"Ezhya has it. Natanu has a copy."

That Natanu who was spoiling for a showdown with Asha and his guards. Oh shit, I could see where this was going.

"Don't look like that. She can't use it unless she enters the command room, and even if she manages to get to Asto and if she tries to enter, the Inner Circle guards will have orders to kill her. The key is an aid to keeping things running and a protection of the hub when the Chief Coordinator is away. It's not a tool for taking over power. Each Chief Coordinator develops their own."

"Wouldn't it be smart, then, to store a copy on-site?" I asked. Frankly, I had no idea if this command key was a physical thing or merely a file on a computer. Coldi rarely spoke about these matters.

"Not if the Chief Coordinator is not on-site. It belongs to *him,* not the Inner Circle. In fact, if it were available freely, his competitors in the Inner Circle could use it to inflict much damage on him."

"But a supporter could use it to strengthen his rule?" I wasn't sure anymore if there was such a thing as a supporter in the Asto system, especially if the system was under stress.

"In theory, yes, but I can't think of anyone who could use it. The Inner Circle would be in lockdown. Anyone who lives in the Inner Circle would be considered a threat to the position and would be kept out of the hub by Ezhya's backed-up orders. Anyone from lower ranks could never even enter the Inner Circle."

"But if they did, they could use this key?"

"In theory, maybe, but how would they get the key?"

The system baffled me. Why have this key if no one could use it?

"Surely, there is a backup plan in case something happens, if the Chief Coordinator is sick or unable to work."

"Yes. The backup is that one of his seconds takes over."

Permanently. Ezhya's seconds were Risha and Taysha.

I understood that Asha's superior, Risha Palayi, was quite old. I hadn't had any involvement with him. Taysha I'd had more involvement with than I'd ever wished to have. I'd horse-traded with him for Thayu's contract, and I did not want to be reminded of this rude man.

If there ever was a fight between the two, I had no doubt Taysha would win that tussle, and then his ascent to power might upset Thayu's networks, too, not to mention my relationship with her.

Damn.

"So what would actually happen if someone could get the command key into the Inner Circle hub?"

"They can't."

"No, but suppose for one moment someone could."

Thayu said, "If the key was activated, it would delay the shift of power, because all of Ezhya's automatic order routines would receive a boost. Eventually, things would happen that would require his input for decisions, and processes would falter, first a few, and then more and more, until the system breaks down, allowing someone to come in."

"Would it last until the Exchange comes back?"

She shrugged. "Perhaps. I don't think anyone has ever tried how long the command key keeps the Inner Circle together. But it's irrelevant because I don't know anyone who could take the key in there without having their heads cut off."

Seriously? "But how would a successor enter the hub then?"

As I said that, I already knew the answer, and it wasn't a nice one. Most likely, it was how Ezhya had taken power because, when the Inner Circle locked down, there *was* only one way of getting in if you weren't the Chief Coordinator. A way that involved a lot of people with guns and a good number of dead bodies.

Damn. There had to be something we could do.

I got up from the table and went into the hall. Ezhya's guards were again fixated on their makeshift receiver. They had attached a screen that lit their faces with a blue glow. It displayed blocks of text that looked like code. Not something I could make out; I left anything to do with technology to Thayu and Nicha.

"Mashara."

The woman Natanu rose and faced me. Her face twitched as if she didn't know what to do. She looked like she would *like* to use the subservient pose, but I didn't even rank in Coldi society. She didn't want me; she wanted Ezhya.

"Can I have a word with you?" I asked her.

I used professional pronouns and studied the other guards while I spoke. One or two of them looked unsure whether they could trust me.

"Delegate, *mashara* again apologises for the intrusion. *Mashara* will aid the household as much as possible."

The tone of her voice chilled me. For a woman said to be after Asto's top job, she sounded too demure. I didn't buy it.

"I understand that you have Ezhya's command key."

She looked startled. "I do."

"I understand you can't use it."

"Not from here, no."

"Excuse my ignorance, but I'm rather unfamiliar with this key. Is it a physical thing?"

She opened the front of her jacket, giving me a glimpse of the armour she wore underneath. Seriously? Wearing armour to breakfast? Oh, I certainly saw Eirani's point of protesting against display of weapons in a private situation.

She pulled out a metal cylinder about the diameter and length of my pinkie. It lay in the palm of her hand, with the light from the screen reflected in the brushed metal surface. A tiny blue light blinked near what I judged the top of the thing.

That was it? The key to Ezhya's hold on power?

She tucked it back into her jacket without saying a word.

"Seeing as we have radio contact with Asto, would it be possible to somehow upload the commands to Ezhya's hub?"

"No." Very definite. "It needs to be physically inserted."

I nodded. We clearly had a problem here. I watched whatever communication the guards were receiving roll over the screen.

I thought for a while, fingering my upper lip.

I remembered my discussion with Ezhya yesterday and his mention that with some planning, a visit to Asto might be possible. Because of the eclipse, Asto was the closest it would be to us all year. A space-enabled ship would cross the distance in days. There happened to be such a ship in orbit. Asha owned it.

I said, in a low voice, "Supposing I could get someone to take this key to Asto and into the hub, would you be committed enough to Ezhya to help me?"

She eyed me as if she thought I was mad. My heart hammered in my chest. She said nothing.

I licked my lips and plunged in further. "Supposing again this person was someone not from the Inner Circle and not interested in taking Ezhya's position, but purely to help secure his position until the Exchange comes back online and he can return."

"That could happen any moment."

"Let's not kid ourselves about that." Oh, that was actually a pretty rude pronoun form. "We heard what the Exchange owner said. It may not be back for days." Many days, I guessed.

But she didn't flinch. She glanced at her colleagues, and then nodded, once. Did that mean *go on* to me, or was it a sign for them to bundle me out of the room?

I waited. Nothing happened.

I continued. "So, supposing what I just said, would you give your commitment to securing Ezhya's position in favour of trying to obtain the position for yourself?"

Well, shit, I'd said it.

I held my breath waiting for her answer, wondering if that answer would be a knife in my heart or a pledge of support, or . . . more of nothing.

She stared into the distance. Her lips twitched with deep emotions warring inside her. I knew I was asking a lot. Declaring loyalty to a *non-Coldi* person, to a position that might prove untenable, while in doing so throwing away all her own chances of securing her future in case we failed.

If Ezhya didn't come back or didn't come back in time, she would be an exile.

For too long, I thought she wasn't going to respond at all. Then she re-opened her jacket. She stuck her hand in and brought out a closed fist, which she held in front of me.

I held my hand out, palm up, and she dropped the metal cylinder into it.

I breathed out heavily.

Shit.

While I tucked this treasure in the inside pocket of my own jacket, her eyes met mine squarely. "I have . . . other interests tied up with Ezhya's leadership that are important to me."

Love was a funny thing in the Coldi. They liked to pretend that their relationships were all rational and existed for a reason. But the emotions that flowed within associations were deeper than appeared on the surface. I would have sworn I saw love in her eyes. Was she Ezhya's lover?

I left the guards fiddling with their rigged-up equipment and went back to the living room, where Nicha and Thayu sat drinking tea. Someone had been in to clear the table, probably Eirani, and likely I'd have to hear her complaints of people not wanting her food for days.

I halted at the door and felt keenly how lucky I was to have the two of them. They got along so well, even though the situation of a group of three *zhaymas* was unusual.

I sat down and took my cup.

"Any luck?" Thayu asked. As part of my security, she had made studious efforts to stay away from Ezhya's guards.

I poured some tea. "They seem fragile."

Nicha nodded wordlessly.

"What can we do?"

Thayu shrugged. "From here? Nothing."

I debated whether to say anything about the key. I had the security of Asto in my pocket.

I said, in a low voice, "I would like to speak to your father as soon as possible."

~

I EXPECTED them to ask questions, but they didn't. In the train on the way into town, after I'd changed into my most official *gamra* clothing, I asked why.

Nicha replied, "When you have that look on your face, you have a plan. I can say whatever I want, but you will do it anyway."

"But you are my *zhayma*. You can try to talk me out of it."

He nodded and said nothing. I couldn't get over the niggling feeling that something in our relationship had shifted since he'd been falsely accused of President Sirkonen's murder.

It was a sad feeling. I wondered if he blamed me for any of it, or whether he just blamed Earth people, of which I happened to be one.

He'd told me he didn't, but telling and believing were two different things.

We got off the train at the airport. With the Exchange out of action, there was not much reason for people to be at the airport, and the platform was eerily quiet. A bored guard stood at the top of the stairs, stifling a yawn.

"Not much action here, Delegate," he said.

We walked past the guard to a square that was normally far too crowded to see its intricate floor mosaic, which depicted the five-pointed star that adorned every damn thing in Barresh, from official correspondence to guard uniforms to family emblems. Each point had a white side and a black side, which symbolised the two native Barresh people. This version of the star had been in use since the liberation of Barresh after the occupation by Miran.

See? I spent way too much time listening to these councillors.

The square was the home of businesses associated with the airport, such as the quarantine and customs offices, the headquarters of the Courier Guild, the Pilot Guild and the Trader Guild. We were just walking past the latter when the door opened and someone came out.

"Good day, Delegate Wilson."

Marin Federza.

He was at his peacock best today, in full Trader uniform with all his shiny decorations for various awards of service. Underneath the sheer Trader cloak, he wore the turquoise of the Barresh Traders. The cloak was held at the top by a bejewelled clip.

"I've just been trying to contact you," he said.

I looked at my comm. So he had. I must have missed the message when we were in the train. That was right. He was going to contact me when he had spoken to his fellow Aghyrians. With all this mess about Ezhya, I'd almost forgotten about it.

"Have you got time now?" he asked.

I glanced at Thayu and Nicha. We hadn't told Asha that we were coming, although I did want to talk to him as soon as possible. "I do."

"Then let us go upstairs."

He preceded us back into the building. I had been inside the Barresh Trading Office before, but never on the top floor.

Federza's office was a light-filled room that overlooked the square, with soft carpet, old book cases, a beautiful and grand timber desk and luxury chairs.

It reminded me, of all things, of the place where my adventure had begun: the old office of president Sirkonen at Nations of Earth, where I'd signed my documents and where I had almost been killed alongside Sirkonen.

It was eerie.

He gestured for me to sit in one of the armchairs away from the window. I did, still observing the room and its lush furniture. On the back wall, behind Federza's desk, hung a close up portrait of a man I recognised. He had a soft, expressive mouth, dark mournful eyes, a finely-sculpted jaw and loose curls that danced about his head like a halo. This soft, melancholy image was in complete contrast with the iron grip with which he was said to have set and ruled the Aghyrian community.

It was Daya Ezmi, founder of the Aghyrian enclave, owner of half the Hedron mines, the reason why the Aghyrians existed as they did today, and the reason why they had so much money.

"My grandfather," Federza said, when he noticed me looking at it.

That figured.

I was highly tempted to ask the question everyone wanted to know: is he still alive? But it was pointless to ask because he would never answer it. No one really knew how long Aghyrians lived. Chief Delegate Akhtari was said to have been over a hundred when I was a little boy, and ages of one hundred and fifty were definitely not uncommon. There was a chance that I'd retire before she did. Awesome.

"So. You spoke to your fellows?" Let's talk about slightly less depressing and more explosive things.

"The claim comes from Asto," he said. "At the moment, we don't have the communication to establish who has made it, as you will understand."

No, I didn't understand. "We have spoken to Asto." I had no doubt that, given their technology, the Aghyrians would have done the same.

"Do you understand the extent of deprival of the *zeyshi* people of Asto? They do not have anything of a nature that would allow them to communicate with us when the Exchange operates normally, let alone now."

"You have never been in contact with these people before?" I returned his belligerent tone.

He glared at me.

"The *zeyshi* are not easy to deal with." Defensive.

"Surely you throw money at them and they'll cooperate."

Federza was one of those gnarled and knotted blocks of wood. You could swing the axe at it, but most blows would just glance off, and, if you were unlucky, injure your own toes.

"They have never given us any reason to 'throw money at them.' " Meaning: they didn't have anything the Aghyrians wanted. The Barresh Aghyrian community tended to have a cool relationship with those who chose to ignore their calls to come and join them. Their promises of a good life, a guaranteed job, good health did not sway everyone who passed their blood tests for "Aghyrian markers". They tended to act miffed towards these people who snubbed their noses at their offers and who preferred to stay in their places of birth.

"But you knew about their existence?"

"Yes we did." That was about as terse an agreement as I could get from him.

"They have every right to make this claim?"

"They do."

"They perhaps have more right to make it because Asto is their home?"

Was that a flinch?

"Mr Wilson, I understand that you don't like us and that you're an instrument for the Asto colonisation machine, but—"

"You claimed to represent all Aghyrian interests. You assured me that there would be no claims, for the sake of peace. I don't care who is on which side. I care that there was a promise that's been broken. So either you do not speak for all Aghyrians or you are not truthful with me."

"Look, we don't know!" He spread his hands. "You probably won't believe me, but we don't have any contact with these people."

"Then get in contact with them."

But I saw it in his face: the claimants did not want any contact with this group of pampered, foppish, self-indulgent people. They were part of a different movement, one that targeted the established structures of Asto more than anything. And somehow these people, whom everyone had written off and ignored for centuries, had crawled out of their desert hole and struck at the heart of *gamra,* in the middle of another crisis.

I'd worked for months assuming that I'd eventually have to deal with the Barresh Aghyrians, that we'd settle their right to claim amicably over a sumptuous lunch somewhere on the island.

And we had been wrong.

Of course we had been wrong.

Stupidly wrong.

There was not that much more I wanted to say to Federza. I left after a few more empty lines of conversation, picking up Thayu and Nicha at the door. I gave them a brief rundown of the conversation on our way out of the building.

In a way, I felt sorry for him and for all the other Aghyrians in Barresh. Their moment in the sun had been stolen by another group. That cemented my plan in my mind.

And hell, it was as far removed from a leisurely lunch as possible.

Asha Domiri's shuttle stood at the high-security end of the airport.

We walked to it across the empty spot where Ezhya's craft would have been.

Asha's craft was a typical run-of-the-mill Asto-built model. Nothing fancy, nothing military except the emblem next to the door which depicted two stylised suns circled by a planetary orbit with the planet drawn in. As with everything in the Asto military forces, the emblem was tense with understatement.

One of Asha's guards stood outside, in civilian guard clothing. He greeted us with a small nod. Coldi could be oddly intimate and could also behave oddly distant after sharing situations that should afford a bit more familiarity. As it was, this guard acted like he never shared breakfast with us at my dinner table.

After all these years dealing with Coldi, my first reaction to this strange habit was still one of finding it rude, despite the fact that I knew it was not. He was a lower-ranked member of the guard association, and only the highest-ranked member would communicate with someone from outside the group. That particular guard now came out of the craft.

"I'd like to speak to Asha," I said. It was also inappropriate to use family relationships for this sort of thing. In official situations, Coldi tended to pretend that they had no family. Even though I had come with his two children, I was expected to make contact, because I wanted to speak with him.

The guard acknowledged me and went inside. He came back a few moments later and gestured for us to come into the craft.

As I had expected, the interior of the craft was not at all like the basic passenger shuttle it resembled. The rows of seats that would normally occupy most of the cabin had been taken out and replaced with a few bays of tables and chairs, like meeting rooms. There was a huge bank of screens towards the back, many black and waiting for input prompts.

Asha sat at one of the tables, reading something on a screen.

He looked up when we came in, and, without acknowledging either of his children, gestured me into the seat opposite him.

Smalltalk was wasted on this man, so I started bluntly, "Would you be prepared to take us to Athyl on board your ship?"

The sharp intake of breath I heard had to be Thayu's.

Asha squinted at me. "You?" It was a pretty direct pronoun form. "You're aware that we can't travel right now?"

"That ship of yours in orbit isn't a long-distance space-enabled craft?" I used similarly direct pronouns, because this was going to be one of those discussions that would be fought through sheer bluff.

"Hmmm." He could do nothing except acknowledge the truth. "Do you have a wish to be cooked alive?"

"Ezhya told me that we could consider a visit. In fact, he encouraged me to start planning for one."

"Did he?" He raised one eyebrow.

I had a feeling that he disagreed with Ezhya about telling non-Coldi people about the possibility of visiting. But being subordinate, he could not express this opinion.

Ezhya's absence had removed that barrier. *That* was how the breakdown of power would work. If you had a superior, you did not have an opinion. With the superior gone, all bets were off. How long would it take for that shift to take place?

Asha seemed more bemused than anything. "And what are you planning to do in Athyl?"

"I intend to take Ezhya's command key to the hub."

Another sharp intake of breath from Thayu.

"You'll be killed," he said.

"Yes," Thayu said, her voice full of horror.

"Not if I can get into the Inner Circle under some sort of excuse. I can arrange . . . an invitation."

Perfect eyebrows went up. "Who from?"

"Ezhya tells me that Risha should be able to inform me about these *zeyshi* and the Aghyrian claim. It is my job to act as intermediary between Asto and any claimants under Ezhya's mandate."

"Hmmm," he said, not in a convinced way.

"Risha does live in the Inner Circle."

"He does."

"He does look after the relationship with the *zeyshi?*"

"Ezhya gave him that task, yes."

"So, he'll be able to tell me who these people are who are making the claim."

"I'm not sure about that. I would suggest that this comes from a rogue element with their own agenda."

"Risha has talked to you about his dealings with the *zeyshi?*"

"Insofar as the army is concerned, yes."

Oh well, that wasn't a good starting point for peaceful talks. I was guessing that he probably wasn't in favour of talking with the *zeyshi* in the first place.

I plunged on, like a blundering drunkard. "Yet, if anyone knows, Risha would. He is your superior. You can introduce me."

He gave me a calculating look, as if deciding whether I was shitting him or I was serious. As if taken aback by my direct pronouns. Deciding how much of a *curious fellow* I really was. Oh, no, I didn't doubt for one minute that he'd shunt me off to someone else if he could.

"What makes you think that Risha will see you in the middle of a crisis?"

"Nothing."

He raised his eyebrows.

"Nothing but the famed *gamra* narrow vision. Of course I know about the crisis, but I am a *gamra* delegate and as they are wont to do, I go about my business unhampered by the world crashing and burning around me."

"Hmph. Guess that would work."

"The heart of the matter is that I get into the Inner Circle. He'll be curious. He'll talk to me, precisely because he'll see me as stupid and harmless. I'll be his entertainment. But never for one moment will he expect me to have the key. So I'll go for a bit of friendly conversation to satisfy his curiosity, and when we're done, I make for the command hub."

I met his eyes, silently giving him the same challenge I'd handed Natanu: help me and protect what we worked for together and forget about your own ambition. Except if we lost and he kept quiet about this plan, he might keep his job. As the head of the armed forces, his association would still be intact. The same could not be said for Natanu.

"Who would be coming on this stupid mission?" But his face showed that he was thinking about it. In what way, I could only guess.

"Thayu and Nicha, and Ezhya's guards."

He stiffened. "I'm not having them on my ship."

"They promised me loyalty. I can vouch for them that they will stay out of the way of you and your crew."

"I don't believe anything that woman says. They're not part of my association. They'll endanger the ship, compromise our security and encourage fights. They are only going back to Athyl so that she can challenge—"

I inserted my hand under my jacket and drew out the key. The metal cylinder lay inoffensive as could be in the palm of my hand.

His eyes widened. Both Thayu and Nicha gaped at it, too.

"If Natanu wanted to challenge, she would not have given me this."

He glared at me, nostrils flaring. "You're serious, aren't you?"

"Damn right I am."

～

I DON'T KNOW how I did it, but he gave me his word. He'd take me and the team into Athyl, leaving tomorrow.

On the train on the way back to the apartment, I had to bear Thayu's anger.

"Why didn't you tell us about this ridiculous plan? You remember last year? Well, you're doing it again. Nicha and I are here to *help* you, not to be kept in the dark about your plans. What is the point if—"

"Thayu." I put my hand on her arm. "You would have told me that this is too dangerous or too stupid—"

"BECAUSE IT IS!" She spread her hands and rolled her eyes. "Nicha, you tell him."

"I'm not going to waste my breath," Nicha said. He seemed quite relaxed, leaning back into his seat. Underneath his mask of calm I suspected he was amused and excited. He'd done his fair share of stupid things with me, like going sailing on the bay on a blustery day. Coldi had a deep-seated fear of large bodies of water, and until their adaptation had settled, they were quite sensitive to temperature extremes, especially in the low range. I still remembered the panic of being in the middle of the bay with flapping sails, water spray and having Nicha collapse on me.

I guess it was my turn.

He said, "Thay', it will be all right. We'll give him two suits and some emergency crew's breathing gear with coolant."

Thayu rounded on her brother. "You've been thinking about this for a while, haven't you?"

"Why not?"

"You're *both* stupid."

"I take it you're not coming then?"

"Whatever makes you think that? *Of course* I'm coming."

7

———

I REMEMBERED weightlessness.

In my youth I had travelled along the natural anpar lines in huge, Earth-built space liners, massive vessels which were even then close to a hundred years old. Some of them were still in operation, since Earth ships could not use the Exchange, and the reach of Earth's colonisation effort was extremely limited as a result.

There was one natural anpar line which Earth people used in getting from Saturn's orbit to Midway Space Station, then another one to Taurus. Each time, those trips involved covering fairly major distances to get to the anpar entry point, a journey of many months, which was why the ship had to be so large.

As long as the ship accelerated or decelerated, there was a measure of gravity. Cabins were designed so that one could live on the ceiling just as well as one could live on the floor. But when the acceleration stopped . . .

I'd been a passenger as a ten-year-old, on my way to Midway Space Station, and I remembered those confusing points of change, where the pilots shut down the ion drives and took most of a day to reverse the direction of thrust, where the floor became the ceiling, where anything not tied down floated around. I remembered hanging in my sleeping bag with my eyes closed, or watching movies on a screen that still had an up and a down. I remembered not eating and drinking when that happened, and regretting the one time I did eat something before a change. Puke does funny things in weightlessness.

Unfortunately, going without food or drink was not an option for a trip lasting sixteen days, and in our hasty planning of the trip I had been more concerned with surviving the impending heat than with the sixteen-day lack of gravity. In fact, I hadn't considered there would be a lack of gravity, but apparently the design requirements for artificial gravity resulted in a ship that was either too large, or else unsuited for firing weapons. So, no gravity. Which meant that my movement was somewhat restricted immediately after dinner. This was not helped at all by the fact that the ship was kept at a temperature range suitable for Coldi, which meant that most of the time my clothes were soaked with sweat.

I swear I lost a lot of weight in those days. Coldi were immune to motion sickness, and Thayu was rather puzzled by the whole affair.

So now we were on this military tin can hurtling towards a pink hothouse planet, with a crew of an unspecified number, weapons of unidentified types and a ship of unspecified dimensions.

I hadn't seen the ship from outside. On the way up in the shuttle, the viewscreens had blacked out soon after take-off. Oh no, they didn't trust us, not one bit.

Once we were out the air lock and inside the white corridor—with the obligatory maroon on the doors and in a stripe over the wall—a crew member had taken me, Thayu, Nicha and Ezhya's guards to a section of the craft separate from the crew. Inside the two dorm rooms, tiny washing cubicle and common room, we had everything we needed, but at the end of the corridor there was a solid sliding door with a panel that required input of a code that none of us had.

The word *prison* was on my tongue most days.

"It's a *military* ship," Nicha had said, by way of apology.

And I'd hardly ever seen any Asto military display out in the open. Asto's leaders and representatives strutted and bluffed like peacocks, but their real striking power remained in the shadows. Shielded, blacked-out and secret. Their armed forces wore no uniforms when they were out. You didn't know who or where they were, although, over the years of dealing with Coldi, I'd developed an eye for picking out military people.

The two dorm rooms we'd been allocated each had six sleeping bays, leaving barely any space for personal belongings—or bulky suits and cooling equipment. Thayu, Nicha and I went into one dorm, six of Ezhya's guards in the other, which left Natanu a spot in our dorm, which she hardly ever used.

It was cramped, claustrophobic and, as usual with Coldi accommodation, always too hot.

There were also no outside viewscreens and we had no passenger feed with information about the journey or anything that gave us outside news.

We played a lot of games, told each other stories, and only knew how much time had passed because of Nicha's timer.

The only link we had to the outside world was Asha's daily visit to us. I could understand his wariness towards me and the guards, but his own children?

Every time he came, I expected to be told that the Exchange was back up and that our journey was no longer necessary, that Ezhya had returned to Athyl to take care of his own position.

That news did not come, and as the days passed I resigned myself to the fact that I would actually have to complete what I'd set out to do. I took my air tank and coolant off the rack and studied the apparatus' operation. I practiced putting it on and moving around with it. It was firefighters' gear. In a place like Barresh, where the fine oil-like substance exuded by the megon trees stopped most fires, firefighting gear was hard to find. This gear I'd borrowed off a Kedrasi merchant who was stuck in Barresh.

I made myself familiar with putting on and taking off the helmet, putting on the breathing mask so that the flaps blocked any air coming in through the cracks. Our impending arrival in Athyl began to fill me with dread. This might be the stupidest thing I'd ever done in my life.

"You can breathe Asto air," Thayu said. "It's not as if it's poisonous."

I was going to say that I read it *could* be poisonous, if an ocean wind carried humidity with acidic droplets. Rain could be lethal, so could the thunderstorms and the sand storms, and flash floods in the aquifers. But maybe I'd read far too many meteorological articles about Asto. Maybe I worried too much.

I started myself on double doses of adaptation medication. The resulting increase in body temperature made me hallucinate, for which I took other medication that made me hyperactive and I spent two days bouncing off the walls. I couldn't sleep and couldn't sit still. On board the ship, there was barely any difference between day and night, and to make things worse, the ship kept an Asto day, which was shorter than the Ceren day and further mucked with my sleeping patterns.

Time was getting horribly blurred—I remembered that from the long-haul trip, too. I hung in my sleeping mat, reading if I felt well enough or watching information about Coldi government if I did not.

ONE DAY, about ten days after departure, Asha came into the cabin. He dipped his head to me, gave a hand signal to his son and daughter and treated Natanu with a wary look.

She hung in the sleeping mat opposite me, on her back, her legs crossed at the ankles and her arms folded behind her head. Her eyes were closed, but I didn't mistake her rest for sleep. I don't know that Natanu ever slept.

Asha held onto one of the wall/ceiling railings next to the door and anchored his tether.

He regarded us with the humourless expression of a military officer. As he had been since entering the ship, he was impeccably dressed in his uniform, which involved a stern jacket with protective shoulder pads of that mysterious bendable material, used in body armour, that wasn't plastic or metal. If you moved slowly, it bent, if you hit it hard, it was rigid.

The fabric of his dress uniform, underneath the patches and decorations, was creamy pink. I'd wondered, on occasion, how pink looked to the Coldi, given their inability to see red. What made it different from white? In any case, I'd never seen anyone carry off wearing pink in such a stern and humourless way. Never mind the pink; everything about him said, *Do not mess with me.*

In all the time that we'd camped in close quarters aboard this ship, I had not gotten to know him any better than I did at the start. His visits were brief, business-like and impersonal.

This man, my father in law, was a mystery to me.

He shut the door of the dorm room, something he didn't usually do.

I tried to work myself out of my sleeping bag without my reader flying off through the cabin. One hand on the railing next to the hammock, the other hanging onto the cord. I needed a third hand for hanging onto the blanket.

Oh, tether. Right. I clipped the magnetic fastening onto the railing, retrieved the blanket and tucked it in the hammock. By now, Asha hung sideways. I hated this. My stomach had gotten tougher, but my balance was pretty much a lost cause. These cabins needed a sign with an arrow saying, "This way is up."

"Is there news?" I asked, trying to distract him from my clumsiness.

"We intercepted some surface broadcasts from Asto." His expression was even more grim than usual.

Thayu must have detected that same grimness because she gave me that hyper-alert look that meant, *Watch out.*

"There are a few general transmitters broadcasting, mostly for local use, we suspect, but we can listen in. They report that chaos has broken out near the airport. The Third Circle has been forced to close it."

Damn. I hadn't considered that possibility. Third Circle airport, wasn't that where we were going? "What sort of chaos?"

"People in the streets, riots. Now that the Exchange is out, people are nervous about food supplies and fair distribution of the stored resources. Many people are hanging around near points where food enters the city to make sure they get their share. The airport, the aquifer entry points. The stores keep at most a month's worth of non-perishables in stock, and people are panicking. It seems an order went out that people could collect food packages from a store in Third Circle. When they came there, no one knew anything about it. A fight broke out. Guards dispersed the crowd, but the troublemakers took their fight to the airport."

He took out his comm-reader. I gave my feeder the command to connect to it, and heard the recording he had made earlier. On it, a garbled voice was barely audible over the sound of shouting. It took a fair amount of training for Earth people to be able to distinguish male Coldi voices from female. I'd gotten pretty good at it, but on this transmission it was impossible. There were a lot of voices in the background distorting the sound and the reception kept floating in and out of focus.

"The groups led by Nayu have advanced into the third circle. Taysha is trying to hold together the First Circle representatives, but some of them have left the compound to defend their own associations."

After a burst of static, a second person asked, "How is Taysha holding up?"

"Still in the Inner Circle, trying to run his side of the network . . ."

The connection cut out.

Both Nicha and Thayu frowned at their father.

He gave a nod, his face grim.

I struggled to put together the information all the others obtained from this snippet.

Taysha Palayi I knew better than I was comfortable with. I'd never seen him, but our discussions over how much I owed him for Thayu's contract had been bad enough that I'd hoped he'd never cross my path again.

"Who is this Nayu?" Dang the Coldi for not using last names. A clan name would be a great help to me. As it was, I knew only Nayu was female.

Thayu said, "She is an activist from the Outer Circle. *Zeyshi.* A troublemaker."

"So the *zeyshi* have become involved already?"

"It is their reason for existence to try to put holes into our society. As soon as there is an imbalance, they create trouble. If there is a conflict, there are *zeyshi.* They explore all the cracks in society and try to force them open. People in outer circles support them quite a bit."

And that was the odd dichotomy of Coldi society, how they could, at any one time, support the existing structures of power and support those mechanisms trying to pull those structures down.

I tried again, "But what about the backed-up commands from Ezhya that should have kept everything running as normal?"

Asha said, "Should have, yes, but obviously stability hasn't lasted that long. Something appears to have happened, and we're still trying to establish what. In any case the guards tracked the false information about food parcels in Third Circle back to the Inner

Circle. Something in the command hub has been giving nonsense orders."

"Ezhya's command hub?"

"So it seems."

I asked, "Would that be a malfunctioning part of the routines he left running or something new?"

Asha replied, "Hard to tell from a distance, although it's too early for his regular routines to start malfunctioning."

I felt a chill at this statement. I had understood us to have some time before Ezhya's order routines would start falling apart, and now it looked like we didn't. I asked, "Can anyone stop the faulty routines?"

"They can't, because as happens when the Chief Coordinator is away, the Inner Circle has gone into lockdown and the guards are under strict orders to let no one in."

"What has caused this?"

"Could be anything." I sensed he'd said about as much as he was going to say, or at least with Natanu in our cabin, or maybe to me full stop.

I became more worried then.

"There is no need for panic." Asha said, his voice decisive. "The airport is out, but we'll have other places to land."

"You're not planning to set us down in Beratha?" Nicha said. He met my eyes. That would pretty much ruin our plan. Beratha was on the other continent and its climate was definitely too hot for me to visit.

"At the army compound in Athyl," Asha said.

"That's in Second Circle. There is no train anywhere close." Thayu's face was concerned.

Asha held up his hand to ask for silence. "We'll walk, or commandeer transport. Listen. This is our plan." Seriously, which father used *chi* pronouns to speak to a group of people that included his children? "All communication we've had so far comes from Taysha. He has access to the radio transmissions we've made to the surface. I'm sure he knows that we're coming and he knows who is on board this craft. He will also know that Ezhya is not, since Ezhya has not communicated with the Inner Circle since the Exchange outage. He will suspect or know that we have the key and that this is the reason we're coming back now instead of waiting for the Exchange to return to full function. He would also know that I am coming back because I cannot risk upheaval in the armed forces." His dark eyes met mine. "He will want to meet us. I believe you wanted to discuss something with him?"

"I wanted to see Risha, not Taysha." I didn't want to engage in any kind of discussion with that man, certainly not in Thayu's presence.

"Taysha and Risha are *zhaymas,* so one will know what the other knows."

Yes, but I don't want to speak to that man! Wasn't Risha Asha's immediate superior? Well, I suppose he had no control over communication. Damn.

I blew out a breath through my nostrils. "I suppose that if Risha is unavailable, I'd have to speak with Taysha—"

"Good. We will request an audience with him on your behalf. He'll be most interested in meeting you, the man who forced him to capitulate his contract with the lady. He has already said so."

I glanced at Thayu. She frowned at me, and a seed of anger grew in me. There should be no need for her to face this man. If he still had any gripe with me, and goodness knew I'd paid him enough already, the standard protocol was to raise the issue with me. "I will go and talk to him about the *zeyshi* or about keeping the command hub running, nothing else."

He gave me a sharp look. "You'll find that he will have different ideas."

He had already spoken with Taysha? Where was Risha and why couldn't I speak to him?

I said, "I don't care what ideas he has. I'll talk to him about Ezhya and about the *zeyshi* claim, if he knows anything about it." *Forced him to capitulate his contract with the lady.* He was talking about his own daughter, for fuck's sake. What was more, Asha *had* agreed to me taking over the contract.

He went on, oblivious. "He will invite you, but he will know it's *shenya.*" A lie for political purposes. "It will be very polite and genteel. I will send two of Ezhya's guards with you."

"Thayu and Nicha will come with me." If I had to face this manipulative arsehole, I wanted only them with me. And what was with this *I will send?* Whose idea was this whole expedition anyway?

"Taysha expects us to come and try something with the command key. He knows we have it. He will think I have it and he will think that I have taken you as a curiosity to distract him. He will play the game and meet you while he directs his best guards to stop us. We will pretend to have the key and we will initially go to my quarters and stay there. They will be puzzled and hang around to see what we're doing next. They might come to question us, in which case we will deal with them, or they might grow bored and leave. After that, we will try to enter the building through another entrance."

A chill crept over my back. In Coldi parlance, *dealing with them* usually involved weapons and dead bodies.

"Meanwhile, you will talk to him until we provide a distraction. I won't tell you what it is, but you will know when it happens. From Taysha's quarters it is only up the next floor to the command hub. Once Taysha ends the discussion and is forced to react to the situation created by us, you will walk up the stairs and into the hub."

The plan was not bad and probably close to something I would have thought up myself, but the way he was ordering me about annoyed me. It annoyed me that I had repeatedly said that I wanted to see Risha, not Taysha, but everyone seemed to have ignored that request. "I want to say one thing, though."

He glanced aside.

"I request to go to the on-board communication hub to speak to Taysha and tell him about this visit. *I* should talk to him and make the arrangement. If you do it, it's going to look like I work for you. I work for Ezhya, not for him, not for you. I should act on Ezhya's behalf. If I were in an association, I would not take orders from anyone except Ezhya."

Asha said nothing. His face was blank as always and I could only guess that underneath that mask, he had to be annoyed at this upstart who not only cost his family money, ran off with his daughter, refused to back down and was much more chummy with his big boss than he was. And why did Thayu look so much like him?

"We'll see," he said. "But Thayu and Nicha can't come. We don't want to make Taysha nervous. He knows both of them too well." He sounded irritated. Judging by how Thayu and Nicha treated him, he was used to being obeyed without question, even by his own children. Worse, he was probably right.

He unclipped his tether as if the discussion was finished.

I wasn't finished, though. I pushed myself across the room so that I hit the door before he did. I stopped the bounce back by grabbing the handle to the emergency hatch. There. I'd had a lot of practice doing this over the past week.

"I want a reply to my request. I want to speak to Taysha as soon as possible to discuss my visit." Goddamn royal-I.

I met his gaze squarely, wiping the sweat from my lip. A vent in the wall blew hot air over my face. It was only going to get hotter.

He nodded, pushed off so he floated around me and floated back towards the door. "Can I get through?" It was phrased as question, but it was an order.

On his ship, at his mercy, I could do nothing except move aside.

Inside, I was seething.

He thumbed the lock code to the door and left us, his face still impassive.

Shit.

Not only was I going to have to go into that building alone with some guards who didn't know me and didn't owe me anything, I wasn't handling the father-in-law too well, either.

I glanced at Nicha and Thayu, and none of us seemed to know what to say. I did not want to be bait for Taysha, putting my relationship with Thayu up as a discussion point to do it. *The man who forced him to capitulate his contract with the lady.* What the actual fuck. I didn't want to have to tell her about the horse-trading I'd been forced to do over her with this foul man, and I especially didn't want to tell her just how much I'd paid to buy out her contract. She'd be horrified. Hell, *I* was horrified.

I re-settled in my hammock, wrapping the stiff outer support layer around me so that I didn't float away.

"You know Asha's going to challenge, don't you?" The voice that broke the tense silence was rich and undeniably female. Natanu pushed herself into a sitting position, as well as one can sit in zero-g. Of course she hadn't been asleep at all and she'd heard everything.

Thayu gave her a sharp glance without looking into her eyes. "So? That's his right. Are *you* going to challenge?"

Nicha let out a low hiss.

For a moment I thought there would be a fight, but Natanu said, her tone surprisingly flat, "I gave up the key, didn't I?"

The object in question felt like it was burning a hole through the inner pocket of my jacket.

Natanu snorted. "Unlike all you people, I sit still. I watch. I do not enter a fight unless I am pretty sure I can win." She met my eyes. "Unlike some of us."

Thayu said, "In case you haven't noticed, he's doing his best to help us. He doesn't even need to do it at all."

Nicha warned, "Thay', please."

I pushed myself from my hammock and floated in the middle of the dorm room. "Please, can we stop making allegations?"

Natanu looked me straight into the eyes, her expression humourless. "Allegations will be made, whether we take part in the making or not. No matter what Asha's told you, he intends to challenge, because Taysha will challenge and he cannot let that challenge go unanswered."

In all truth, I didn't know what Asha wanted. I just assumed that because he agreed to carry us, he supported our action at least somewhat. Or, I hoped he would.

"Well, *we* all want to maintain the current power structure, right?"

No one said anything.

I glanced at Nicha and Thayu. *Come on, help me.* But I knew they weren't going to, not while facing someone far superior. Thayu had already tested the boundaries by speaking up against Natanu.

And Natanu had never said that she wouldn't challenge. If she wanted to make a grab for Ezhya's position, she didn't need the key.

I felt like punching the walls, but with the lack of gravity, I didn't even know which the walls were, and punching walls, floor or ceiling would just make me bounce through the cabin.

Nowhere in this tiny shoe box did we have a place where the three of us could talk and not be overheard by Ezhya's guards. Even my feeder was useless here because there was no Exchange and on-board networks didn't support many of its features, including direct lines into other feeders. Or, more likely, didn't give us access to those features.

Did Asha speak the truth? Was Natanu's promise worth anything?

Was anyone free of this instinct to dominate?

Where was Risha?

Thayu and Nicha were probably too far down the hierarchy to be in contention for the leadership, but everyone else around us seemed to consider themselves in the running. And while they were prowling around and eying each other, they'd given me the hot potato. Increasingly, I was feeling like everyone could pounce on me at any moment.

WE BUSIED ourselves with preparing dinner.

Even though the ship had a food lab, the food on board consisted mostly of freeze-dried things that had been packed and stored so long that it was impossible to determine what they had been. Most of the rations were red-coded, so the choice in diet was even more boring for me, not to mention bland. When heated up, Thayu's dinner smelled a lot nicer than mine, but I knew better than to try to eat some.

We'd just finished eating when the door opened and a crew member came in. It was a woman I hadn't seen before, one of the lower-ranked ship crew.

She looked at everyone in the room, stopping at me. "Delegate. Come."

I glanced at Thayu and Nicha. Should they come with me?

She pre-empted that with, "Only you can come."

"For what purpose?"

Asha was going to *deal with me* to keep me or both his children in line. He'd been severely put out by my use of pronouns and my demands. He was going to demand compensation—

Stop it, Delegate. There was no reason to believe that he would do any of those things.

Living cooped up in this tin can was getting to me.

Heart thudding, I followed the woman out the solid door. Two other crew members waited outside. They both wore flight pressure suits and one wore a jacket over the top that had attachments for monitoring equipment. As far as I knew, these jackets were worn by weapons operators.

We floated through the ship, and I was once more reminded that moving around so much after eating was not a good idea.

We passed through a long corridor that had doors on all four walls: sides, ceiling and floor. While obviously Exchange-enabled, this ship was designed for deep space. There had often been rumours at *gamra* about Asto's spy ships shadowing important delegations and monitoring industrial projects from the cover of deep space. At various points in time, groups of delegates would rally in favour of the setting up of more space telescopes to pick up this kind of activity. Within *gamra*, Asto was the major force, but it absolutely owned deep space, and this ship was one of those vehicles for that domination. I eyed the doors on either side of the passage. Most of them were unmarked, although some had security panels or warning lights. I suspected that more than a few would be locked, providing access to the ship's engines, its reactor or weapons systems. For all I knew, the ship possessed an Exchange sling, which was said to cut out the need for a local Exchange reference point. That meant that there had to be some kind of Exchange core on board. All of which meant that the Asto military probably had an unhealthy interest in the activities of the Aghyrians in Barresh. Alternate Exchange systems, some of them suitable for use as weaponry. Press a button on one planet and an explosion happens on another planet.

I shivered. Damn, being shut up in this tin can *really* started getting to me. The fact that we were here, in mid-space, meant that the Asto military *had* no alternate Exchange system, right? Because otherwise they would have used it, right?

At the end of the passage we came to a tube with metal rungs that led at right angles to the corridor. It was dark inside, with thin rings of blue light encircling the passage. The tube was only wide enough for one person and we pulled ourselves through. The female crew member first, one of the guards second, then me and then the crew member with the weapons control vest.

One of the blue rings flashed when I passed. No doubt assessing the risk I posed. Scanning me for weapons, or some such.

The top of the tube opened out into a larger area which was quite dark, but a strange glow of light hit the wall just outside the tunnel. I followed my guides out of the tube and, to my great surprise, onto the ship's bridge.

I floated in mid-air, taking in the huge banks of controls, the large window or viewscreen at the far end, where the glow of a huge half-lit planet hung to the left.

The rest of the sky was dotted with millions of pinpricks of stars.

Oh, wow. Look at that view. Look at the detail of shadows and mountain ridges on Asto. Look at the cloud formations billowing into the atmosphere.

In my amazement, I let go of the handholds and floated through the cabin. One of my guides took my elbow and attached my magnetic tether to the wall.

Don't be dumb, Delegate.

There were at least six people in this room, all of them strapped behind their work stations. Two of them sat at the very front row of controls. The next bench back held four work stations.

The single chair behind that, on a slightly elevated platform, was Asha's. He sat leaning back, with a small portable console on his lap. He glanced up briefly and met my eyes, still emotionless.

"Use that terminal," Asha said, gesturing at an island bench to the left-hand side of the room, unoccupied.

I floated across, trying not to hit anything this time. I aimed for the seat, which was more like the seat of a bike with straps on the "pedals" to keep the occupant in place.

The bench had two screens and a whole bevy of input controls.

Both screens were empty. The three crew members who had come to get me took up positions between me and the front two rows, obscuring much of my view of the window. Heaven forbid I might actually see anything on the pilots' controls. Little pinpricks of blue or white on black screens that would tell me so much, pardon the sarcasm. I suppose I might also see the weapons station on the other side of the cabin.

One of the crew handed me an earpiece.

When I attached it, I was blasted in the ear by a burst of static.

Ouch. Asha fiddled with his controls and spoke in his earpiece.

The static in my ear died and a fairly clear voice said, "So. You come to visit us, hmmm? Making history for yourself, bringing in the hordes of foreigners."

Taysha. Damn it, even his tone was patronising, just like I would have expected from his correspondence.

"In light of the Aghyrian claim on Asto, it has been brought to my attention that a meeting was warranted." Only the most formal pronouns would do, even if to show how much I disliked his manner. We were into bluff territory now.

The time delay had decreased a lot and I didn't have to wait too long for his reply.

"Ha, the Aghyrian claim. The cowards won't talk to us themselves, and send a foreign diplomat? No, no, no, I don't fall for that. I would very much like to know what matters *you* could like to discuss with *me*."

Actually, I really don't want to talk with you.

I'd made an attempt to be polite, but his tone and pronouns rattled with belligerence. *He's only needling you.* He'd done the same in his correspondence, talking about Thayu in the crudest possible way.

"Ezhya has sent me as envoy, because I look after these matters at *gamra*. I had hoped to speak to Risha and I hoped he could put me in contact with the *zeyshi* claimants."

I waited for the reply. It seemed odd that no one had mentioned Risha, even more so because he was Asha's superior.

Was I imagining it, or did the silence last longer than the previous ones? "You choose to do this now, at this time of crisis?"

"The next sitting of the assembly is in one solar. It is of utmost importance that I prepare my address to the assembly and that I have input from all the parties. We've attempted to contact the claimants, but haven't been successful. I was assured that Risha deals with the matter of the *zeyshi* and that he can help me locate the people I need to listen to."

They called this *shenya*, mutually-accepted bullshit that was a cover for something else. It was seen as a rude thing, but a skilled leader or businessman could hold an entire conversation in *shenya*, get his meaning across and not once mention the actual subject of the conversation. Coldi often appended the adjective *shenya* to non-Coldi conversation. Dishonest, something done by non-Coldi bureaucrats, whom everyone despised.

His reply came with a snort. "You can discuss this with me also. As it is, I have a wish to see you. I shall be expecting you. I shall look forward to seeing you."

Did he really? To do what? Poke me around a bit more? Show off what he did with all the money I paid him for Thayu's contract?

He signed off and I relaxed fists that, without my realising it, I'd been clenching so tight that my nails had made impressions in my palms. I peeled off the earpiece, feeling drained.

I glanced sideways at Asha, who regarded me as if he wanted to say, *There. Happy now?*

He nodded, briefly. There was something in his expression that I hadn't seen before, but it was gone just as quickly.

I wanted to ask him why I couldn't see Risha, but I began to suspect that the subject was *zharu,* under a gag order from Risha himself, and I'd had enough of dealing with rudeness masquerading as honesty for today.

I let the three crew members escort me back to our prison, becoming increasingly certain that I'd made the biggest mistake in my life.

In our section, I found Thayu in the tiny hallway using foldout fitness equipment that we were all meant to use every day but that I found offered too much resistance for my weak, non-Coldi muscles. She was panting and her face was sweaty.

She smiled when I came in. It was impossible to get into the room without going really close to her. I bent to her and kissed the skin on her neck as I passed. Coldi sweat smelled of dry earth and baked salt.

"What was that about?" she asked softly, running a sweaty hand over my cheek.

"I spoke to Taysha to officially announce our visit." I shrugged. The whole thing had a feel about it as if it was a token gesture from Asha to appease this annoying human. "I wanted to speak to Risha, but I don't know what's happening there—"

"Spoke to Taysha—where?"

"In the communications hub, I guess."

"He let you up to the bridge?" Her eyes widened.

"Um—yeah?"

"The real bridge, with the control benches and the window?"

"I guess that's what it was." Was that special?

"Do you know that non-military people never get to fly on military ships or get anywhere near command centres?"

"Not even you and Nicha?"

"Not even us. And you just walk in, invite yourself and . . ." She spread her hands. "This is not the first time you've managed to pull that off. How do you do that?"

"Um . . ." How was I supposed to know? "It's amazing what you can get when you act as if it's the most normal thing in the world."

"I could never do anything of the sort."

That was part of the Coldi make-up, too. I'd tried to get Thayu and Nicha to be more assertive, but as long as I spoke to people who were their superiors, they would never do as much as ask a question. Thayu making snarky comments to Natanu was about as far as I'd seen either of them challenge a superior.

"Do you know that your father is planning anything we don't know about?"

She shook her head.

"Does he ever talk to you?"

"Not about his work, no. I don't see him a lot anymore. You can ask him."

Why not you? "He doesn't seem to like me very much."

That brought a look of utter surprise to her face. She stopped moving. "Why do you think that?"

"Well, he . . ." I shrugged. I was going to say, "He's rude and ignores me," but that was the sort of thing a high-ranking Coldi would do and she wouldn't think that was unusual. The fact that Asha had allowed me on this ship—with Ezhya's guards whom he didn't trust—probably said more about his opinions of me than his manner did, even if he was one of the most overbearing, authoritative, arrogant dicks that I'd been forced to interact with recently.

I balled my fists in my pockets with sheer frustration. What sort of relationship did this man have with his children? What sort of father would use formal language to his children? Sometimes Coldi family relationships looked like ours, sometimes they were distant and cold like this. I wanted to ask her why my assessment surprised her so much, but Natanu and the guards in the other room were probably listening, so Thayu would never reply honestly.

Natanu might have promised not to challenge, but I don't think any of us believed her. If it came to a challenge, Thayu and Nicha would be supporting their father. Well, I thought they would, at least. That's how I understood it. If, in fact, this stupid human understood anything about Coldi relationships—and any certainty I'd ever felt in that regard was receding fast.

I didn't fucking understand anything.

And come to that, why did it have to be so fucking hot in this tin can?

8

—————

I WENT back to reading and playing games and staring, bored, into nothingness. Sometimes I caught Thayu looking at me, with a worried expression on her face, and I worried, too. I hadn't mentioned anything about the trouble I'd had getting Taysha to release her contract. I just couldn't bring myself to do so, especially not with our lack of privacy. But she wasn't stupid and knew something bothered me.

When action finally happened, five days later, it came suddenly.

I was attempting to concentrate enough to work on a report when Nicha, in the other hammock, said, "Am I imagining it or did the engine just turn on?"

No, he didn't imagine it, because there was the slightest vibration in the walls that hadn't been there before, and not much later, a faint measure of *gravity* returned. Except of course it wasn't gravity but the backwards-pointing force from deceleration and it pulled me annoyingly to a side of the cabin I had for the past two weeks considered to be the wall. Over the next few hours, this force grew stronger before ebbing again, and then movement alarms came on. *All non-essential crew at their stations.*

The clock next to the door went into countdown.

I strapped myself in my sleeping bag and watched the numbers tick down, hanging sideways. At zero, lights went off, the craft started vibrating and pressure increased in the direction of my feet. The safety harness cut under my arms, but I couldn't even lift my hand enough to stuff a bit of fabric in between my skin and the straps.

I concentrated on my breathing, letting the noise wash over me.

As quickly as it had come on, it was gone, and so was the associated gravity.

There was a clang against the hull and with a weird lurch, another force took over, pushing me against the wall. My borrowed firefighting gear and tanks dangled above me and the wall that held my mat had decided to be the floor.

"We've docked at the orbiting base," Thayu said. Her hammock had conveniently ended up low enough on the wall for her to easily climb out.

She did that while I clumsily wrestled myself out of the harness, resembling a stranded whale. Damn; after only two weeks in zero-g, I felt like I was made of jelly. Thayu helped Nicha down since his sleeping bag now hung high up on the wall. We unstrapped and gathered all our gear near the door. Well, sort of near the door, because the door was now in the ceiling. Fortunately, a set of metal rungs on the wall would allow us to climb up there. I kept glancing at the bags and tanks, expecting them to float away.

Natanu and the other guards sat in the other bedroom, talking in low voices. They didn't seem to have brought any bags and I'd never seen them with any personal gear. Those suits they wore must be self-cleaning or something. They didn't look dirty to me despite two weeks of constant wear, and didn't smell either.

Some time after all movement and clangs had stopped, the door to the rest of the ship slid aside and a crew member stuck his head down into our section.

"You need to disembark here. A shuttle is waiting."

We struggled up a ladder of narrow rungs with all our gear. I was exhausted just getting to the top.

What was it with this damn thing called gravity? I cursed it when it wasn't there and cursed it when it was.

The "here" mentioned by the crew member turned out to be the orbiting military base of which I had heard whispers but never had its existence confirmed. The ship had soft-docked. We entered through a wobbly access tube—I was still unsteady on my feet—to an entrance lock guarded by a couple of troops wearing what I'd come to recognise as security corps uniforms. On the other side of the lock we came onto a walkway so wide that it seemed absurd to my ship-adjusted eyes. There was a railing opposite the tube entrance, but the far wall beyond that was entirely transparent, giving the illusion that we hung in space with nothing to protect us from the vacuum. The pink scarred surface of Asto filled the entire view, appearing overhead from where we stood.

"Whoa." I stopped to re-gain my balance. Another re-assessment of what was up or down. It looked like the planet was about to hit us.

Most of the ship's crew appeared to be staying aboard, but Asha and an entourage of guards were already waiting.

He led us along the walkway to the left at a brisk pace, accompanied by a couple of uniformed people on scooters.

Natanu walked next to me, and Ezhya's other guards in a pyramid formation behind her.

A number of troops stood on either side of the walkway, each in a subservient pose. Had they been waiting for their superior? Did they snap into position as soon as they saw Asha coming?

As we progressed, I noticed that all the doors to the gallery were kept shut. Sometimes personnel stood before the closed door as if to make sure that no one got in. Everyone wore charge guns, and I even spotted some heavier weaponry. They were all watching me and our party.

The walkway was smooth and glass-like and curved gently up, so that the floor disappeared behind the ceiling ahead. The parched landscape outside the window had rotated as we moved over it. Damn, we were in a ring structure so big that the floor of the outer ring seemed almost flat. This had to be one of the largest space stations in existence. Much, much bigger than Midway.

What did they do up here? How many military personnel were stationed here? The thought of the sheer power in this place sent a chill down my spine. I'd never understood why Asto seemed so reluctant about using its military, or even admitting that it existed. Seeing all this made me even more puzzled. They had all this and didn't use it? What was the function of this station in the power structure of Asto?

Next to me, Thayu's face showed absolute wonder, as if her eyes were drinking this all in.

"Have you been here before?" I asked her in Isla.

"No. No one gets to see this."

Which explained Asha's terseness.

And that, when you came to think of it, said a whole lot more about my relationship with a man who, with my non-Coldi senses, I would have described as a first-class arsehole.

A group of military came towards us, and Asha stopped to talk. His guards kept us just out of hearing as if we were naughty children.

The newcomers cast suspicious looks at our ensemble. I suspected Asha had told them about the key.

I pretended to ignore both the conversation and the slight and concentrated on the view.

The station floated directly above a brown and orange tinged ocean. Wind whipped the water into white-capped waves that showed as tiny ripples from here. Sunlight glinted off the surface. On the horizon, coming into view, was Vaneyi, Asto's main continent, with a brown and pink-edged shoreline caked with foam and yellow encrustations, some of which had formed net-like patterns in the shallow areas amongst which there were pools of many different shades of yellow and orange.

The continent was pink, with outcrops of grey, dark brown and red. A narrow mountain ridge bordered the ocean. Small puffs of clouds hung above those mountains and where I could see between them, the land-facing slopes were covered in dark fuzz of vegetation and bright azure lakes.

Deep scores crisscrossed the land beyond the mountains. From directly above, I could see into these natural aquifers, into the green oases within.

The meteorite that had struck the planet more than fifty thousand years ago had broken up. The main piece had formed the crater that was now the roughly circular, virtually land-locked ocean between the continents. The other was a much smaller piece and it had made a neat circular crater in the desert. The land between the crater and the ocean was known as the Crystal wastelands, a hot, sun-baked plain strewn with sharp-edged stones.

The crater lay just to the south of Athyl and was filled with a grey-purple gas that looked almost like water from this height.

It was sulphur-hexafluoride, a heavy gas that occurred on Earth only through industrial activity. It had formed immediately after the meteorite strike, because of the high fluoride content of Asto's rock. It was a strong greenhouse gas and its breakdown was the main trigger in the change washing over the planet.

The mega-city of Athyl lay in the middle of the landmass, like a fat spider in a web of roads. Even from this far up, you could clearly distinguish the circles: concentric rings around the middle of the city, marked by a wall or a stretch of vacant land. Agriculture happened in the aquifers, small strips of brilliant green on the banks of rivers or holding basins. Industry occupied most of the Eighth Circle, followed by administration, education, services, until you reached the Inner Circle, the secret domain of Ezhya and his immediate association. That association which was on the brink of fracture.

"Cory." Thayu touched my arm and held the temperature-retaining suits under my nose.

I tore my gaze away from that amazing landscape.

"It's time to get changed." Her voice was soft and gentle, the way I loved it so much. I wanted to hold her in my arms and kiss her.

"Oh. All right." I took the soft material from her. Our hands touched fleetingly. Sixteen days since I'd last slept next to her, since we'd made love in our bathroom and then again on the bed by the light of Ceren's moons. Those sixteen days screamed at me. If I died on the planet below, would it be without ever touching my wife again?

"You got the key safely tucked away?" she whispered to me when I passed, in Isla.

"I do." Although the weight of it in the pocket of my jacket seemed to be growing.

Everyone in a position of power wanted that thing. How long would it be before someone tried to get it by force?

When the hell was the Exchange going to come back?

I followed her to a small, windowless, featureless room where she helped me into all the gear we had brought. A double temperature retaining suit, the outer layer silver, with the distinctive maroon sash that signified Ezhya's association. The fabric was too long for me, and she had to wrap it a few times around the belt. I looked at myself in the reflection of the wall: too puny for these clothes, already sweating before I even got to this hot place.

"I will look like a cyborg once I put on my tanks and helmet." It was a lame attempt at levity which fell flat.

She ran the tip of her nose over the skin under my ear. I held her with one arm while holding the helmet with the other. I kissed her with all the passion I could muster. Her muscles tensed under my hands. Yes, I knew everyone was waiting for us.

"Do you think I'm stupid to do this?"

"Yes. But also very brave."

"I'm not looking forward to it," I confessed. I wanted to say so much more, like *What is your father up to?* and *What do you know about these guards he's sending with us?* or *Does he hate me or expect anything from me or is he trying to push his own take-over bid?* or even just *Do you know what the fuck is going on?* but this room was probably bugged and we didn't have time for long discussions.

She stroked my hair out of my face. "You'll be fine." But there was no conviction in her voice.

I took a deep breath and let it out slowly. "All right then, let's go."

9

FROM THE LITTLE ROOM, we were escorted down the walkway and through a long corridor to another part of the station facing away from the planet. Via an arched entry hall, we came into a huge docking bay carved across at least six levels into the station, as with the slash of a giant knife. Along both walls, there were hundreds of shuttles stacked in rack-like structures. The ceiling and far side of this hall was open, displaying the brilliant firmament of stars. The view was so clear that it looked like the bay opened directly into space. How on earth would they keep the pressure in?

It was dark and quiet in this hall. Not even our footsteps made any sound, as if the floor and walls absorbed all sound. I had started to wonder if all the ships up there were lifeboats when a craft floated through the middle of the hall and settled into a shelf with a merest minimum of noise. It was strange. I knew those downward jets were noisy, but it was like watching a movie with the sound turned down.

Two of Asha's guards were talking to each other, but I couldn't even hear their voices, let alone understand what they said.

How the hell did they do this?

Thayu mouthed to me, *Sound-cancelling waves.*

I nodded, and now started looking for the equipment emitting those waves; not that I saw any, or knew what to look for.

We went into a lift in the right-hand wall, which took us up to the second level, a broad gallery shrouded in semidarkness with small pinpricks of different-coloured lights.

The craft that was taking us down stood at the end of the gallery, a regular Asto-built shuttle. As with the craft Asha had used to come down to Barresh, the only indication of military ownership was a small emblem next to the door. Lights winked on and off in the darkness, showing that the pilot was going through pre-flight tests. The rest of our party were already on board and strapped in, and once we arrived and climbed in, deck crew shut the door.

The interior of the craft seated about twenty, in rows of two or three. There was a little drink bar at the back and tables interspersed with the seats. To my surprise, most of the craft's side walls were transparent. The cabin looked like a glass bubble.

Every seat had a fold-down display and a comm outlet, now all lifeless.

No sooner had I strapped myself in than we were off. The craft lifted off the gallery and flew slowly into the centre of the hall, then it went straight up and *through* the glass. I could see it glow as the craft pushed its way through it with a slight shudder.

"Biosynthetics," Thayu said in a low voice.

Bacterial glass, just like the screen on my reader, which I'd bought in a regular electronics shop in Rotterdam, but which clearly used Asto technology, no doubt financed through Earth-based banks owned by Asto bigwigs.

I knew that this interlinking of technology was going on. Everyone at Nations of Earth knew it, and there was not a damn thing we could do about it. People wanted fancy new technology. Coldi brought their knowledge, first through refugees, then through businesspeople. And now the two were inextricably intertwined with technology on Earth, especially after the wars.

Those people at *gamra* who said that Earth was being turned into a Coldi colony by stealth were not wrong at all. Whether it was a good or bad thing didn't matter. It was happening. We needed to be aware of it and let our laws reflect it.

As the craft drifted away, I strained in my seat to catch a glimpse of the station; but that part of the cabin had gone opaque and I only saw a shadow tracking over the cloud deck below, which was actually over the top of the cabin as we were flying upside down. I had to close my eyes because the brief foray into normal gravity had already upset my ability to cope with weightlessness.

As soon as we were far enough from the station, the pilot opened all the outside inputs so that we could appreciate the magnificent kaleidoscope of colours. There was not a colour that wasn't represented on the surface of Asto. The oranges and reds of the desert, the yellows and browns of the oceans, the greens of the mountain ranges and the floors of the aquifers, the blues and aquas of the mountain lakes. The landscape was scarred and chemically tainted because of the meteorite impact, but seen from above, deeply beautiful. The sky overhead was deep blue, with a very bright and pale blue speck that was Ceren.

When I had come here with Ezhya, we'd been nowhere near as close. Also, there had been no huge cumulus cloud formations stacking cauliflower upon cauliflower over the mountain ranges. Those clouds hung huge and towering to the west of Athyl, tinged blue with the haze of ozone. It also seemed to me that the atmosphere was clearer, less hazy. It could be the season, but I had a feeling that the planet was changing rapidly.

Re-entry into the atmosphere made the craft shudder. The light and screens were turned off. The transparent sides of the craft glowed with the heat.

I hung onto my chair. This was the part that you didn't get to see on commercial flights. Not only did they have solid walls, but the Exchange didn't take craft this far above the atmosphere.

The orange glow faded and was replaced by the unfamiliar sound of rushing air past the craft's wings. The pilot turned us the right way up.

We flew over endless expanses of canyon-scored desert, plains of featureless pink, with crevasses a few hundred metres deep where water flowed, sometimes above ground and often under it, and where people grew things. The little settlements along these waterways grew more abundant until we came over encampments in the desert, then a jumble of shacks and simple stone buildings. That had to be the Outer Circle. Then we crossed the wall of the Eighth Circle with checkpoints at the entries, followed by neat houses and streets, larger buildings with storage yards that looked like industries.

We flew over a few more circle walls, the density, quality and height of buildings increasing with each one.

I could spot the airport in Third Circle, a huge, multi-pronged building with landing platforms set in a circular arrangement surrounding the main hub, and attached to each other through curving arms that made the structure resemble an opening flower. It was a fabulous building, one of the architectural wonders of the universe, but we weren't going there. Our destination was the army headquarters.

As we neared, the craft sank deeper and deeper into the haze that coloured the sky white at ground level. The vast cloud-stacks over the mountain ranges disappeared from view.

Thayu had been rummaging in our packs and slipped into the seat next to me while doing up her harness. "When we land, we need to get you into a building as soon as possible. We will rush you through as a special guest from Ezhya. After that we'll have to leave you. Sheydu and Veyada are good guards and they'll look after you well." But her eyes said, *They're Ezhya's guards, so don't trust them too much.* "Please, Cory, be careful. Taysha Palayi is not a nice man."

I nodded, fully aware of that fact, probably more than she realised.

"Don't let him know that you have the key."

"I know, we've been over this."

She sighed. "I wish I could come with you."

I did, too. On the other hand, she shouldn't have to face this man now that I'd bought out her contract with him. I still couldn't believe that I'd actually done that. On the other hand, Thayu knew a lot more about him than I did and might pick up on things I missed. Were these two guards going to give me subtle warnings if I was about to do something stupid?

The craft was going down fast. My ears were popping. It felt like we were in freefall. There was no stopping it now.

I clutched my chest through my protective suit, hoping this had been a wise choice, hoping that Ezhya had been right about the temperature.

We flew very low over roofs, many in pink stone, but some were structures of metal or glass.

Forward movement slowed and slowed further. We drifted over a high wall into a complex with many low buildings interlinked with footbridges or covered walkways. The craft's engines were now roaring.

Then the noise stopped, I felt a thump and the only sounds were the ticking of cooling metal and the rush of air out of the ceiling vents. Thayu rose from her seat first.

"Are you all right?"

I nodded, my mouth too dry to speak. At the press of a button in the arm rest, the safety harness retracted itself into the seat. I pushed myself up, wobbled, dizzy. My legs felt like they were glued to the floor.

"Whoa."

I took a few careful steps. How was that for gravity?

"Be careful."

A few deep breaths. "I'm fine. Really." The first non-Coldi on Asto for thousands of years.

I put on the vest that held the cooling tank. Nicha helped me attach the hoses.

Damn, it was so *heavy*.

Thayu handed me the protective hood and mask, and I slid both over my head. Turned on the coolant supply from the tank. A cool breeze wafted over my face. Beautiful.

"Ready?"

I gave her the thumbs up.

Someone had opened the door and the guards all lined up ready to go. There seemed to be some sort of entry tube involved.

I followed Thayu to the entry hatch. Ezhya's junior female guard and a companion followed us like little ducklings. They had to be Shcydu and Veyada.

The inner door opened, and then the outer door. I walked through, feeling awkward with the weight of all this gear in the high gravity.

The tube was short, nothing more than a covered ramp from the craft entrance to the ground. I took that last step, onto the dry packed earth, with the seriousness of this occasion pressing on me.

Once, many lifetimes ago, a man stepping on the surface of the Moon had said, "One small step for man, a giant leap for mankind." This occasion had that kind of feel about it.

Asto.

Humanity in all its various forms had originated here, on this planet, in a different era.

We had landed on a dry and desolate-looking stretch of concrete-like paving. A number of aircraft like the one that had taken us from the station sat in one corner. Low buildings surrounded the field, some with windows overlooking the area.

And shit, the light. No one can tell you what twenty percent more solar interception means until you see it. If people could go to the surface of Venus, this is what I imagined it would look like.

The air shimmered with heat and the scent of hot stone seeped into my helmet. Like everyone had always said, the sky was white and the ground pink. A few pink-tinged grey clouds hung over the horizon.

To come to Barresh from Earth was a big difference, a huge adjustment. This was something different altogether.

For a moment I staggered, feeling unable to breathe. Somewhere deep inside me, the fear told me: *This is Asto. You're not supposed to be able to survive here.* I sucked deep breaths of cooling air from the tank.

A number of people came towards us. They walked in a classic association formation: one at the front, two behind and four behind that. They wore silver suits and big belts bristling with weapons. They were wider than me, some of them taller. Asha went up to them. They welcomed him with subservient greetings, nods and hand signals.

After a few exchanges of words, he waved me closer.

I went up to the group, facing emotionless expressions which I had come to associate with the Asto military, even though none of these men and women were in uniform.

"The Delegate needs transport. He has an audience with Taysha," Asha said. "It is of utmost importance." I'd never heard military pronouns used before. They were to indicate rank but were only used by military to speak to other military. As if the Coldi pronouns weren't hard enough, they chose to add a whole extra layer to the issue.

Nods all around.

The man at the front of the association said, "Come with us."

I guessed this was the part where our group split up.

I looked over my shoulder at Thayu. I had no idea if she could see my face behind the visor. Probably not. She looked at me, but her gaze searched the faceplate, trying to look beyond her own reflection.

I didn't like the expression of worry I saw in her face.

She put her hand on my arm. "Do you want your travel bag?"

She carried it over her shoulder. It contained spare clothes, shoes, some toiletry items. Nothing I needed for talking to Taysha.

"You carry it. I'd look silly visiting Taysha with all that gear."

"True. All right. I'll see you soon."

"Yeah." The sound of my voice echoed back at me inside the helmet.

I lifted a hand by way of goodbye and followed these new guards. Ezhya's two junior guards were behind me. Thayu's touch lingered on my arm.

Belatedly, I thought I understood part of Asha's reason for not sending Thayu and Nicha with me. They clearly weren't bodyguards, and if they came, Asha would have to lend me four of his guards so as to send me with a complete association, and that would make a sizeable hole in anything he might plan to do.

Creating a disturbance required more people than talking. I should have thought of that earlier. Stupid.

Still, as I crossed the paving, I wished I could see where the rest of the group was going, especially Natanu and Asha. The helmet's visor restricted my vision and turning my head with the hoses and the weight of the helmet might make me trip.

When I caught a glimpse of the party, they were so far away that I couldn't make out Thayu and Nicha anymore. I was really on my own.

The air was full of noise of my own breathing.

The heat seared the inside of my nose even under the mask. I pulled the cloth of the hood up to close the gap between the helmet and my face, but could still smell the hot-stone scent that I often smelled on Thayu's skin. It was engrained in the air. The whole planet smelled like it.

Sweating, and heart pounding, I followed my guides in the direction of one of the buildings, a low blocky and functional structure made of pink stone with square windows at regular intervals.

In front of the building waited a bullet-shaped vehicle, and this was where the out-of-uniform troops took us. One of them opened the door. I stumbled up the steps into a typical maroon interior. Whoa, that gravity really dragged me down.

My head was reeling. Not coping very well right now. Inside the cabin it was even hotter than outside. Sweat trickled over my back under my layers of clothing.

I dropped into the nearest seat and I fiddled with the setting on my tank to increase the cool air flow.

And I was meant to survive this expedition?

One of the local men took the controls of the vehicle. Ezhya's male guard Veyada sat next to me and the junior female guard Sheydu sat opposite me. She was of Thayu's build, a bit more heavy than normal for a Coldi woman but quite a bit older than Thayu, evidenced by white streaks in her hair. Her flat chest told me that she'd never had children. Many high-ranking Coldi forfeited their two allocated children.

The vehicle started moving and left the military compound through a forbidding gate with sentries on both sides. We entered a wide street of the Second Circle lined on both sides by magnificent buildings: made out of stone, blocky or domed, with glass rooms, elaborate towers, metal support arches, cables, leaf-shaped slate, carbon fibre plating, and those were just the materials I recognised. There were dozens I couldn't identify. I'd only ever seen pictures of the rich and varied architecture of the inner circles of Athyl. Even in those pictures the arches, the domes, the blocky or flowing and elegant structures had amazed me. Reality made it so much more wonderful. No two buildings were the same. Glass buildings with clean lines stood next to stone buildings with intricate carving and steel structures with impossible curves. And then the colours. The stone was mostly pink or ochre, but doors, fittings and window frames had every imaginable colour, including lurid purple, bright green and sky blue.

After passing into the First Circle, the houses grew even more intricate, and then the Inner Circle complex came into view.

Seen from a distance, the building looked like a pile of domes stacked in a pyramid, built on what was probably a hill in the landscape that was now completely hidden underneath the structure. There were towers and balconies and stairs, all interlinked and stacked so that no two corners, entrances or sections of wall were the same.

We had to leave the carriage at the Inner Circle gate, so we went into the searing heat and through another checkpoint with humourless guards. They spoke to Ezhya's guards in subservient manner and eyed me and all my gear like I was something out of a curiosity cabinet—which I probably was.

On the other side we had to cross a wide and glaring expanse of paving. The heat radiated through the soles of my boots. I glanced at the little temperature gauge I had attached to my belt. Fifty-eight.

Someone had mentioned that this was a mild day.

We went up a wide set of stone stairs and into a hall.

Fortunately, it was cooler inside.

We walked through a long curving corridor, where natural light filtered through a semitransparent ceiling. The material of the floor was soft and bouncy. People in uniform rushed past us, disappearing into the constant curve.

A group of people came the other way, wearing silver suits with splashes of red. Someone shouted an order I didn't catch. My guards stopped, too.

"Who are these people, *mashara?*"

"They're Taysha's guard," Veyada said. "Don't get involved if you don't have to. This will be between guards."

I had no intention of doing so, but the key in my pocket felt heavier. The suit was doing a good job of keeping me alive, but if this was a mild day, I didn't think I wanted to know what a hot day was like.

There were seven guards in classic formation: the leader first, the seconds following to the sides, the thirds at the back. All guards wore silver suits with a thin red belt, not the sash. The suits were sleeveless, the guards' arms tanned and muscled.

In their midst walked a stocky man in a maroon robe. I had never seen him in the flesh but recognised him from the pictures.

Taysha Palayi.

10

DAMN IT. Straight into the fire.

Trust a Coldi to face a situation head-on.

Taysha was a lot shorter than I'd imagined. His face was unusually narrow, with the darker skin which I'd heard was more common on the island of the second major city, Beratha. His hair was, in typical Coldi style, tied back behind his head with not a wisp of hair out of place. Was it the visor or was his hair duller than that of the average Coldi? He had small, deep-set eyes with a fair bit of gold flecking.

He wore a loose robe with flowing sleeves that hid most of his arms. His hands looked quite young, and he wore the traditional rings and jewels of an important clan figure. I couldn't stop the thought: had he bought any of those things with my money?

He addressed the guards. "So. *Mashara,* you bring our foreign visitor. Let me see him." His voice sounded belligerent and his pronouns were commanding. I associated vhi forms with talking to young students or children. Condescending, really.

Ezhya's female guard Sheydu greeted him in the subservient position. "This is *gamra* delegate Cory Wilson, representing Ezhya."

She stepped aside a fraction so that he could see me, and I sure as hell wasn't going to bow for him. I might have considered it had he been polite to the guards, but not now.

He eyed me up and down.

"You." His voice was disdainful. That was a very accusatory *you*. "You thought you could step in the history books, huh?"

"I have come for a reason." My voice echoed back at me. I wish I didn't have to speak through that blasted helmet. What would happen if I took it off? Fifty-eight degrees? Maybe not.

He came towards us and stopped a few paces away from me. Didn't bow. Looked me in the eye through the visor. I held my breath. When I had met Nicha, he confessed later that his dominance instinct had fired. It didn't often happen facing non-Coldi people, but it seemed I was one of those exceptional cases where it did happen sometimes. Just my luck.

"Ha, you're a cocky one." Taysha snorted and turned around, retreating to the company of his guards.

"I was hoping to see Risha."

"You're out of luck."

"Is he out?" Risha's continued absence bugged me perhaps more than it should, since no one else seemed to care. Was he stuck in Beratha, perhaps?

"Of sorts. But come. I had rather not let you faint, because that would mean I'd have to forego your interesting replies to the questions I'm going to ask you." His voice held a hint of laughter—and laughing in Coldi was a rude thing.

He waved his hand.

Without a word, his company turned and set off in the direction from which they had come.

I glanced sideways to the female guard Sheydu. Her face showed no emotion.

"We follow?" I asked her.

She nodded and we set off. I couldn't say I liked the wary expression on her face. This woman was hard-faced and wiry, older than most guards. She had probably been with Ezhya most of her life and I should pay attention to her cues, especially where Taysha was concerned.

While we walked, I noticed there had been a subtle change in the exposed skin on her face since we'd arrived. The surface had gone matte and velvet-like as if she wore a crapload of powder. I'd heard that this would happen on Asto. This was another adaptation of the Coldi people, in addition to their ability to vary their body temperature. The skin became really rough so that it had more surface area to lose heat.

Taysha and his party led us through a maze of corridors to an underground station. Here, Taysha commandeered a vehicle for us, a sleek, bullet-shaped carriage that, like the trains in Barresh, seemed to come with its own engine. Through wide doors and a floor that adjoined the platform so precisely that there was hardly a gap, we entered into a spacious interior. Cloth-covered seats lined both walls and we sat down, Taysha and his guards on one side and our group on the other. I'm sure it was no accident that Taysha sat opposite me. While the doors shut and the carriage started moving, he took in each of us, letting his gaze rest on Sheydu.

I felt her tense next to me.

He said nothing, just stared at her.

She avoided his gaze by looking at her hands in her lap, but her back was straight and she held her shoulders in a tense position.

Taysha had a full association of guards with him, all seven female. Two of them sat between Taysha and the window; two more on the other side of the aisle. One stood behind us in the aisle, another ahead. The last one, probably the leader, sat across the aisle from Sheydu.

She had the distinctive cross-hatched scars on her upper arm that marked her as having been a member of the Hedron guard. Hedron, the world settled by *zeyshi*. My gaze lingered on her, but not too long. These Hedron guards were said to be highly-strung and dangerous.

Five of the other guards were mothers, as I could tell because their breasts were developed. None, except for the ex-Hedron guard, had Natanu's build. The others were more slender, more female.

So, the shapely creatures were supposed to be guards, huh?

Just the thought of this creep getting his hands on Thayu made me angry. She must have been desperate when she agreed to that contract.

The uncomfortable silence lingered. Sheydu fidgeted. Taysha stared at her as if undressing her with his eyes. The only sound in the cabin was the whine of the wheels on the rails. I wanted to tell him to stop staring at Sheydu. I wondered why he'd come to meet me if he wasn't going to say anything.

To get me away from other people, including Risha?

I was hot. I was angry. Neither were a good state to be in, if my experience was anything to go by. Damn, I wanted Nicha and Thayu here.

A few stations zipped past, with people waiting on the platforms. The train weaved its way between tall buildings, underneath underpasses, over streets. All of this I only saw out the opposite window, because I didn't want to look away from that man. I didn't want him to think I was afraid of him or that I would back down from whatever he was going to throw at me.

The train slowed down approaching the huge Inner Circle complex. From all the time I'd spent studying the upper levels of Asto's society, I recognised the tower of the Inner Circle and the domed area at the very top that was the Chief Coordinator's residence. The hub where I needed to take the key was up there.

The train shot into a tunnel and came to a halt not much later. The doors slid open.

I followed Taysha and his party onto the platform which was in an underground hall. The cam in my helmet showed the air to be quite humid here and reasonably cool. Only forty degrees.

I unclipped the helmet and lifted it off my head. Then I took off the mask.

A hot breeze that smelled of wet stone wafted across my face. My hair felt damp from sweat. Tangled strands had escaped my ponytail and stuck to the skin of my cheeks and neck. I teased them off with my fingers, rolling my head. That helmet was not very comfortable.

The ceiling and walls of the station consisted of exposed rough-hewn rock. That and the humid breeze made me think that this passage was part of the system of underground aquifers.

We walked across a long platform, past a number of bullet-shaped carriages similar to the one that had brought us here, all standing idle.

A few screens hanging over the platform showed messages about delays and cancellations. We were the only people at the station. I had no doubt that this place would normally be buzzing with activity. It was hard to comprehend that the absence of one person could have such a huge impact on society, but there it was in front of me: the evidence that one person was the glue that held all these loyalty networks together.

The thought chilled me. How long would people be happy to stay home and wait for Ezhya to return?

A group of silver-clad guards came towards us out of the passage that led off the platform. A ripple of alertness went through Taysha's guards. They rearranged themselves into defensive positions, in front and to the sides and back of their leader. Sheydu and Veyada walked closer to me, both with alert looks on their faces.

When we came closer, the other group split and the members lined up on both sides of the passage. All of those guards also wore the thin maroon belts, but the patches on their chests were different to those worn by Taysha's guards. I made a guess that these troops belonged to Risha.

Taysha ordered his own guards, "At ease."

The guards' faces showed no emotion.

We progressed between the two lines of the group in tense silence. None of the newcomers moved, although their eyes followed us all the way down the passage. They didn't look at Taysha, but they sure looked at me.

Phew. What was all that about?

The corridor opened out into a well-lit hall where we went up a sweeping staircase into a circular hall with a number of doors.

A pompous affair it was, too, with white stone floor and walls, thick doors and a high ceiling. A hall where our footsteps sounded like thunder, a hall that meant to say, *You are puny—enter at your own risk.*

Taysha went through a door at the far end. A house servant stood next to this door, and he stopped me when I tried to follow.

What the heck?

The man didn't meet my eyes. He looked like a doll dressed up in a stiff maroon coat with gold piping.

Sheydu said in a low voice, "We need to be invited in first, Delegate, after we have freshened up. *Mashara* advises taking off as much gear as you can."

So, things were going to be that formal, huh?

On the table next to the servant stood a bowl with water and a stack of cloths.

I unclipped the hoses to my helmet, which I had carried on my arm, and lifted the vest with the tank off my back. There was a slit window next to the door where we had come in. The wind chose this moment to blow a gust of sharp tangy desert air into the room. Holy shit, that was hot. I coughed.

Sheydu gave me a concerned look. She spoke softly. *"Mashara* will take the tank in with us if you need it."

"I'll be fine." I dragged my hands across my face, half-expecting to find blisters on my skin.

"We can't risk you fainting on the job."

I shrugged, feeling both annoyed and flustered. Everyone kept saying that.

But I didn't protest when she picked up the tank and the helmet.

"Do I take off anything else?" I could feel the sweat rolling down my stomach. Not coping very well with the heat all of a sudden.

"The outer layer only, if you feel you have to."

Yes, I did. I had to appear strong and in control in front of this man.

I undid my belt and almost dropped it. Then I undid the arm bracket that held my gun, slid it from my arm and looped the belt through it.

Now I was free to peel off the suit and found that, indoors, it didn't seem to do much against the heat anyway. The material fell to the floor like a silver puddle.

The servant eyed it, but didn't move. *Protocol, Delegate, observe the protocol.* Not that there was any-bloody-where to hang it. Normal visitors here didn't, of course, wear such ridiculous overgarments. Never mind that normal visitors could stand the heat outside.

I glanced around, hopeful of finding some piece of furniture to hang my suit. The servant still didn't move. The dark eyes didn't even blink, and the glistening green blue and pink highlights in his hair didn't twinkle with the merest movement.

I spread my hands. My eyes met Veyada's while he was washing his hands in the bowl. *Where the fuck do I put it?*

He dried his hands on one of the towels and took the suit from me, hanging it over his arm. Well that was embarrassing. They were my guards, not clothes horses.

I stuck my hands in the bowl, quickly, because I remembered that the water might be too acidic to be safe. My hands tingled when I dried them, so maybe the water wasn't safe, or maybe my senses were just too screwed-up to be of much use.

Apart from the table, the hall contained a single piece of furniture: the obligatory long and narrow table against the far wall with the customary decorative arrangement on it: a couple of simple rocks in a bowl on one side, and a vase with a single closed flower in the other.

I had learned to observe those signs that influential people put on display for visitors to indicate their mood. The rocks signified something uncultured, probably me. The closed flower was no bud but a flower that had finished. It could signify that the time for business was past, or that he waited for me, but I failed to show.

If so, it wasn't a good start.

I missed Thayu's sharp interpretation of these arrangements.

The door to Taysha's domain opened. Another servant gestured for us to come in.

I walked first, with the two guards behind me.

The official room was smaller than I expected. Low couches stood around a square table. The carpet and all the fabric upholstery was in the same maroon colour. I recognised this setup from Ezhya's room in the *gamra* complex. It was about the same temperature, too, and the same colour. I didn't get the Coldi's obsession with maroon. Their eyes didn't see the colour red and my lenses showed that without red, the colour was an ugly kind of purplish black.

I stopped on the rug in the middle of the floor, and held myself in the traditional subservient position—looking down, my hands by my sides, hating every bit of this, but I could not risk upsetting him.

Taysha gestured for me to sit down.

I sat on the couch, feeling the fabric of the bottom layer of my suit stick to me.

Sheydu and Veyada went to stand behind me. Both of them still wore Ezhya's red sash and I wondered what they made of being forced to act like subordinates to a man and association they normally far outranked.

A servant came in with a tray. This was yet another woman. She wore a long and flowing dress of a type I'd only ever seen Coldi wear for official occasions and showing more skin than was normal for Coldi women in professional positions.

She bowed to Taysha first, then to me, then his guards and, finally, Ezhya's guards despite their higher rank. Both Veyada and Sheydu refused the drink on her tray.

There was probably a message in that.

Then the woman came to me and held out the tray. I hesitated. The glasses held a pale yellow liquid that looked safe enough. There was also a plate with parcels wrapped in fried pastry and fried curly things that didn't quite look the same as the fried worms that were so popular at the markets in Barresh.

The most important warning about red-coded food was: stay away from the mushrooms. Which was pretty useless advice when food had been processed.

Was this food safe or red-coded?

Sheydu leaned over my shoulder and studied the plate. She said while not meeting Taysha's eyes, "The Delegate eats only green-coded food."

Taysha pursed his lips. "I have not catered for delicate stomachs."

The woman retreated.

When she passed him, he beckoned her over. He took a parcel from the tray and stuffed it in his mouth and loaded a few more pastries on a small plate. I sat as quietly as I could, kept my face as unemotional as I could. All right, the game was on. Let's play it.

In silence, the servant left again, her hips swaying.

Taysha took his time eating and said nothing while he did so. I had to forcefully remind myself that I was in no hurry. The less I spoke with him, the better. Asha, Natanu and the others would create their diversion soon, and maybe I would not have to speak with him at all. Wishful thinking.

Apart from the couches and table, the room contained a glass-fronted cabinet against the back wall which contained a number of clay pots with sigil-like inscriptions—I hated to think what was in them, somebody's ashes probably—and also various objects that seemed decorative. Vases made of glass and metal, statuettes depicting people and animals, quite a lot of them of voluptuous women, and also a white porcelain coffee cup. In faded paint, on the front, it said, *I [heart] NY.* Next to that stood a garish silver-painted model of the Eiffel Tower, and on the shelf below, a whole army of plastic figurines in garish colours depicting late twentieth or early twenty-first century Earth culture figures. From where I sat, I recognised Superman and Pikachu, but none of the others. All those things had to be more than a hundred years old. I knew that some of those statuettes were worth serious money to collectors.

Taysha put down his plate with a soft and definite *chink* that seemed to end the "eating" part of the visit and start the "talking" part.

"Anyway, Delegate, I am glad that you have decided to come here so that I can meet you in person. There is a desperate need to deal with some business." He waved to the motionless servant in the corner.

The man promptly left the room.

Damn, I really didn't like his choice of pronouns. Accusatory almost.

A different woman now came into the room, bowed to Taysha and then to me. She carried a small tray with a piece of card on it and held it out to me.

What on earth was this?

No, not liking this at all.

I took the card, square, folded and about the size of my palm. I unfolded it. Across the inside was a paragraph of Coldi text in calligraphy.

Shit. It was a writ.

Hereby, I, Taysha Palayi, declare financial injury and loss of respect from the claimant who pressured me into signing away a contract I had negotiated many years ago and was much looking forward to taking up. I demand compensation or will revoke my permission for the woman in question to be released from her obligations to my family. I demand that such will be completed or agreed to be undertaken to my satisfaction within ten days of this statement having been read by the recipient.

I stared at the loopy text, its exquisite calligraphy belying the seriousness of the message. Coldi sent writs for serious legal matters. I didn't know enough about Coldi law to judge the validity of this claim, but Taysha's rank alone would demand some sort of response.

Normal writs dealt with serious grievances. The recipient was meant to respond adequately to the claims made or risk assassination.

Shit, that was not part of the plan. This had nothing to do with my job or Ezhya or the *zeyshi*. This was a direct and personal attack on me.

Why? What was this about? We'd finished with that business.

"I don't understand." I had to do my best not to sound completely bewildered.

"You don't understand?" He cocked his head and regarded me, as if his looking at me would somehow instil me with understanding.

I stared back at him.

"Do you know what contracts are for?"

"Partnership."

He scoffed and waved his hand at me. "Don't give me any of that rubbish. Contracts are to beget children. Heirs."

It was true. Contracts were rarely for love.

His eyes continued to meet me. "So. Tell me, when is your heir due?"

"I . . ." *What the hell?*

"There isn't one, is there?"

"No."

"There isn't ever going to be one, is there?"

"Well, I don't know about that—"

"There isn't."

"Well, I . . ." I seriously did not want to discuss it with this man. And even so, why the *hell* hadn't he brought this subject up previously? Surely he had to have known?

"My brother and I selected Thayu from a long list of candidates to be the mother of our children. She gave my brother a son, as you will probably know. It is imperative, for the sake of the business interests of our families, that we have a family heir. The child in question needs to be a daughter. We have specific requirements for the mother of this child. Thayu meets them. We have been unable to find a replacement."

And you have looked, how long?

"You are not going to use her allocation for one more child. You did not mention this in your negotiations."

"That would have been fairly self-evident from the fact that I'm not Coldi."

"You didn't play fair with us."

And giving me writs is fair?

"So this is our injury: the fact that we have already given her tests, and we have selected parts of her genetic make-up that we are going to activate with custom-made markers. This is work we have already done, at great expense to us. The only stage of the process that remains is for her to become pregnant and give birth to this child. I could let it rest as a matter of honour between two men, but you're not even going to use this right. It is an insult, a slap in our face by an upstart foreigner who makes me look like a fool."

"I'm sure I didn't—"

"A fool, you hear me? I do not take kindly to being laughed at by my guards. Knocked out of the bed by an impotent bureaucrat I've heard them say. You have insulted me."

"I haven't done any—" Wasn't that what I paid him for?

"So, here is my deal: I absolve you from any further favours to me if she has the child, fulfilling her obligation to me. She can continue to live with you if you want. I don't need her to be here."

What the fuck?

Through clenched teeth, I said, "Thayu is not some sort of breeding . . ." I was going to say *cow*, but Coldi didn't keep domestic animals, much less bred them for anything. ". . . animal." The Coldi word for animal wasn't strong either. An animal was something curious and exotic, because few vertebrate species lived on Asto, and Coldi didn't entertain the very human notion that animals were worth less than people. Nor was breeding a bad thing.

I glanced over my shoulder at Sheydu and Veyada, both of whom wore their unemotional faces and were not going to be any help. Hell, they might even agree with him.

"I'm afraid I don't find that acceptable."

"Then I will require compensation."

I re-read the card in my hand. Sweat trickled down my back. I had trouble thinking through my anger. "What . . . what sort of compensation? I paid the amount you asked."

If he was going to ask for more money, I was dead. Come to think of it, I was pretty much dead anyway. Whatever he wanted, I didn't have the money or the power to give it to him. I didn't *want* to give anything to him beyond what we'd agreed on.

A corner of his mouth lifted. Coldi didn't normally smile and I'd come to associate smiles with bad news.

"I would have asked favours from you from within your world. You will know that I hold interests in a fair number of financial institutions and I could use some help with the facilitation of certain processes I want to complete—"

Such as illegally moving money to criminal organisations. "I don't have any of that kind of power."

"I am aware of that. Strange that such a populous world would send a delegate who has so little power. That shows how important they think we are, doesn't it?" He laughed.

The rudeness of it stung almost as much as the impotent remark. I managed to remain quiet.

"Well, in that case I have to ask for money—"

"After what I've already paid? There is no justification that allows it. I have proof. It will never stand up under scrutiny."

"Whose scrutiny? I could *make* it stand up to scrutiny."

Oh, shit.

He continued, "But then again, things could get messy with our laws and their laws, and I want to keep my financial interests out of the court."

I expelled a breath.

"So, we're back at the original request." His voice lifted. It sounded like the bastard was enjoying himself. "You are not going to make use of her allocation to have one more child. So she's going to have mine."

No. Fucking. Way. Was he going to get his hands on Thayu.

The corner of the mouth went up again. "This prospect distresses you?"

I breathed in deeply, trying to hold in the insults I wanted to hurl at the man. Or the insane urge I had to pull the gun out of its bracket —had I not left it with my suit that hung over Veyada's arm—and shoot the bastard. I had often experienced the bluntness of Coldi correspondence and mistaken it for rudeness, but this man took the absolute cake.

He continued, "Do tell me about this curious habit you people have of choosing a partner for life. That must be incredibly boring and restrictive. If you would only understand the custom of *nethana* instead of trying to claim possession of everything you fuck. That seems a very tiring way of living to me."

I don't take possession— I clenched hands into fists so tightly that my nails dug into my palms.

And then I decided what the heck. The heat was probably getting to me, and this was probably the most stupid thing I'd ever do, not to mention the last thing I'd ever do. But my mother, who had died when I was eight, had not raised me to be a doormat, and if it was with her memory that I would end my life in this hellhole, then so be it.

I rose, crossed the room in a few steps and deposited the card on the table.

He stared at me.

I stared back.

He blinked.

My heart was thudding so loudly that he should be able to hear it. A drop of sweat was threatening to run into my eye, but I resisted the urge to wipe it away.

I spoke slowly, letting every word hit the right spot. I chose the most accusatory pronouns I could find. "You have no right to give me a fucking writ. You will not touch Thayu in any way. If Thayu has another child, which she well may if she wishes, she will select the father, and the child will live with us. I don't see why you need additional concessions. We negotiated, I paid. We're finished. I don't have the power to give you extra business concessions on Earth even if I wanted to do it, which I don't. I don't have any money I can give you that you don't already have. We're fucking finished with this business—"

He laughed. "A very apt use of soldier's language. To me, this only proves the depth of the sentiment. If you people have a particular attachment to a sexual partner, you become very defensive if anyone looks at that person."

He was using me as a fucking guinea pig. *Shut up, shut up. And shut up, Delegate Cory Wilson.* Before I got myself into more trouble. Before I yanked the suit out of Veyada's hands, got the gun and shot him, because there was certainly not much to stop me doing that.

I breathed out heavily. It was so hot that I could feel the breeze from my nostrils track over my skin.

Taysha continued. "So you'd rather I didn't touch the lady. That leaves me little alternative but to ask for something that shouldn't cost you anything at all."

Another one of those dreadful smiles. Shit. He knew I had the key. My heart hammered against my ribs. Sweat was running into my eyes.

Sheydu stood in the corner with my tank. I longed for the protection of the helmet and the cool air over my face but by hell I wasn't going to appear weak and ask for it in front of this man.

"You have Ezhya's command key, don't you?"

There it was.

"I'm here as his supporter." That didn't translate well. The word I used, *yetha,* meant that I was part of his association, which of course I wasn't. I was dropping stitches and needed to stay alert, but if he kept teasing me like this, I would die of heat stroke before he got to the end of the conversation.

His eyebrows rose. "Do you have the key?"

"He has given the key to us to be taken to the Inner Circle and only to be handed over within the command hub."

"Yes, but do you have it, personally?"

Deep breath. "No. Why would someone from the Inner Circle trust me with it, someone from outside?"

"Someone like you would be an excellent choice to carry it in a party like the one that accompanied you here, because you are the only one in that group who could never use it."

"I don't have it, and I can't give it to you."

I glanced at the window and the part of a roof and wall I could see there, despairing when and how this distraction of Asha's was going to happen, or even if it was going to happen at all.

"But you know who has it?"

"The same person who would normally have it. They have not discussed those matters with me. I am here to discuss the Aghyrian claim with Risha and whoever else knows about the *zeyshi* Aghyrians."

"Hmmm. That useless rabble. Do you think I believe that?"

He said nothing for a while and I eyed my tank and helmet in Sheydu's hands. I needed those things. Now.

"Hmm," Taysha said again and neither his voice nor his face showed any emotion. "Well, in that case, allow me to offer you hospitality in the guest rooms of my quarters. I am rather busy right now, but we can continue this conversation later, after I've caught up with the rest of your party. Don't worry, I've sent out staff to buy food for weak stomachs and all your needs will be catered for. Unfortunately, I am not sure what you hope to achieve with your visit and your actions.

I cannot help you. Unless you had rather cooperate with me in the matter of the lady." They were all direct and rather rude pronouns.

I glared at him. The arsehole.

He rose and flicked his hand at the guards who had remained at the door. Those men opened the door for him. I followed him back into the foyer. I met my two guards' eyes, wanting to ask them what they thought had happened to the diversion Asha had been planning to create, and that any time now would be a good idea.

Taysha watched bemused while I put my gear back on. My hands were so sweaty and trembled so much that the guards needed to help me with the helmet and the mask, but once I turned the cool air on, it was beautiful. I could think clearly again. Bliss.

We went back into the corridor where we went around a corner into another corridor, where a guard in silver with a red belt stood in front of a set of double doors. She opened the doors at our approach.

On the other side was the hall to the guest quarters, neatly appointed with the customary red rug and small table containing another arrangement of rocks, this time with an oil light on a stand.

Taysha showed us a sitting room, a bedroom and a modest bathroom. The sitting room contained the customary couches and low table, the latter with a couple of trays with food and drinks with the green-coded label attached.

"Make yourself at home," Taysha said. "It is an honour to have you here." We were back to professional pronouns and the whole mockery of the occasion annoyed me.

He and his entourage left, shutting the door behind them with a click.

Shit.

11

———

THE FIRST THING Veyada did after the door shut was walk to it and hold his reader up to the lock. He shook his head.

I didn't know what he meant or what he was doing, but I had no energy to deal with this now. I collapsed on the couch, alternately hot and shivering. I took off my helmet, but kept on the mask, sucking deep breaths of cooling air.

Sheydu went to the window, which overlooked the front of the building. She ran her comm along the sill and then all the room's walls, corners and furniture. Seated on the couch, I could see the electrical activity readouts jump on the screen as she passed over certain spots. That was where the wires and bugs were hidden.

She nodded and sat down with me.

I knew all the signs. We were being monitored. The door was locked.

We were not guests; we were prisoners.

For some reason, Asha's diversion had not worked.

Worse, I needed my adaptation medication, and Thayu had it.

Veyada also joined us on the couch. A sense of unease hung between us. I didn't know these guards, didn't know how much I could trust them and they were not at all the people I would have chosen to be locked up with.

Sheydu said, "Do eat something, Delegate."

I dragged one of the trays over the table. On it lay some nondescript doughy-looking morsels whose identity did not become clearer by eating them. I don't know if it was because I felt tense, but the food sank straight to the bottom of my stomach and proceeded to sit there in an unmovable lump. At least the water was cold and safe.

We made small talk. I asked what the food was and Veyada explained about some sort of grain that grew in the aquifers. He also explained how the water had been filtered, because a lot of surface water on Asto was too acidic to qualify as green-coded.

I asked if there was any chance of visiting these fabled aquifers because they intrigued me, and Sheydu talked about which ones were closest. There was indeed a passage connected to the station where we had entered the building.

I suspected the latter was the only important bit of information exchanged in this conversation. It meant, *Here is a way to flee, if you need it.*

Veyada and Sheydu ate from the other tray. Veyada was fiddling with his reader. After a while, he handed it to me. On the screen was a diagram of the building. He had pointed out where we were and the position of the command hub on the floor above us and to the left.

But how would we get there if the door was locked and there were bars across the windows?

He made a hand signal. *Don't worry.*

Then Sheydu said, "I think the Delegate would like a bath to cool off."

It did sound like a good idea. In Barresh the bathrooms were like indoor pools: they were always full and constantly flowed over with hot water from the springs.

In Athyl, you had to fill the bath from a tap that filled up via an outlet in the bottom of the basin. The water had a brown tinge and smelled earthy. I hoped it was safe. At least it was quite cool. It was lovely to be free of all those layers of clothing.

Of course there was more behind the decision for going into the bath. Security monitoring was always weakest in the bathroom. That was the case in my apartment and all others I'd visited. There would probably be a camera somewhere, but it couldn't be anywhere close to the bath or it would be visible and sounds in this room echoed too much to provide a good recording.

Before he came into the water, Veyada unfolded a kind of spindly device from his pocket. He set it on the ground, where it looked like an absurd spider with only five legs, and positioned it while lining up its "body" with the corner of the room above the door.

"What's that?" I asked when he joined us.

"It's a disruptor, Delegate."

"Please, everyone calls me Cory."

He nodded, but still didn't look me in the eye. I wasn't sure how to react to him, because as Ezhya's guard, even a junior one, he ranked far higher than me or Thayu. Now he had been contracted to protect someone of lower status. How did that even work?

I continued, "Is it safe to talk?"

"As safe as it will ever be inside this building."

Sheydu nodded. She sat on the seat opposite me, her legs stretched out so her feet touched the side under the bench where I sat. She had the body shape of a teenage Coldi girl: more slender in the waist than usual, and a flat chest, her arms wiry and corded with muscle. The skin on her upper arms had lost its youthful softness. I judged her to be well in her forties.

"You have a plan?" I asked.

She held her hand up. *Be quiet.*

All right, not as safe as I thought.

Veyada said, "I think you're right. He doesn't have any grounds to make more demands from you. Your contract was settled and paid, and if there was going to be any financial hardship on his part, he should have calculated that in his original claim."

He was putting on an act, but I found myself getting angry all over again. "I paid enough—more than enough actually. His first claim was ridiculous."

"There have been some rumours about that, yes."

Blood rose to my cheeks. Damn! It was hot enough in this room already, and I didn't need to be reminded of what might well have been a very stupid decision. "Tell me, what can I do? He holds us hostage here. I have no great knowledge of Coldi law, and even if I had, I still couldn't think what—"

Sheydu was pointing at Veyada.

I mouthed, *What?* And at the same time I thought I understood. *He knows about law?*

She nodded.

Veyada continued, "Taysha takes advantage of you because you've shown emotional attachment to the lady. He seems highly amused by the way you form relationships in an irrational way."

"Irrational?"

"So it seems to us. When you choose a life partner, there is no evidence of instinct at work, no reason, yet when you form such a relationship, it is for life, and you protect it with everything you have. He exploits that."

That's because I love her.

And love crosses boundaries.

And . . .

Damn. He was right of course. Coldi described their official relationships in contracts and any other relationships that formed were either hormonally determined or were *nethana:* loose, didn't mean anything and could be discarded at will. Love certainly happened, but rarely between contracted partners.

I breathed out heavily.

"So what should I do about these new claims? I can't pay him any more. I can't give him what he wants. I don't want to give him any more—"

Veyada opened his mouth.

"No, and don't even think about suggesting that Thayu should fulfil her part of the contract. That's not happening. You can say these contract relationships are purely rational for you, but I see fear of that man in her eyes." Besides, if she had her second child, that child would live with us.

"I wasn't going to say that. I understand that the notion of Thayu going back to him to complete his contract is offensive to you."

"If I agreed to that, I'd want my money back," I said in a low voice. Damn the man and his rude intrusions to hell. "Then what were you going to say?"

"The current circumstances justify your issuing a counter-writ."

What? "But I don't . . ." *give ultimatums to kill people, no matter how offensive they are* ". . . belong in your justice system."

"But you do. Taysha has determined that through a diviner, and their judgements can be binding in some circumstances, clan matters being one of them. You can claim official membership of the Domiri clan."

"How do you know that? Did he tell you that?"

"Because I have access to the ancestry diviners' legal records. It's there for all to see."

What the fuck— I'd heard of those diviners, but I'd thought them to be part of superstition in lower-class Coldi, and didn't expect them to make legally binding statements.

Veyada continued, "I would take it up, especially if you're planning a long-term relationship with the lady. It could be very advantageous."

Now he did look me in the eye, and he was serious. Me, a member of the Domiri clan. I didn't even know that was possible.

Right. Here was another re-assessment of Asha's opinion about me. He had sent me to a man whom he knew was my nemesis, not with two random junior guards because he had no use for them himself, but two people whose knowledge I was likely to need.

Come to think of it, Ezhya didn't have any guards who would be of no use to me. Like Thayu, they would all be graduates of the security academy and would have one or more specialities.

And obviously Asha didn't mind having me in his clan either.

Right. So rather than being an obnoxious boor—well, he was that, too—he was helping me, or, more likely, handing me tidbits to see what I'd do with them. What a typical upper-class Coldi thing to do. And damn it, I should have realised that, too, rather than let him rile me with his behaviour.

Deep breath, Delegate Wilson.

"So. This counter-writ. How is that going to work from here, while we're locked up? Who would carry it out? To be honest, I'm not a fan of sending someone a piece of paper with an order to have him killed for a minor transgression."

"Another strange habit of your people. This thing called *mercy*." He used the Isla word. "If someone has committed an offense, why lock them up, feed them and then release them when they're angrier than when they committed the offense and will only re-offend?"

"We have a forgiving nature."

"And you also have some of the most violent conflicts in all of the settled worlds, some of the greatest mass murders of people by people, by their own leaders, or by other leaders."

And Asto's colonisation had been aggressive, but they had barely shed blood and despite the fearsome size and know-how of their army, had rarely fought any wars.

Touché.

I'd had this discussion with Nicha so many times and he always won it.

There was something about Coldi nature that Earth people could learn a lot from, if we could only determine what it was.

"Please, Delegate—Cory—listen to this because it is important advice. Taysha has offended you deeply. You have played along with him to appease Ezhya. But through offending you with these further requests, Taysha has offended Ezhya as well. Our laws are very clear in this respect. Trust has been broken. You have the right to issue a writ to Taysha. You should do this, so as not to set a precedent that people in power can mess around with foreigners unused to our laws."

"Is that what you would do? I don't mean if you were Ezhya, because . . ." *Ezhya rules everything.* "But if something like this happened to you, or Natanu, would you send him a writ?"

"No. Any of us would go straight to his private rooms and shoot him."

Crap.

I looked down at the surface of the water, expelling a breath. I knew he was right and I'd known that something was seriously wrong in the relationship between Ezhya and his seconds once Asha started deflecting my questions about Risha. Taysha had tried, but failed, to take the command hub and Risha had fled?

With a chill, I remembered something Amarru had told me when I was training for my job at the Exchange in Athens: "Chief Coordinators don't retire, generally speaking. Most of them never make it to old age. As their years in power increase, so does the importance of a loyal security network that can go into absolute lockdown to see their leader through the worst crises. Still, virtually all Chief Coordinators die by the hand of a fellow member of the Inner Circle."

So the fight was on. I'd never expected to be caught up in it.

Veyada went on in great detail about possible wordings for a writ and their precise meanings. I knew that people had special interpreters for these things, people who specialised in writing the exact amount of offense received and intended with their choice of pronouns and tone.

The wording of Taysha's writ to me, he assured me, had been very offensive, designed to provoke.

I didn't like talking about this while in the man's apartment, and certainly didn't like the suggestion that I should kill him without giving him the opportunity to respond, but we did settle on a text for a potential writ to go out as soon as I was near a place where I could find a calligrapher. Since that was not going to happen any time soon, I guessed I was safe from this arcane custom for a while. When Ezhya came back, he was welcome to "deal with" Taysha in any way he saw fit.

That probably made me a coward.

Meanwhile, Sheydu had gotten out of the bath, wrapped herself in a towel and sat in the corner reading something. The loose texture and dark spots of the skin on her legs made me re-assess her age. She was likely closer to sixty than forty. A veteran with vast experience in her field. I had an ominous feeling that I'd soon find out what that field of expertise was. It probably involved the subject we'd studiously avoided talking about: how to get out of this room.

So, was this talk about writs a smokescreen, too?

Once we got out of the bath, I was uncomfortably reminded that the water was cooler than the air in the apartment. My clothes stuck to me with sweat by the time I'd dried myself. I put on my suit over my clothes, but it seemed to give me little comfort. If only I had that adaptation medicine.

While we had been in the bathroom, the last of the hazy daylight had departed and the white sky was now dark.

A brown tinge hung at the horizon from the lingering daylight. The slice of the city visible from the window twinkled with a kaleidoscope of colours. There were street lights on posts or strung from wire, and lights attached to walls, functional lights and lights that created multi-coloured patterns on walls and roofs. Taller buildings and towers or spires sported patterns of smaller lights: curved or blocky in intricate colour combinations. Some flickered as if to some inaudible beat.

"It's very pretty. Is that taller building over there the armed forces base?"

There was no reply from the guards. I looked over my shoulder.

Neither of them had sat down, but lingered near the door, both looking at screens. Veyada had to have a feeder, because a feeder log scrolled over the screen.

Sheydu came to me and showed me her reader. The screen said, *Put on your outside suit. Take everything.*

I mouthed, "What's happened?"

She gestured, *Later.*

I pointed to the ceiling. *We're going up?*

She nodded, still listening to something in her earpiece. Sounds of bumps and thunks came from elsewhere in the building, nowhere close to us. Was this finally the promised diversion?

That was it, then. No idea how they thought they could get out and past Taysha's guard. Likely, there was some more "dealing with" involved, but deep inside I'd known that when I decided to come here.

12

I WENT to the bedroom and wrestled myself into my second suit. I checked the key in my pocket before I did up the fastenings. Then I strapped on my belt and bracket with the gun after checking the charge level. Then the tanks and that hot helmet. I slipped the breathing mask over my face and turned on the cool air supply, something I'd sworn not to do indoors, but I was so damn hot. It was night, too, and I had no idea how long it would be before I could get to my adaptation medication.

Back in the hall, Sheydu crouched next to the door with the spindly spider thing that Veyada had also used in the bathroom and whose function wasn't quite clear to me. When I came in, she looked up, rose and took something from her pocket.

"Take this." She handed me a parcel in waxy paper with something in a clear bag stuck to it. That piece of electronics I recognised: a detonator.

"You know what to do with it?"

"Think so." *Gamra* had made me do a weapons and self-defence course.

Explosives were for getting oneself out of locked rooms.

"Put it away somewhere safe."

I opened the fastening to my suit and slid the parcel inside my inner pocket of my outer suit, separated from the key by a mere layer of fabric.

Sheydu sat down facing the door, poking some very thin and stiff wires between the door and the frame. Veyada stood behind her, leaning against the wall. He had unclipped his gun from his arm bracket and held it, half-raised pointed at the door. He gestured for me to stand behind him.

I pointed at my own gun.

He gestured *leave it*. Quite relaxed.

Sheydu clipped on an earpiece, connected some wires and listened. Then she said something in code. She jumped to her feet and retreated to the other side of the door. There was a brief fizzing sound and the door popped open.

Someone outside gave a surprised exclamation.

Veyada jumped through the doorway and fired once, twice, three, four times in rapid succession.

Sheydu calmly swiped her gear off the floor and stuffed it into her pockets.

"Quick, get out of here."

We ran out, Sheydu leading the way, then poor old me, sweating, struggling with all my gear, then Veyada. I spotted a couple of people on the ground. I hoped Veyada had used the stun setting, but knew he likely hadn't. The dealing had well and truly begun.

We ran down the corridor the same way we had come in, around the corner, another corner and up a flight of stairs. The gear was heavy. I didn't seem to have put on the tank properly, because it bumped against my back. I was so hot and felt sick. Dizzy, in a just-go-away-and-let-me-die-here kind of way.

By the time we were on top of the stairs, I was ready to black out. The fact that night had come didn't seem to have made it any cooler.

Sheydu crossed the upstairs gallery and led us into a long corridor with windows on one side that looked out over some sort of internal courtyard. There was a roof over the top and lush vegetation lit by a couple of lights along a path.

Ahead the corridor ended in a set of double doors. Three guards stood before them. These ones wore silver suits and red sashes, like Sheydu and Veyada. Thank heavens, we were back on Ezhya's territory.

As we came closer, one of the guards shouted, "Hey, there."

Sheydu stopped. Her face showed apprehension.

Next to me, Veyada tensed.

"We want to get into the hub," Sheydu said. "We've come from Barresh with Ezhya's personal approval."

The man's face showed no emotion. His left hand had moved close to the gun bracket on his right arm. From that position, he could pull the weapon out in an instant.

"We have Ezhya's command key," Sheydu said.

"We don't need it. We're fine."

"Ezhya may not be back for a while. The Exchange needs to re-align the nodes. Some may be damaged. Let us through so that we can install Ezhya's running routines and secure our positions."

The guard's hand went closer to the gun's grip. "Stay away."

"On whose orders?"

He didn't respond to that.

Sheydu whispered, "What's up with him?"

Veyada whispered, "No idea, but we've a got a problem."

"You got any smart ideas?"

"Maybe." Veyada glanced aside past where I stood. There was a plain and unmarked door in the wall. In one step, he opened this door and pulled both of us inside a dark and narrow hole like a broom cupboard. He slammed the door shut behind him and locked it.

To my surprise, he vanished into the darkness at the back of the cupboard. Sheydu pushed me after him.

I stumbled along following the walls by touch. The helmet and visor hampered my vision at the best of times, but now I only saw the annoying projection of the atmosphere biometrics in the corner of my visor. There was a way to turn off the display, but right now, I couldn't remember how to do it.

The passage seemed endless. Our footsteps sounded muffled in the cramped space. Every now and then we passed a small light mounted on the ceiling. It was hot here. The helmet display showed increasing temperature. Where the hell were we going?

After a while, we got to a set of steps going down—I almost tripped and fell—and then a door that was made of thick concrete. It reminded me of the war shelter dug into the back yard of the house in New Zealand where I'd grown up. As kid, I'd found it a scary place, where my mother kept a supply of cans and packaged food just in case. The war had never come to New Zealand, but I could still see her setting down the box to open the fat concrete door with both hands and then disappearing inside its dark maw.

We went in. Veyada shut the door and locked it. Then he led us out the other side of the shelter, into a larger room.

Here, he halted.

I took the opportunity to sit down on a bench and take off the helmet. I studied the outside but couldn't see or remember any place to turn off the interior display.

Sheydu turned to her colleague. "What's going on? Why didn't he let us through? These are our people. Natanu's association. They should let us in. We have no one higher-ranking with us who could be a threat to the hub."

"I don't know," Veyada said. He was panting. "Something tells me there has already been a re-alignment of power."

"But who could have done that? Risha?"

"Risha's guards were at the station, remember? They let us through."

"Then who? Asha never made it into the building, Taysha is still in his apartment, Natanu is with Asha . . ." She spread her hands. "Anyone else coming up here would have had to fight their way in, and there's been no fight. He can only refuse us entry if someone is using the hub, and it's not Taysha, although he would very much like to get in, and it's not Asha, although he would also very much like to get in. It's definitely not Natanu, because we're her association and we would know."

Shit, the leadership struggle was in full force.

I asked, slightly out of breath, "Ezhya lives alone, doesn't he?" I'd never heard him mention a woman or any other kind of partner.

Her eyes met mine in a blank look. I wasn't quite sure what she thought I'd suggested, but the notion that family should be protective of a family member's position was not so out-there for Coldi to be unable to understand; or was it? Or, based on what Veyada had said, maybe not.

"Yes, he lives alone." Her voice had an odd coolness to it.

What? Jilted lover? Unrequited love?

All right, all right, I wasn't going to go there anymore. "Could it be any of his domestic staff?"

"They are all accounted for in the domestic quarters. They don't have access to the hub anymore. They wouldn't know how to use it. They wouldn't dare enter the hub room."

What about cleaning it? But I was sure that would also be a stupid question.

I tried again, "How do you know it's a person, not one of the routines gone haywire? Maybe it could have been caused by the Exchange outage."

"No. For orders to have changed at this level, someone would have to have gone into the hub with a key or an approximation and accessed the command structure. It would have to be someone from the office or domestic staff who not only has the right to be inside his quarters, but knows how the hub works. The domestic staff doesn't know that. The office staff can't get in when Ezhya is not here."

I didn't know what else to suggest. No had had ever spoken to me about the arrangements of the Chief Coordinator's position. I doubted even many of the people immediately under Ezhya knew those things.

"Then who knows how to use the hub besides Ezhya?"

"Not many," Veyada said.

Sheydu said, "I do."

That's why she had come with me.

And then a niggling voice inside me said, *What if she wants to challenge?*

But no, I had to believe that at least some people would remain loyal to Ezhya when it mattered, or this would drive me mad.

Veyada jerked his head. "Let's keep going."

He ducked into another passage. Seriously, how big was this building? It had more secret passages than an Egyptian pyramid.

I needed all my energy to keep up with them and to stop any embarrassing stumbles.

At least we were out of that claustrophobic tunnel and ran from one room into another. Storage, offices, communication hubs, all abandoned. I had no idea where we were going.

Down the stairs, through another hall and out an arched doorway into the plant-filled courtyard. Across the path. Shapes of strange plants and giant mushrooms flashed past—Asto had plants that could move, and most of them had gathered on the ground to catch the lingering heat of the day. Some of them had moved onto the path and

I had to make sure I didn't step on them. I'd seen these odd things before, curiosities in the hothouses of the rich Barresh councillors' mansions.

On the other side of the courtyard Sheydu crouched at a small door and folded out her spindly machine while Veyada and I waited in the shadow of the wall.

Lights had come on in the wing opposite the courtyard where we had come from. Faint sounds of shouts drifted on the air. People were looking for us no doubt.

Sheydu sprang to her feet. The door opened.

We bolted outside. Up a set of steps, across another the courtyard. Did I imagine it or had the sky really turned a livid orange?

Sheydu ran ahead and I followed as best as I could, but I was so hot my vision was starting to blur. When we climbed another set of steps to a kind of footbridge that led across a dome roof, the floor of the bridge suddenly seemed to fall under my feet. My vision contracted to a narrow tunnel. I stopped, grabbing onto the side railing.

"Stop, Sheydu, please stop."

I let myself sink to the floor against the railing, gulping deep breaths. The hot air seared my throat. Veyada crouched next to me. He turned the air flow on my tank up as far as it would go.

"You're all right?"

"Just . . . a little rest," I panted, gulping cool air.

I leaned back against the railing, trying to calm my racing heart. I needed to calm down because being agitated made the heat stress worse. But I needed my medication and damn it, where were Thayu and Nicha and why hadn't the diversion happened? Why had we been separated in the first place?

Sheydu had stopped a little further, alert as a predator ready to spring.

She said something I didn't catch.

"We need to keep going. Are you ready?" Veyada asked.

I wasn't, but attempted to push myself up anyway. A little voice in the back of my head said that I shouldn't be stupid and let them assist me. Both guards were much stronger than me and had no trouble with the climate. I should stop being stubborn and—

"Come!" Sheydu called, her voice urgent.

Veyada dragged me up.

A small object hit my arm with a *plock* as if someone was throwing pebbles.

"What—"

Another object hit my helmet. *Plock!* And then another fell on my shoulder—

"Hurry up!"

Plock, plock, plock. A little dark circle formed on the stone in front of me.

Rain.

And rain on Asto was nasty business. Very high in acid and poisons.

The wind brought a waft of wet stone that wormed itself between the helmet and my face mask.

We started running again across the footbridge. I managed to find some strength to move my feet. Veyada was close behind me.

The footbridge seemed endless. I couldn't help thinking of that time I had dragged Thayu along the streets of Far Atok in Barresh, suffering hypothermia and barely able to think coherently. That was how I felt. The air rushed through my helmet and I felt like there was never enough, leaving me light-headed. Several times Veyada had to hang onto my arm so that I didn't fall.

We reached the end of the footbridge at a kind of porch-like structure in front of a door. It was pitch dark underneath the overhang of the roof, with walls on two sides.

The wind picked up, carrying clouds of dust and grit.

Sheydu knelt near the door. Part of her hair had escaped her ponytail. It was flying across her face, defying her attempts to tuck it behind her ear. She shouted orders at Veyada who joined her in fiddling with the spider-thing and the wires.

A gust of wind nearly knocked me off my feet. Grit and sand grazed my helmet. More and more large drops hit the pavement of the footbridge which, seen from here, seemed to lead into nothingness, the courtyard having been obscured by dust or droplets, I couldn't tell which. I could taste dust in my mouth despite the helmet.

"Hurry up!" Sheydu said.

Veyada opened the door to a dark room. We stumbled inside just as a sheet of rain lashed the building. I stood, panting, inside the door, looking out over the footbridge, which became drenched in seconds. My helmet display indicated a sharp drop in temperature. Only forty degrees C. I slowly lifted the helmet from my head, breathing the humid air that smelled of rain after a hot day.

"I love that smell."

With heat like that, the scent was very strong. So strong, in fact, that the very stone was breathing. Steam rose off the paving and formed a mist over the ground. Wait—that wasn't part of the normal state of affairs. That was . . .

Holy crap. Acid.

I coughed and slammed the door shut, but could still smell the scent in the back of my nose. How damn acid was that rain?

"Got a nose full of burning air?" Sheydu asked, her voice barely hiding a smile.

"Urgh, that's terrible. Is it always like this?"

"Often. Although of course it never used to rain when I was young."

I'd never truly understood why rain frightened people on Asto so. Rain was supposed to be a good thing, right?

But if this stuff got into the aquifers and the fragile agricultural systems, it had potential to do great damage.

The smell of rain after a hot day would never again be the same.

13

———

WE HAD ENTERED what looked like a guest apartment and, by the crunch of grit under my boots, it hadn't been used for some time.

I put my helmet down on a bench against the wall and turned off the air. It was pretty hot inside, but I'd better conserve the cool air for when I really needed it. Things weren't exactly going to plan.

A steady thrum against the windows indicated that it was pouring.

"I wonder what this much rain does to the buildings."

"It's not been good," Veyada said. "It does a lot of damage to stone and metal structures. The first drops are always the worst."

I looked out of the window, which offered a view over the city.

"Those noises we heard, was that Asha and his disturbance?" It was on the bold side asking him this, and he had no reason to tell me. This could be filed under *stuff the politician or diplomat is better off not knowing.*

He put a finger to his lips and pointed at the ceiling.

Oh. Bugs.

I shivered involuntarily.

Sheydu lingered by the door on the far side of the room. She kept glancing at her reader and had opened the door a crack so she could see out.

"Any signs of movement?" asked Veyada.

She shook her head and kept fiddling with the reader.

Veyada went to have a look. She pointed at the screen.

"Are you serious?"

She looked at him, chin up.

"Damn. You know I have no love for those things."

"You got a better suggestion?"

He said nothing.

She sniffed, made a hand signal and went back to fiddling with the screen. Veyada prowled around the room a few times looking at the screen of his reader before he yanked his gun from the bracket. I ducked, unable to muffle a squeak. He fired at the ceiling three times. Plaster and bits of stone rained down.

One of the hits had left a hole in the ceiling where blackened wires had fallen out of the plaster. Veyada climbed on a box and pulled the lot free with a further shower of plaster, some of which went into my hair.

I gave him my best *What the hell?* look.

"We're forced to stop being subtle about this," he said, dumping burnt wires on the floor. "As of now, this is an official attempt to gain control of the hub. Everyone in the Inner Circle will be after us anyway. We need to move fast if we have any chance of reaching the hub. We need to talk without being overheard."

Hence the wires on the floor.

Sheydu said, "You do that while I open this." She was at the window, and had stuck her threads between the frame and the sill.

"We are going outside again?" The rain lashed against the glass.

Veyada nodded, solemnly. "They won't expect us to do that."

"Does anyone go out in this rain?"

"It's not about the rain. It is because there are drones."

"Drones?" I was starting to like this less and less. Climbing over the façade of a building in the dark was one thing, but doing so with increased gravity was another, and so was climbing while wearing cumbersome gear, and while acid rain pissed down on you. What the hell were drones? I seriously didn't want to know.

Just didn't.

Veyada said, "Listen. There are a few things you need to know about the drones. They're about as long as your arm and they crawl over the outside of the building, detecting movement. When they find it, they will come and investigate. They have a biometrics sensor and will scan your ID. When they ask you a question, you should give a code while pressing the two middle buttons on their 'heads'. Because of who we are, we have the code. I'll send it to you now."

My comm pinged. A sequence of six numbers appeared on the screen.

"When a drone comes, read it out slowly and clearly. Don't make any mistakes."

"What happens if you get it wrong?"

"They'll kill you."

"No way. I'll kill it first."

"Sure, but that's not going to help you much. If you attack a drone, it will attract a general security alarm and will bring all the guards on us. If the drone doesn't kill you, they certainly will. So please get this right."

Sheydu was yanking at the grille that covered the window. Three sides of it were loose already.

I repeated the number sequence a few times. *Six, nine, four, twelve, two, seven.* It was a long and awkward number combination, because in Coldi only exponentials of two were whole numbers and the rest were all composite numbers made up out of the exponential plus the number of times the residual was divisible by lower exponentials of two. The notation for twelve was 32: two to the power of three plus two squared. I guess making the code awkward was the whole point. They could have made it 321—fourteen—or 3210—fifteen. It was a system that did my head in at times, but reflected everything about Coldi society: pairs were paramount, and the larger numbers became, the less importance was placed on their accuracy, because the numbers became too long and awkward. Also, with increasing numbers came vastly increasing complexity.

Sheydu said, "I'm ready, let's go."

She had cut away the grille and forced the window open and jumped onto the windowsill. Veyada handed her a thin rope from his pack and a sticky pad about the size of an orange, wrapped in clear foil. She peeled the foil off, scrunched it up and put it in her pocket. Meanwhile, in her other hand, the contents of the foil reshaped into a baseball-glove-shaped blob, which oozed and sloshed around. It was covered with brown bristly hair. A metal eyelet went through the middle. Sheydu attached the rope to it, and stuck her hand out the window. She flung the thing up against the outside wall, keeping the end of the rope in her hand. She pulled it taut, and yanked harder. She seemed satisfied with the sticking power of the pad and edged out of the window. Where she went and how she hung onto the outside wall, I couldn't see. Veyada prepared a second pad, looking unconcerned for his partner's safety.

The rope swung back to the window.

"Your turn," he said.

"Where to?"

"Climb up. You'll see Sheydu up there."

"What about the rain?"

"It should be just water now. It's usually just the first drops that are high in acids."

Nothing for it.

Getting onto the windowsill in my gear wasn't that easy. Veyada gave me the final leg-up and came to stand next to me. He gave me the helmet, helped me put it on and turned on the tank. Then he attached the rope to my belt, gave me a second rope which he had attached to the second pad. He flung that pad up into the darkness where it hit the wall above the window with a thud and stuck there.

He yanked the rope, apparently satisfied.

I peered out into the night. The city of Athyl stretched out underneath me, twisted rows of lights and a variety of architecture reaching all the way to the horizon. Concentric lines of red lights marked the circle boundaries. Occasional spotlight beams showed the intensity of the rain that was still coming down.

So the rain was safe now, huh?

The window was on the second floor of this side of the building. There was a domed roof on the ground floor level, probably some kind of foyer.

I could see the shape of Sheydu ahead. She had walked along a ledge that led from our window to a balcony on the corner facing away from us. The ledge passed a few windows, all of them dark. She had strung the rope along the wall, with sticky pads holding it at regular intervals.

I stepped onto the ledge. A waft of hot, acid-tinged and droplet-charged air blew up from the courtyard. It fogged up the visor of the helmet, and all of a sudden I couldn't see where I was going. Shit.

Hanging onto the rope with one hand, I pushed the visor up. Did my eyes prick because of the acidity or because I expected them to prick with acidity? Sweat rolled down my back.

Keep going, Mr Wilson.

Slowly, I shuffled along the ledge. Wasn't I lucky that I didn't suffer a great fear of heights?

I got into a pattern: move my right hand along the rope, then my right foot along the ridge, then my left foot and left hand. Repeat. Slowly, I came closer to the balcony. The courtyard downstairs remained empty. I saw no drones.

Veyada followed a few steps behind me, pulling sticky pads loose by gently tugging them and tucking them away in his armoured jacket as he went.

I reached the balcony without much trouble, helped over the railing by Sheydu who waited there.

I had expected her to go into the door on the balcony, but it seemed we hadn't reached our destination yet.

Sheydu took the sticky pads Veyada had collected and flung a couple against the wall on the other side of the balcony. She climbed over the railing again.

My heart sank. I was hot and sweaty and my arms were screaming from holding on in the higher gravity. I was also carrying a lot more equipment on me than they were and was less suited to carry it.

Veyada helped me over the railing.

The ledge here was thinner. Sheydu disappeared around a corner. When I edged around, I couldn't see her anymore. A light burned behind one of the alcove windows she had apparently already passed. Maybe the light had come on after she passed. Maybe the guards inside knew where we were and were waiting for us.

In any case, I was too hot to worry about it. If someone shot me, at least I wouldn't be hot anymore.

I shuffled over the ledge, doing my best to concentrate on each step.

The lit room turned out to be empty. Shuffling around the corner of the alcove window was tricky, but once I passed the window, I spotted Sheydu, waiting in the next alcove. She pointed to the other side of her, where the wall joined up with a larger dome than the one that formed the foyer to the building below us.

I couldn't see what she was pointing at. Wait, I could. Something moved up there. The light from the city glinted off a shiny object, black and about the size of a child, cresting the curve of the dome. A couple of lights blinked on the side that was pointed towards us. It was coming our way.

Shit. I pulled my comm out of my pocket and had one more look at the number I was supposed to give this drone.

"Stay here until it has passed," Veyada said softly behind me. "Don't move."

We waited. My heart was thudding so loudly that I was sure Veyada would be able to hear it.

The thing came to Sheydu. It blinked a yellow light and sent out a blue scanner signal that traced Sheydu's outline. She touched the machine. A couple of blue lights blinked and the drone trundled off, towards me this time. My heart sped up even more until I heard nothing except the roaring of blood in my ears.

From close up, the thing was much more bulky than I expected. Too bulky, in fact, to believably crawl over a vertical wall without falling and without any visible means to hold it up.

It resembled a black shiny spider. Its "body" had four wheels at the base. Its six "feet" were constantly moving, sensing and tasting. A dull red glow issued from a round window at the front.

Press buttons on its head, Veyada had said. That would be the two slightly outward-bulging things above the window?

It stopped in front of me with a soft whirring noise. The blue beam tracked over my suit. A little light flashed red.

Shit. What did that mean?

Text appeared on the round window: *Speak authorisation code.*

I reached out and pressed the bulbous buttons above the red glowing window. I spoke clearly.

"Six, nine, four, twelve, two, seven."

The red light kept flashing. Come to think of it, those buttons felt really solid, not like buttons at all. What about the two little dark spots above them?

I pressed those spots, which were soft and felt more like buttons. I repeated as clear as I could, "Six, nine, four, twelve, two, seven."

Come on, listen to me, you fucking thing.

The red light stopped flashing. Something whirred. The blue beams tracked over me again. It hadn't done that with Sheydu.

Text popped up in the glowing red window. *Input sequence.*

"Six, nine, four, twelve, two, seven."

The screen replied with, *Unauthorised language detected.*

"Six, nine, four, twelve, two, seven." I couldn't believe this. This thing was going to make a fuss over the fact that I spoke *gamra* Coldi with a more formal intonation than the locals?

"Six, nine, four, twelve, two, seven."

Unauthorised language detected. Warning expires in 12 . . . 11 . . . 10 . . .

"Six, nine, four, twelve, two, seven!"

9 . . . 8 . . . 7 . . .

Fuck it. I fumbled to tie the rope to my belt.

6 . . . 5 . . .

Closed my hand on the gun and pulled it from its bracket.

4 . . . 3 . . .

Turned it on. A green light flashed *fully charged.*

14

T ook off the safety and turned up the power as far as it would go.

15

Fired.

The kickback and subsequent explosion nearly blew me off the ledge. The drone exploded in a fireball and dropped from the wall to the roof below. On its way down, it broke into flaming chunks that rained down onto the pavement.

"Shit!" Sheydu called. "Why did you do that?"

"It wouldn't recognise my accent. It was giving warnings."

"Damn it. We're gone, finished."

"No, we're not." I remembered this chilling sense of determination that came over me when under threat. We were going to get into that room, and I was going to use that key. "Where is the command room?"

"We need to climb into the last window on the ledge. It's right behind that wall, on the corner."

Which wasn't all that far. "Come on, let's go. Go, go, now. Shoot everything in our way."

16

S FAST as we could, we shuffled along the ledge. Two more drones came to check us out, and they were shot down in flames by Veyada as soon as they cleared the corner.

Sheydu reached the window first. She yanked at the safety grille that covered the window but it wouldn't come out. She retreated a bit along the ledge and fired at it at maximum power setting. The metal glowed red hot and then the whole thing disintegrated. Bits of metal exploded everywhere. The explosion left a ragged hole which she had to clean up with the cutting setting. Sparks flew into the air and rained down over her arms and down the side of the building.

Guards were streaming into the courtyard below.

Sheydu heaved herself onto the windowsill and disappeared inside. I was the next one to reach the window.

Someone on the ground yelled, "Up there!"

A gun discharged. The charge hit the window frame next to my hand.

Veyada grabbed me by the legs and unceremoniously tipped me over the windowsill. A charge flashed across the window. I landed hard on the floor. Veyada fell on top of me.

Oof.

He rolled off me. "Damn it, did you hear that? That was Reynu's voice down there."

"Your association?" I asked.

"Ezhya's. Those guards should have been loyal to us."

Sheydu cursed. "Should have been. Like the ones at the checkpoint. What the fuck is going on?"

Veyada said, "I guess we'll find out soon, because *something* has happened in that hub room."

Sheydu pushed herself to her feet, "There is going to have to be so much sorting out of associations when this is all over."

We had come out in an empty corridor. I took off my helmet so that at least I didn't have to peer through fogged-up glass. Sheydu set off at a brisk pace. Veyada grabbed my arm and more or less dragged me along, around the corner and into another corridor that ran at right angles and then to the right through an open door.

They stopped. The circular room beyond was shrouded in semi-darkness. In the middle stood a circular bench with a tall stool at its centre. Around it were two tiers of benches of controls, screens and holo displays and a bevy of sensors and feeder stations. Huge screens on the walls showed fast-scrolling text and images.

"What the fuck?" Sheydu whispered. "It's on and operating."

"Shhh," Veyada said.

They frowned at each other. Sheydu mouthed, "There's someone here."

Veyada whispered, "You two, walk calmly to the middle. I'll cover you." He inched into the room, his gun aimed at the empty command chair.

Sheydu took one step, but there was a noise, a soft *snick* somewhere in the room. She froze, gesturing me back to the door.

Veyada called, "Come out and we won't harm you."

There was no reply, no movement.

He turned around and scanned all the walls—made from white material floor to ceiling. There was nowhere to hide in the room except in the middle of the circular hub benches.

Sheydu unclipped her gun.

"Stay here until I tell you it's all right to come in. Get the key ready." She inched past me, also with her gun raised in her left hand. In her right hand, she held a small object that I guessed to be a sleeping gas bomb.

"We are not here to harm you. Come out please. We can help. We have the command key."

I stuck my hand into the pocket of my jacket and closed my fingers around the smooth metal of the key's casing.

There was a small noise, the scuffing of a foot, or a sniff.

Veyada said, "Show yourself now or I'll have no option but to fire. The entire Inner Circle security force is about to come in. There are at least three challengers in the building." His voice sounded strained.

There was another small noise, a faint squeak as if a frightened animal hid under the stool and behind the benches.

I noticed that the outer casing of the circular bench didn't quite reach the floor. I sunk to my knees so that I could look underneath the casing through a gap as wide as my hand.

There was a bed of sorts on the floor. Pillows. A maroon blanket. A couple of small devices, one of them bright yellow. A floppy thing made from dirty rags.

That looked suspiciously like . . . The head of a doll?

"Wait, Veyada. Hold fire."

I went a few steps into the room, bending down so that whoever hid behind the bench couldn't see me.

"Cory, be careful," Sheydu warned me.

I reached the gap in the circular bench that allowed the user to enter the hub, and crouched on the floor.

Tucked away under the bench sat someone small. Two bare feet belonging to a little girl stuck out of the shadows. Two trembling and dirty hands held a very lethal gun, turned to a wide-spray setting, pointed at me.

"Hello. We come here to help you. What's your name?"

Eyes blinked in the darkness. "My daddy says anyone who comes in this room is bad. Why didn't the guard stop you? I said they should keep everyone away."

Oh shit. I didn't even know Ezhya had a daughter. How old was she?

Wait. "*You* told the guards not to let in anyone?"

"I used Daddy's feeder, up there." Her gaze flicked to the bench above her.

I almost laughed. The whole of the Inner Circle guard had been confused because of one cute little girl?

"Where is my daddy?"

"He's safe. You're safe now."

"I'll sit here until he comes back. No one comes in here."

"I won't be happy until we have that gun of hers," Sheydu whispered behind me. "The little brat should be disciplined. He's always too soft on her."

"Shhh," I hissed at her. That was no way to talk to a frightened child.

The girl glanced aside. "Who are you and who is there with you?" She used disturbingly mature pronouns.

"Your daddy has sent us to fix the hub before he comes home."

"My daddy?" She had come a little bit further into the light.

I guessed she would be about seven or eight in *gamra* years—which were shorter than Earth years by a couple of days.

She wore a child-sized silver suit and red sash. Her eyes were wide, and her irises spotted through with the gold flecking that was so distinctive of Ezhya's eyes.

"What is your name?"

"Raanu."

"Raanu, I'm Cory. I'm one of your father's associates. Please put the gun down. There are a lot of bad men on their way here. I can stop them if you let me."

"Only Natanu can. She has a key."

"She gave it to me."

She frowned. "My daddy says that anyone who has a key except him or Natanu is someone who will try to kill him."

"Not me. Natanu trusted me with the key. Come out. Look at me."

A small silence. She shuffled forward a bit. And then, "Why does your hair have that funny colour? You talk funny, too." Well, hadn't I just paid the price for that. Somewhere in the building an alarm was going off. Those guards in the courtyard would be on their way up here.

"I'm not Coldi, which is why Natanu trusted me with the key. I have no interest in taking over or killing anyone. I am an associate of your father's, from Barresh."

She frowned. A flicker of interest went over that sincere face. She had a smudge over her forehead and her skin looked sallow.

"Come, please put the gun down so I can use the key and we will all be safe until your father comes back. We have food." There were shouts somewhere closer in the building. "Please, hurry up, before the guards come."

She still looked dubious.

I held out my hand.

The people were definitely in the corridor now.

"Please . . ."

She shifted forward. Then she saw Sheydu. Her face became suspicious. "You're with the nasty woman."

"Sheydu is not nasty."

"Yes, she is. She calls me a brat. I heard it."

"She's not—"

"She always does that. She says I am annoying. Well, puh, my father is more powerful than she is, and he—"

"Please, come with us. There are angry Inner Circle guards coming." I held out my hand motioning for Sheydu to retreat.

At the same time, Veyada, of whom I'd lost sight, came into the hub area from the other opening between the circular benches. He looped an arm around her chest, while grabbing hold of the gun with the other.

Raanu screamed. "Let go of me. I order you to let go of me!"

A whole line of lights flashed on the control bench. An alarm started beeping in the room.

"What's that?" Veyada called. "Sheydu, what's that?"

Sheydu studied the screens. "Oh, fuck it. She's still wearing his feeder." And it tapped into the hub and was now probably sending all sorts of distress signals to the Inner Circle guards.

Veyada did his best to hold the girl with one arm and search the back of her head between her hair with the other.

"Ha, got it." His hand came away with a dark spidery thing that dangled off his fingers.

Raanu screamed. "Let go of me. That's mine. You have no right to take it. Give it back to me!"

Sheydu shut off the alarm with a few touches on the panel. The beeping stopped but the lights still flashed.

"Cory, quick, the key. I have no idea what orders just went out with her alarm call."

I scanned the array of screens and buttons. Hell, I was glad she was with me. I had no clue what to do with this key.

"There," she pointed at the top left-hand side of the panel.

Something flashed at the door. Veyada yelled. He handed the girl to me and flung the feeder onto the bench top. He and Sheydu ran for the door with guns raised.

With one hand, I reached over the bench and slotted the metal strip of the key into the hole.

The entire bench in front of me lit up. A holo display sprang up and asked for input. *Key sequence.* What was that?

Sheydu and Veyada had disappeared out the door. Flashes went off outside the room.

Damn I needed to get this thing working.

A small voice said next to me, "It's the number on the display up there."

She pointed a chubby hand at the screen next to the slot where I'd stuck the key.

I sat on the stool and lifted the girl onto my lap. "You help me."

"I need that." She reached out, scooped up the feeder and put it back in her hair. It took a second or so to connect, at which time a solemn look came over her face.

Her chubby hands went over the controls as she typed numbers. The holo input vanished, having accepted the code. Text and images scrolled over the walls and ceiling. Orders carried given, completed, carried out. Pre-programmed routines by Ezhya.

Phew.

We did it.

Only then was I aware that the disturbance in the corridor had stopped. Sheydu and Veyada were standing wide-eyed by the door with a group of guards. I realised what this must look like to them: a foreigner in the chair normally reserved only for their absolute leader, with a child on his lap.

I set the girl on the ground and pushed myself off the stool. "I'm sorry, I . . ."

All those guards had come to check out the breach of security, and were soldiers loyal to who knew whom within the Inner Circle. They were all staring at me, not all of them in a friendly way.

Sheydu said softly, "Cory, let's get out of here. The hub is stable now. Put on your helmet."

I had no idea what the urgency was, but we'd done what we set out to do, and we could go and find Thayu and Nicha.

I put on my helmet and attached the tank.

Then looked back to the hub, where Ezhya's daughter stood, looking lonely and abandoned. "What about her?"

"Cory, hurry up, the building is secure now, but Taysha is furious. I'm getting a lot of bad language on the comms. He's let it be known that you refused to accept his writ and all troops loyal to him will want to kill you."

I'd also just stifled his chance of taking the job he so desperately wanted, not to mention killing some of his personnel and taking his woman without even being capable of using her for the only purpose he'd wanted her for.

Damn, what was wrong with this man? And Sheydu hadn't answered my question. Although I already knew the answer. She didn't care about the girl.

A deep anger welled up in me. How could a little girl like this be left alone? Why hadn't she come with Ezhya to the wedding? She was the heir of Ezhya's estate. She would have been more than welcome in my apartment.

I ran back and took her hand. "Come."

"Why? You said that my daddy would come back when you fixed the machine. You fixed the machine. I want him back now."

"Come on, we have no time for arguments. I'll explain later."

"No."

Veyada looped an arm around her waist and lifted her, struggling and all, over his shoulder. "He says you come. That means you come."

17

RAANU STARTED screaming. Veyada slung her further over his shoulder where she hung with her backside in the air, her fists pummelling Veyada's back. We ran into the corridor, past the guards who still didn't seem quite sure what to do after their instructions had suddenly changed. I was also guessing that those instructions didn't include how to deal with a screaming child.

There was a lift cubicle at the end. Sheydu went in and Veyada dragged in Raanu, who was still screaming and struggling against his grip.

The doors shut.

"Shut up, brat," Sheydu said while operating the lift panel.

"I'm not a brat! I'm not a brat!"

"You're behaving like one."

"Let me go, let me go let me go!" She hit Veyada's back. Her face was red with exertion.

"Veyada, let her go," I said. The lift started moving down.

Raanu pushed herself up and stared at me. Her nostrils were flaring.

"We can't let her loose. She'll attract attention to us," Sheydu said.

And she won't attract attention like this? "She won't. She is a smart girl." I met Raanu's eyes. "Do you understand that? He will put you down, but you have to be quiet because there is danger."

Raanu looked at me, her eyes wide. Somehow through the entire struggle she had managed to hang onto her dirty rag doll.

"Who are you? You're not in Daddy's association. How come you can order Veyada around?"

I chose to ignore that question. To be honest, I wasn't quite clear of where I stood with the two guards myself.

Veyada set Raanu on her feet. He checked the safety on that fearsome gun he'd taken off her and shoved into his belt.

She faced him with her back straight. "That's mine."

"That's no weapon for a little girl."

"I know how to use it. Daddy taught me."

Ezhya was an ace sharpshooter. I suspected she probably knew how to handle a gun better than I did.

"Your daddy would never forgive us if something happened to you because of that gun."

"I can defend myself." She stuck her chin in the air.

"People will shoot at you if you have a gun."

"Just stop arguing," Sheydu said. "You can't have the gun, end of story."

"You're nasty."

"You're a spoilt brat."

"I'm not."

She turned around to me, and then seemed to slump.

"Where is Daddy? Why isn't he with you? You said you came from Barresh. That's where he went."

Fortunately, the lift doors opened before I had to make a decision whether to lie or tell her the truth. We came out in the building's entry hall. At least twenty or so guards were standing around in small groups looking confused.

Sheydu and Veyada stepped out of the lift, apparently confident they weren't about to be shot.

Raanu hid behind me.

"They're not Daddy's association," she whispered, using a pronoun form that I'd hardly ever heard anyone use, and definitely not while addressing me. It was for people who were part of a rival association.

I said, "Come, take my hand. We're going to quietly walk through this hall and not look at anyone."

We needed to cross it to get to the station—presuming there were trains, presuming we'd be let onto them.

"No, they will kill us." She clamped her arms around my waist.

"Stop this nonsense." Sheydu whirled around at her. "Shut up, brat. Do as you're told."

"She's scared." Someone had told me that Coldi children had no ranking and didn't derive any respect from their parents' status. For a child, the Inner Circle had to be a frightening place to grow up.

"We don't have time for this nonsense. Just pick her up and carry her."

Veyada turned around, ready to do just that.

"No, don't touch me!"

"Wait." I stepped in front of Veyada.

He glared at me. I glared back.

There was a tense moment in which I wondered if he'd attack me, but then he retreated a step and looked down.

I breathed out relief, not sure what this backdown of his meant. Damn, I didn't want to mess up Ezhya's relationship with his guards, but it looked like that was already happening.

I put a hand on Raanu's shoulder, hoping she'd listen. "We're going to calmly walk out of this hall and you're going to be quiet and behave nicely. These guards don't know me and will be looking at me in my funny suit. If you walk next to me, they won't see you."

The guards were already looking at me. Some exchanged glances. They looked to me like any other Inner Circle guards. They even wore Ezhya's red sash and based on that, I would have thought they were friendly. But I trusted her instincts more than mine.

She responded by taking my hand. "I don't know what they're doing here," she whispered to me. "They're not daddy's guards. I've never seen them around here."

"I'm not sure what's going on, *mashara,*" I said in a low voice. "Who are these guards?"

"Most of them are Taysha's," Veyada said in an equally low voice.

"Wearing the sash?"

I met his eyes and saw in them what it meant: the noises we had heard earlier in the building had been of a coup in progress, and we had thrown the process in disarray by activating the command key.

Hence the confusion. The guards were suddenly getting strong orders from the hub again, and now they didn't know what to do anymore.

But the fact that they'd come in here meant that there'd be a bloodbath somewhere in the building.

Thayu, Nicha. I shivered despite the heat. "Is there anything we can do?"

"Keep going and hope we can get out of here."

"What about the command hub?"

"Ezhya's key will have triggered further lockdowns. The hub will be his for at least a few more days. We can't stay that long anyway. The rest of the building will be Taysha's, and his guards would shut us in. You need to get out of here as soon as possible. Our work is done until the Exchange returns."

Shit. That had been way too close for comfort. A few more days. Was that worth the risk to my life? Worse, had my stupidity harmed Thayu?

Sheydu increased the pace. I understood that we badly needed to leave that hall, but I had trouble keeping up with my heavy gear. All this traipsing around in high gravity made me feel that as soon as I hit a bed, I'd fall asleep and stay down for a whole day. My entire lower body ached, but I forced myself to keep going.

Not fast enough for Sheydu's liking. She ran ahead, urging us along.

Veyada called out to her, "Come back here. We protect the Delegate." There was an oddly sniping tone to his voice.

Sheydu shot him a glare, but waited for us to catch up. Her face said, *He's too slow.*

Damn it. I'd risked my life for the key, but it might have been too late, because everything was falling apart.

We ran through the long passage and arrived at the station just as a train pulled in. While we walked down the stairs to the platform, it stopped. The doors opened, letting a huge contingent of guards onto the platform. A whole bunch of different guards ran in from behind us, weaving past us and taking the stairs two steps at a time.

The two groups met at the bottom of the stairs. Fist fights broke out. There were shouts, and a weapon discharged. Guards around us fired back.

Raanu screamed. She threw her arms around my waist. I almost tripped with the sudden weight.

"Come." Veyada pulled me along. Down the stairs, onto the platform. We ran, doubled over, past a knot of hand-to-hand fights.

There were people down on the ground. We had to step over a few of the bodies. I was torn between wanting to stop and check on them and wanting to ignore them. Some were beyond help, their clothes burned off and the skin underneath blackened.

Raanu hung tight onto my suit, burying her face in the fabric. She was crying inaudible words. I held my gloved hand on her head in an attempt to both hold her down so that she remained covered by me, and to shield her eyes.

That blood bath I'd been wondering about?

It was right here.

Sheydu reached the very edge of the platform. She jumped onto the rails. Veyada handed her Raanu and, after eying the train, I unceremoniously slid down after her. Discharges flashed over our heads.

We ran into the tunnel, where it was dark and hot. I couldn't see anything with the biometrics display inside the helmet. Raanu tripped a few times and I had to use all my strength to haul her up. That strength was waning with every step. I was sweating in my suit, not coping, worried when a train would come and flatten us. I was gasping for air, never getting quite enough.

Where the hell were we going?

My legs ached, my head pounded. I was afraid to ask the guards to stop and afraid to keep going. Purple spots danced in my vision. For a second, I blacked out—

—Sheydu had disappeared from where she'd just been running in front of us.

Crap. I stumbled to a halt. Purple dots danced in my vision.

Veyada pulled me aside into a niche in the side of the tunnel.

"Train coming?" I panted. I had to slow down, or I was going to faint.

Raanu gave a frightened squeak. I pulled her against me, bracing for the rush of a passing train.

But there was none. Instead, Veyada turned the handle of a door in the darkness of the alcove. It opened with a creak and groan. A rush of cool air wafted out. We went in.

The passage into the rock was uneven, narrow and, when Veyada had shut the door behind me, completely dark.

Sheydu flicked on a light and then Veyada added his, casting stark shadows over rough-hewn rock walls.

We started moving again, down the passage, which went further into the earth. It was much cooler here. I wanted to take off my helmet, but Sheydu kept going.

We walked and half-ran. At one point, the ground rumbled. Raanu gave a squeak and I expected a cave-in, but Veyada behind me said only, "Train."

After having covered a good distance, the passage widened out into a cavern where the floor was more even.

Sheydu finally stopped here.

I sank down on a rock ledge and took that horrible hot helmet off my head. My hair was wetter than it would have been had I jumped in water.

The air in the tunnel was cooler than I'd experienced anywhere since stepping off the shuttle. A breeze wafted over my skin, making me shiver. A wave of nausea rose in me. I leaned against the rock behind me, closing my eyes until it had passed.

The passage led into the darkness, going down. A humid breeze came from that direction.

"Where are we?"

"Aquifer network," Veyada said.

Sheydu had pulled out a reader and was studying the screen. Veyada went to look over her shoulder.

Raanu sat next to me, putting her hand on my arm. "You're all wet."

"Yes." I leaned my head back against the rock. "Yes. I'm sorry."

"You don't need to be sorry for being wet, you silly."

"I'm sorry for . . ." I wasn't coping very well. My body was under stress.

"Are we going to go into the tunnels?"

"I think so."

"But . . ." Her eyes grew wide. "Daddy says you shouldn't go into the tunnels. When it rains, the water comes up suddenly and sweeps you away."

Sheydu gave her a *shut up* sort of glance.

I nodded, glaring back at Sheydu. Was it really so hard to be nice to a child? "I know the aquifers are dangerous, but it's the only way we can get out."

I had no idea where we were going, even if we were going anywhere and if there was any point going to where we were going. "You have to be brave, right, for your daddy."

Her shoulders slumped. "Daddy wanted me to watch the hub."

"The hub is safe, for now." Or so I hoped. "It was not safe to stay there." Not with a take-over in progress.

She drew her knees to her chest and looped her arms around them, staring into the distance. "I'm hungry."

Maybe, I was, too. The doughy meal in Taysha's apartment was a long time ago. I always noticed that I ate a lot when I was on adaptation. Damn, I hoped that we were going to arrive where we were going soon. My head was swimming. I hoped someone where we were going could give me medication.

Sheydu and Veyada were discussing directions.

"Can we go back to the army base from here?"

"There's no point in going there," Sheydu said. "Without Asha, there will be no transport off the surface. Not from the army base at least."

Shit.

And the airport in Third Circle was closed. Then how was I going to get home? Worse, how was I going to survive?

She met my eyes for an intense moment, and then looked down.

I breathed out heavily.

Thayu had my medication.

My tank was running low on coolant.

Without Exchange we wouldn't know what was going on in the rest of the city.

No one would know where we were.

I might as well be dead.

Veyada said, "We're going to attempt to reach one of the open aquifers so that we can have radio reception. According to Sheydu's map, there should be one not too far away. We can rest there, and get some food."

"Food sounds great." Trying to be cheerful. In my current state, I'd have a hard job holding any food down.

Soon after we started walking again, the passage joined an even wider passage, where a concrete walkway ran along an underground river. The water was dark, softly churning, the surface oily and dotted with debris from the rain. Trails of debris also lined lower sections of the path.

I wondered what time it was and if daylight had come yet. My timer was in the pocket of my inner suit and I couldn't reach it without taking off the outer layer.

Raanu walked silently next to me. Strands of hair had escaped her ponytail and were plastered to her forehead. Her hair was dull, having lost much of the typical Coldi lustre, a reliable sign that she was well and truly worn out.

We kept walking. The small stream became a bigger stream and then a smaller stream again. There were racks on the walls of some passages, structures about as tall as me that hung from hooks in the rock. They had shelves of fine mesh where mushrooms grew. The sharp acidic scent of them was much stronger than I had ever smelled in the markets in Barresh.

Then we met a man coming our way. He wore a loose shirt tied with a cloth belt, and loose, three-quarter-length pants. He carried a basket and when he saw us coming, he jumped to the side and pushed himself against the rock wall, looking at the ground.

These Inner Circle guards had a reputation, didn't they?

A bit later, we came to a cavern where a couple of women hanging off the walls in harnesses were chatting while harvesting mushrooms. They fell quiet as soon as we entered, spying on us from their perches with dark, glittering eyes.

The passage widened up further, and through a ragged natural hole in the ceiling I could see sky: yellow-tinged blue with pink streaks of cloud. Dawn, then.

After a couple more such caverns, we came to one that opened right out. The river bed widened and shallowed, the river banks became vivid green with fields of crops. A couple of people worked the soil at the far end of the canyon, oblivious to our presence.

A number of houses stood jammed against the rocky wall. Where the canyon joined the underground passage there was a dam. Water pooled on the canyon side, deep and smooth as a mirror. Droplet trails trickled from the overhanging rock onto a stony beach.

A plain shack stood against the gorge wall, deep in the shadow of the overhanging rock. It was here that Sheydu led us.

The inside of the shack held simple furniture, a low table and a couple of backless benches. And sleeping mats. I peeled off my suit while Veyada inspected a cupboard against the back wall. My clothes underneath were entirely soaked with sweat.

"Ew, that smells." Raanu wrinkled her nose.

"Do you think I could rinse off in that pool outside?" I asked Veyada. My jaw was shivering.

"Yeah, if you like getting wet."

Not only did I like getting wet, I suddenly felt that if I didn't, I'd be dead before night.

I slung both suits over my arm and went outside. Whoa, the light had become a lot brighter suddenly. Without the suits, the wind scorched over my skin, as if I stood in a hot exhaust.

I clambered down the rocky slope to the water and was about to dive in when I remembered the vapour rising off the rocks. How acid was this water? I stuck the tip of my finger in. It looked like normal water. It smelled like normal water.

What to do?

I was so hot, the sweat was running in my eyes. Where was Thayu with my medication?

I sat on the rock and stuck my feet onto the water. It was warm. Did it make my skin tingle? Was it slowly eating away at my feet?

I didn't even care anymore.

Damn, I was feeling very bad all of a sudden. This would *not* be a good place to faint. I turned around. I managed to push myself to my feet, but my knees felt weak and my legs were unable to support my weight. I tried to call for help, but my throat was dry and only a strangled sound came out.

The vision in the corners of my eyes went white. I took a staggering step but lost my balance on the wobbly rocks. I fell. A voice yelled somewhere far in the distance. Then all my senses blacked out.

18

VOICES.

There were voices in my head, hollow and echoing.

I was lying on something soft that held me in a half-sitting position, head elevated. My legs and body felt cool.

I couldn't move.

Why were there so many people around me? Why couldn't they shut up?

I tried to open my eyes, but there was a sharp light above me that hurt my eyes.

Someone close, a woman with an unfamiliar voice said, "He's waking up."

I tried harder and a bright slit opened. Ouch, that light was really sharp.

"Can you turn that off?" My tongue felt like rubber and probably didn't produce the words as I wanted.

The light remained on.

Someone lifted me under my shoulders and held a cup to my mouth.

I drank.

Water. Cool and soothing. There was a splashing sound around me. I could feel more water lapping at my skin.

My eyes opened further now. I half-lay into a shallow bath, wearing nothing more than a loincloth. A thick arm band sat snug around my upper arm. A tube filled with clear fluid went into it. Two patches with leads dangling off were attached to my chest.

There was a privacy screen around me, and to my left stood a bank of blinking equipment, none of it familiar to me.

Well, bugger that. Someone had taken me to a hospital. I vaguely remembered collapsing on the stony beach of a pool. In fact, there was a scrape on my leg that I must have sustained when falling.

At a stool next to me sat a woman in an odd kind of loose garb reminiscent of a Roman toga. It was grey, not white, and she wore an apron over the top. She was tall, dark-skinned, with high cheekbones. The toga left her slender arms uncovered. Her hands had very long fingers.

I wanted to say, "Who are you?" but my throat tickled so much I ended up coughing. She put the cup to my mouth again. When it was empty, she set it on a tray next to the bed.

"Where am I? Can I get up?" My voice was still very fragile.

"If you're well enough." She sounded distinctly female, not like a typical Coldi voice that was too dark to be female and too high to sound male. "Let me take this off first."

She loosened the band around my upper arm and detached the skin infusion patch that was at the end of the tube. Adaptation medicine.

I struggled to sit up.

She pulled the sticky pads off my chest.

"Are you hungry?" she asked.

"I think so."

"I'll get someone to bring you some food." She rose from the stool and left, carrying the arm band and the tube.

"Green-coded," I called after her.

"We are aware of that."

The head of my watery bed was shielded by the moveable screen, but past the foot of the bed I could see others in the room. People on beds, people sitting next to beds, people walking around.

Wait.

Last I knew I was in one of the aquifers in Athyl.

Some of these people weren't Coldi, including that strangely-dressed nurse.

I clamped my arms around me. I'd never thought I'd say this, but it was actually quite chilly in here. That fluid in the basin wasn't water, but some kind of very runny, clingy gel that made a cold patch wherever it dried.

"He is going to be fine," the nurse said somewhere else in the room.

Running footsteps approached.

Raanu came around the privacy screen, pulling herself up on her toes on the edge of the bed. "You have woken up! Oh, I have to tell everyone."

She ran off again.

Her voice drifted through the room. "Come, come here quickly, he's woken up!"

This was followed by quick footsteps in the part of the room that was obscured by the screen, and then . . .

"Cory!"

Thayu. Her eyes bright with joy.

She ran to the bed and wrapped her arms around me. And kissed me. Not caring about the inappropriateness of the intimacy or the fact that most Coldi didn't kiss, or that I was wet with disgusting gel.

I clung onto her, feeling the heat of her body through her clothes, and the heat of her mouth and her breath over my skin. Her heart beat under her chest, I could feel that, too. I was never going to leave her again. Never.

Eventually, when the silence around us had grown too awkward, I let her go. Her eyes glittered with tears. Her chest heaved with deep breaths.

Nicha was there, too. He came to me for a wordless hug.

"What happened? Why are you here? How did you know I was here?" *Where is your father and Natanu? Why didn't the diversion happen?*

"I had your medicine with me. I knew that if you . . ." She swallowed visibly. ". . . if you were still alive, this was the only place you would be, because these would be the only people who would know what you needed."

I digested that for a bit. The tears in her eyes, the equipment around me.

"How long have I been out?"

"Two days. They said the aquifer farmers brought you in after you collapsed. You are very lucky, Cory."

Two days?

And where were we?

The only people who would know what I needed?

The tall brown-skinned woman was now attending a different patient on the other side of the room. The grey garment she wore was not a toga. Thin and sheer as gauze, its many folds wrapped around her legs as well. I thought I recognised it from the pictures. This was a *shayka,* a loose garment made from one length of fabric that was mainly worn by desert rebels.

I frowned at Thayu. *"Zeyshi?"*

Whatever happened to the people who were supposedly so deprived that Marin Federza considered them a lost cause.

She nodded. Her expression had a *careful* expression.

I glanced at the nurse. "Is she Aghyrian?" All the Aghyrians I'd ever seen were pale-skinned, slender, elfin-like creatures I'd come to distrust intensely.

She nodded. "There have always been Aghyrians with the *zeyshi.* It's why the *zeyshi* live underground and why the group was formed in the first place."

The nurse moved to the next patient, an elderly Coldi man. Her actions were competent and her eyes alert; her face lacked the haughty expression that I knew from Federza, Chief Delegate Akhtari or any other Aghyrians I'd met in Barresh.

Zeyshi and many other people in the Outer Circles lacked the association instinct and didn't form loyalty networks in the same way most Coldi did. In hindsight, it was clear that this was the section of the population rich in Aghyrian blood, but ages of discrimination and poverty preceded that discovery.

The hospital was well-appointed and modern. Obviously, the days that *zeyshi* were poor and lived like animals in holes in the desert, killing each other over a few drops of water, were long gone. It also seemed that Federza and the Barresh contingent had completely over-looked and underestimated these people.

A different nurse, this one male, Coldi and also wearing a grey *shayka,* came to bring a tray with a bowl of food.

"Thank you." I sat up, shivered with a breeze going over my wet skin. A bowl on the tray contained a handful of mini-rolls, bread-like things the size of a large marble. They were still warm and exuded a fresh smell. They tasted good, too.

"How far are we from the Inner Circle?" I asked with my mouth full.

"Quite a way," Nicha said.

"And is the situation in the Inner Circle still . . . stable?"

"I think so. It's very hard to get news here, but it seems there is a stand-off going at the Inner Circle. If there had been a take-over, there would have been a lot more violence followed by a very sudden stop in fighting."

Of course, none of us had experienced a change in leadership, so this was pure guesswork. I agreed that the signs were in favour of the status quo.

"Look at the goose bumps on you," Thayu said, trailing a finger over my arm which, ironically, increased the goose bumps. "You should get dressed. I'll go and see what happened to your clothes."

When she was gone, Nicha leaned against the edge of the basin. "There is some good news. The Exchange has made an announcement that they expect to be able to start resonating with Barresh later today."

Thank the heavens. "Anyone heard from Ezhya?"

"Not yet. No one knows how badly other sections of the networks have been affected. It could still be days before functionality is returned."

"We don't have days."

"No, but there is little we can do from here. You did what you could. You were successful. Right now, I think the most important thing for us is to try to get you out of here. Taysha holds all of the area surrounding the hub. He will get in within the next day or two. It's beyond us. The race is between him and the Exchange."

Damn. "Can't your father help us?"

"I'm afraid not. That side of the command has broken down. It seems Taysha dealt with Risha first. We can't raise him and no one seems to know where he is."

And Risha, of course, was Asha's superior, without whom Asha was cut adrift. The saying went that a high-powered Coldi without a loyalty network always gravitated to the top. And Taysha had cleverly neutralised both Risha and Asha.

"Is that why the diversion didn't go as planned?"

"That and other problems. When we got to my father's quarters, Taysha's troops were waiting for us. They took us into custody and interrogated us. We managed to get out, but our father is still held. They'll be testing his loyalties."

"Testing?"

Nicha's eyes met mine, sincere. "You really don't want to know."

Well, then, I guess I didn't, and I guessed that testing loyalties was probably something that involved semi-legitimate torture.

"Are you worried about him?"

"No. If he chooses to challenge Taysha, he will do so because he knows he can win. Otherwise he will not challenge."

"Would your father serve under Taysha?"

"Never."

"So he would essentially take Risha's position?"

"If it is indeed vacant."

I was somewhat pleased with that reply, although it probably did make matters more difficult. If Taysha took over as Chief Coordinator, what did that mean for the entire army?

If that happened, I interpreted from Nicha's tone that Asha would challenge and that it would be a fight to the death, and that quite possibly there would be armed troops involved.

I was trying to digest this in a Coldi way, while a little voice inside me was screaming *do you know we call this a military coup?* and I couldn't convince it to shut up.

But it wasn't. Not yet. Ezhya still clung to power. I had to maintain hope.

Nicha said, "There will be a time of turmoil. Associations have been ripped and everything needs aligning."

I nodded. I felt the same about what had happened with our small group. Coldi had a word for that: *denaryi*. It meant "everyone is OK, but the associations are a mess." It described our current situation well.

"What happened to you?" Nicha asked.

In a few sentences, I described the meeting with Taysha, and the writ—

"You're serious? Did he want that?"

I switched to Isla. "Would I joke about that? You know how much I hate horse-trading over partners."

"He's got to be kidding. You know . . . you should write a counter-writ."

"That's what Veyada said."

He snorted. "Veyada would just go and kill the bastard if this happened to him."

That's what Veyada had said, too. "What do you think, Nich'? What should I do? I don't want to get involved in this justice system I don't understand—"

"You understand better than many Coldi."

"You know what I mean."

Nicha sighed. He nodded. "You don't want to give orders to kill anyone. But, you know, you're going to have to make a decision. Since you have clearly violated the laws of your own world, *gamra* will want to see you obey some law, not pick and choose whatever law suits you."

Ouch. "Thanks, Nich'. "

"I mean it. This is what people say to me: is he Coldi or what jurisdiction does he fall under? Everyone saw clearly how you stood up to Danziger."

I nodded. I could pretend I didn't, but I understood perfectly well. The concept of democracy was alien to these people. What a leader said was law. You did not argue with a leader. Also, what Veyada had said resonated with me. If I didn't act, future powerful Coldi people would try to bully other foreigners into submission because they knew they would get away with it.

"So I should send the writ?"

Nicha nodded. "That's what I would do."

My heart sank. "Who would carry it out?"

He gave me an are-you-fucking-kidding look.

"You?"

"And Thayu."

"But you're my *zhaymas*."

"Delegate Cory Wilson, it is time that you stopped holding yourself to illusions—"

"Nich—" He had never spoken to me like that.

"—We are a complete association. There are two *zhaymas* and a superior. The *zhaymas* are my sister and I."

I stared at him, wanting to protest, but knowing deep inside that he was right. When I challenged Ezhya Palayi in his apartment in Barresh last year, something had changed in our relationship. I'd not wanted to see it.

"Don't look like that. There is no reason. This is the way it is. Associations change all the time. You moved up. We are both honoured to work with you."

"But I don't—" There was no point in arguing. *Wanting* had nothing to do with it.

I knew. It had probably been like that for some time already. But then he looked down and took up the subservient position.

I cringed inside. All the friendship we had, the times we'd laughed and did things together, were they all gone? Moreover, what did it mean for my relationship with Thayu?

I swallowed hard.

"All right, I'll accept that. Two things, Nich'. This writ . . . If there is any acting to be done on my writ, I'm not going to send both of you to do my shitty jobs. If there is no other option but to kill him, I will do it myself. Secondly, I want you to never, ever act like a subordinate in front of me again."

19

WHEN I TURNED away from Nicha, Thayu had returned with my clothes. She stood to the side, just behind the end of the privacy screen. I wondered how much of the conversation she had heard. Raanu was with her so I couldn't ask.

I met her eyes and I wondered if she saw any of the pain I felt.

Damn it, these associations would ruin everything I'd built up with Nicha and Thayu. The closer I came to Ezhya, the further I ventured from them. Yet I should have known. When I first met Thayu, she had shown a subservient reaction to me. Nicha had shown a latent reaction to me.

Who was I? What was I? What right did I have to do these things and mess up these people's lives? What did it mean for me to support a leader whom everyone already seemed to have considered having lost his position?

I climbed out of the water. Thayu handed me a towel. I still felt a little light-headed and sat on the stool where the nurse had been sitting earlier.

"I'll help," Raanu said. I wanted to protest but hadn't the energy. Guess Coldi didn't worry much about their children seeing naked adult men. I let her dry my back.

"It's funny, you have hair here." She pulled.

"Ouch!" That was very low on my back.

"Raanu!" Thayu warned.

There was a tense silence in which I couldn't see what went on behind me. The drying resumed. When Raanu came to the front, she was pouting.

After a while, Thayu said, "Now we're done. Get his clothes."

Raanu bowed awkwardly and took a neatly-folded bundle of cloth from a set of shelves behind her. She gave them to me with that same stiff little bow.

I said, "Thank you." I had to clamp my jaws in an effort not to laugh.

She went to stand next to Thayu, and Thayu ruffled her hair.

I got up and unfolded the bundle.

Someone had washed my clothes and rinsed my temperature suit. I stuck my hand inside the pocket—empty.

Thayu pulled something from her pocket. "If you're looking for this, I took the liberty to remove it before the *zeyshi* got their hands on it." She held up the package with the explosive and detonator that Sheydu had given me.

"Thanks."

"How did you get it? Sheydu?"

"Yes."

"That figures. She's an explosives specialist. Hang onto it. That's good stuff. We might be able to use it later."

I pulled my clothes on. Thayu handed me the helmet, which had been cleaned.

"Careful with the tank. It's been filled up. This fill should last you longer. *Zeyshi* have always been pretty good at finding nifty cooling systems. Put it on. The sooner we're out of here, the better."

"Am I allowed to leave?"

"The nurse says it's all right," Nicha said.

I took the tank and jacket from him and almost dropped it. All this gear was so incredibly heavy.

Nicha put a hand on my shoulder. "Are you all right, Cory?"

"Yes. Just . . ." I leaned over, trying to dispel the dizziness.

"It's not that far from here to a fissure where Thayu has a contact with an aircraft. You only need to last that far."

I struggled with the jacket. It was inside out and the straps to hang the tank were tangled.

Get out. Go home, to safety and a place where I wasn't at risk of being cooked inside my skin.

Wait.

What was I doing? *Think, Mr Wilson, think.*

We were at a *zeyshi* stronghold. *Zeyshi* had made a claim on Asto. Ezhya wanted me to go and talk to them. Taysha certainly would never do that.

"What is it?" Thayu asked.

"I can't leave right now. I need to speak to the *zeyshi* leaders first."

Nicha frowned at me. "I would prefer to get out of here as soon as possible. Besides, I don't know if this is the right time—"

"I don't know if there will ever be another time. By all accounts, Taysha is about to take over the leadership, but the claim on Asto made by the *zeyshi* still stands. *Gamra* is going to have to deal with it. No one from *gamra* can visit the *zeyshi* to assess their claims, certainly not when Taysha takes over, and when he takes over, *zeyshi* won't be allowed to travel either. Federza and the Barresh group don't represent these claimants at all. Taysha very much disagrees with visits from non-Coldi. I must do it quickly, while I'm here." I looked from Nicha to Thayu.

"Then I will arrange it," Nicha said. His face went blank.

I swear he gave a little bow before turning around and walking out the room.

"Nich'?"

He looked over his shoulder.

"Please, don't . . ." *behave like that, or act like a servant.* I spread my hands. There was so much I wanted to say, but every time I thought I was getting close to understanding the Coldi psyche something like this thwacked me square in the face. I couldn't get my head around the thought that the man I had considered my best friend for many years suddenly started treating me as a superior.

Nicha pointed. "The head nurse is at her station right now. I'll be back soon."

I sighed and let my shoulders slump. *Nicha, please.* I didn't want to lose him to this stupid custom.

Thayu massaged my neck. Her hands radiated warm and dry heat.

I looked over my shoulder into her gorgeous eyes, wanting to be alone with her to sort this mess out. I didn't want them to be subservient to me. That kind of behaviour was a step back. You became more intimate with someone when you were closer to them, not the other way around.

But likely neither of them would understand. They would think this was a good development, that an association strengthened us as a unit and—

They were right, in their own way, and I was sending them all kinds of mixed messages. I paid out Thayu's contract, I was sending Taysha a writ, I'd gotten rid on my facial hair. I was sending them—and everyone else—messages that I wanted to be considered Coldi. Even Nicha was telling me that it had to be one or the other. I could behave like I was Coldi and accept it, or I could continue to fight it. I knew what Nicha and Thayu would prefer.

Damn.

Thayu's fingers had moved up to my shoulders. Her palms and fingertips were like little heat pads kneading my skin. "You're not taking adaptation medication?"

Normally, Coldi would take it on short trips, because if their bodies went into adaptation to adjust their internal temperature, they could be quite ill for a number of days.

"I've been across enough times that I'm getting used to quick adaptation. I really don't like taking that stuff. Gives me nightmares."

I nodded. Didn't I know about that.

The only people left in the room were three other patients and us. Two of them were old, Coldi, and the deeply bronzed, dust-engrained skin screamed *zeyshi* louder than anything else could. One appeared to have a broken leg, the other's face was covered in a face mask. Both men eyed me suspiciously.

The third patient, next to the room's only exit, was a young woman. She lay in a similar basin to mine, head slightly raised, eyes closed. The cloth that had covered my private parts lay over her pregnant belly and an apparatus next to the bed spread a constant stream of drops onto the cloth.

Her breasts were swollen and looked painfully firm. Tangles of tubes lay around her, including a couple of them that disappeared between her legs. Neither Thayu nor Raanu seemed overly interested, but for me, as a prude earthling, it was kind of confronting and embarrassing, yet I couldn't *not* look.

"Her child is Aghyrian," Thayu said in a low voice. "Apparently when they allow Coldi to carry these pregnancies naturally, almost all the girls abort."

"She looks ready to burst."

"This afternoon." Her eyes met mine longer than necessary, and I could no longer stand the questions hovering in her expression.

"Did you hear me tell Nicha what Taysha said about you?"

She nodded.

"You are *not* having anything to do with that man."

"But he's right about the allocation, and he did spend a lot of money testing me."

"You are *not* giving in to his demands."

She looked down.

"Thayu?"

I reached out and touched the sensitive skin on her neck. I was aware of Raanu watching, otherwise I would have kissed her. I pushed her chin up with my thumb.

"Thayu, if you want a child, I'll find a donor. I'll pay for the contract with the man. We will have the whole process done artificially, and the child will live with us."

"But . . ."

"That way, you'll cease to have any value to Taysha, and you'll be happy."

A brief smile crossed her face, in which I saw the Thayu I loved so much. Then she said, "What about you?"

"I'm fine with that, I . . ." *am not particularly desperate to pass my genetic material to the next generation.* Goodness knew there were enough faults in my genetic code already.

"I couldn't ask you to—"

"Yes, you can, I'm serious. If you want, we'll start the process when we come back."

She made a small, soft noise. Her eyes glittered. With one hand, she held Raanu, and with the other she took mine. She squeezed my hand and gave me a heart-stopping smile. The tear rolled over her cheek.

Suddenly, I felt all choked up inside. What sort of society allowed women to be used as breeding receptacles without the right to look after their own children?

I was going to do the right thing by Thayu and truly free her from this man's demands. If that meant a writ, then so be it. He was challenging me to play? I would play.

Veyada and Sheydu came into the ward.

Both of them greeted me in the subservient position. "Delegate," Veyada said in a low voice, speaking in the general direction of his chest. I didn't like this, oh boy how I didn't like it. If they now thought I was superior to them, how could they ever return to Ezhya?

Thayu jumped into position. Some looks were exchanged between her and the guards that I didn't understand.

Then Veyada said, "The Delegate is invited."

Nicha had sent them? This was getting ever stranger.

They and Thayu led me out of the emergency room into a neat and well-lit passage where Nicha waited in the company of a stout Coldi man, who had so many *zeyshi* tattoos on the visible parts of his skin that it was hard to make out his face. His eyebrows were exaggerated, the parts above his eyes were vivid green. Vicious spikes extended from below his eyes over his cheeks.

He wore a dark grey *shayka* and a magnificent belt with thorns and native flowers embroidered in silver thread. He did not bow or look down, but stuck his chin in the air—the skin bronzed—an action which made his little plaits dance around his head.

His eyes were almost black.

He set off down the passage without speaking a single word.

I knew this whole area was underground but it looked curiously like many hospitals and medical centres I'd seen anywhere within *gamra,* if possible more modern than that. So much for *zeyshi* being primitive and poor.

Then a chilling thought: had any off-world Aghyrian money gone into this?

Damn. That possibility chilled me no end. While I was negotiating with Federza, another sub-set of Aghyrians funded the *zeyshi* to destabilise Asto society.

We passed an assessment area where doctors sat in alcoves assessing patients. Some patients were *zeyshi,* but many were not. They looked like the mushroom farming folk we'd seen in the aquifers. I even spotted some people in Circle dress, probably Eighth.

Unlike in the Inner Circle, life continued as normal, unaffected by the continued Exchange outage, and there were no guards anywhere.

How far did the influence of the *zeyshi* reach? I'd never heard Ezhya speak about them. I'd heard other Coldi figures of authority speak about them only in derogatory terms.

An Aghyrian claim on Asto would probably be thrown out if unsupported by the Barresh Aghyrians, but the *zeyshi* had a valid claim on Asto. They'd suffered a long and well-documented record of discrimination and ill treatment, and if they teamed up with the Aghyrians, they could form a powerful bloc . . . independent of the Aghyrian section in Barresh. This was weird and scary and very interesting all in one.

From the hospital passage we entered an older tunnel, then went down a spiral staircase with treads so worn, I had to hand the tank to Nicha to free my hands for the handrail, or I'd end up in a heap at the bottom. The staircase wound down into a stone-paved hall where many footsteps had worn a path from the stairs to an arched doorway. Outside this doorway were the first two guards I'd seen in this underground warren. Both *zeyshi,* they wore pale yellow *shaykas,* each with a black belt and silver embroidery.

They held Ezhya's two guards back, standing out as they did in their silver suits and sashes.

Some hand signals were exchanged.

Sheydu said, "Delegate, our host requires that we stay here. This is the only entrance into this room. We will wait here until you return."

The *zeyshi* guard made another hand signal, one I didn't get.

"He says to leave the girl here, too."

"Nooo!" Raanu clung to Thayu's arm.

Thayu crouched so that she was face-to-face with Raanu. "We won't be long."

"Don't leave me with the nasty lady."

Sheydu shot her an angry look. Heavens, what had she done to deserve this treatment from Raanu?

Thayu took Raanu's face between her hands. "Do you want to be big and brave like your father?"

Raanu nodded.

"Then you stand here quietly with the guards. They are not going to hurt you or they'll be in big trouble with your father or with the

Delegate." She gave me a sideways look that said, *Put on your angry face.* I tried not to laugh.

Sheydu rolled her eyes.

"You'll come back soon?" Raanu asked, wide-eyed.

"Yes, we will. We're going to a meeting. It's boring. There will be only adults talking."

Raanu eyed Sheydu wearily. "But it will be boring here, too."

"The man says you can't come in."

The sharp black-eyed gaze went to the *zeyshi* guard. Oh, this girl would not miss anything, even if it was only *adults talking about boring things*.

The *zeyshi* clearly knew who she was.

"If you behave nicely, I'll give you a lesson in wrestling."

Raanu's face grew emotionless. She snapped into position in front of Sheydu, straightened her back and held her arms stiff to her sides.

"All right now?" Thayu asked the *zeyshi* guide, who returned a terse nod.

I acknowledged the guards with another hand signal. Raanu had already forgotten that she was supposed to be quiet and was asking Veyada to explain the hand signals to her.

He seemed to be handling her well enough so I followed the guide through the doorway.

Inside a cavernous room a number of people were sitting around a table. Many were elderly, some were Coldi, and some Aghyrian. Most of them wore *shaykas*. I recognised none of them.

Facing the door in a high-backed chair sat a fierce-looking Coldi woman, broad-shouldered and tall. Her skin was rough as leather and deeply tanned. She wore a full *shayka,* fabric crossed at the front, complete with the embroidered belt. Her bare arms bore the *zeyshi* tattoos of black thorns and stylised flowers.

She met my eyes and held my gaze in a cold, emotionless look. I imagined Natanu would look like her in middle age.

Four seats were still empty. Three for myself, Nicha and Thayu . . . and was there another person still coming?

On the table stood a veritable feast of colourful dishes in equally colourful bowls. A serving boy walked around the far side of the table unloading more dishes from a tray. The smell of food—strong and spicy—hung in the room.

There came the sound of footsteps on stone and a moment later an elderly Coldi man entered the room, alone.

Both Thayu and Nicha snapped into subservient positions.

He looked around the gathering until his gaze stopped with mine. He had to be the oldest Coldi I had ever seen. He was thin, his hair was white and his robe, also white, hung from his shoulders like a potato bag. Around his waist he wore a thin red belt.

Damn, this was Risha Palayi.

What the hell was he doing here?

He nodded to me, showing no sign of irritation that most people in the room, including me, didn't greet him in the traditional way. One of the guards from outside pushed the door shut behind him. Risha walked around the table, attending to each person one by one, touched their shoulders and patted their cheeks. While he did this, his face was kind and expression serious. No one moved; no one spoke.

All the people greeted him with reverence, with bright faces and subservient body language, even the *zeyshi*.

He completed the lap around the table and came to us. With a gnarled finger, he pushed up Thayu's chin so that she looked him in the eyes. "Peace, sister, all will be sorted out."

To Nicha, he said, "You are the steadying force in your family."

Then he faced me.

"So. Ezhya did send you here, as he suggested. I heard a lot about you."

Was it good or bad? I dipped my head, acknowledging him. I did *not* do this subservient greeting thing unless I absolutely had to.

Risha continued, "You're a strange fellow, oddly stubborn. Maybe even more stubborn than Ezhya, if that is possible. I do not say this lightly. Stubbornness is a rare quality. Weak is the sand that drifts with the stream."

Coldi loved their proverbs.

I nodded again, acknowledging the compliment. At this point, a Coldi would rattle the originator of the proverb. I knew a few proverbs with names of the person they were ascribed to, but I had never heard this particular one.

Risha waved his hand and said to everyone, "Be at ease. Sit down. This is not the time or place for formalities."

We sat with the others. Risha took his spot next to the *zeyshi* leader; Thayu, Nicha and I the chairs on the side of the table closest to the door.

I couldn't help it, I instantly liked this man. I *knew* I shouldn't trust my human instincts, much less make decisions based on them, but Risha had just calmed me in all the ways in which Taysha, Asha and Natanu riled me.

The fact that I ended up opposite him at the table was probably not a coincidence.

The *zeyshi* rebel leader was studying me. To her right sat an older woman, tall, slender and white-haired. She reminded me strongly of Chief Delegate Akhtari, even with her black eyes and dark skin.

Aghyrian.

Eying me with interest.

Risha said, while indicating the *zeyshi* leader, "For the newcomers who don't know her, this is Nayu."

I acknowledged her.

She observed me wordlessly as if she were an older Natanu-clone. I couldn't help hearing Natanu's words: "I only take part in fights I'm sure I can win." Had she been human, I would have guessed her about fifty, with white streaks in her hair and no-longer firm skin with spots and wrinkles.

So this was the rebel leader who had been causing trouble in Athyl according to the *shey' shamata* official news service of Asto. And here she was, offering a refuge for one of the Inner Circle's power brokers. He had been talking to the *zeyshi* Aghyrians about their claim when the Exchange went down? Why was he so friendly with them? This was getting really strange and would be interesting if we weren't in the middle of it.

"I'm glad you've come here." Risha said. "These good people are so kind to look out for any Inner Circle refugees and bring them to safety."

These good people? What the heck? The Inner Circle considered *zeyshi* an outcast nuisance.

"Oh, but I see that you are puzzled. Life is a delicate balance of *rimoyu*. We balance the two sides of each situation. I am Inner Circle. I reach out to the statusless people because they are half of what balances us. Without *zeyshi,* we would not be as strong as we are. They expose our faults and drive us to excel."

The woman Nayu took this statement without emotion. In her shoes, I would have found it patronising, but whatever the *zeyshi* were, they did seem to subscribe to that two halves to a whole thing: *ichi* and *ata-ichi*—those who were privileged and those who were not. They were both part of the same society and each accepted their place in it.

A young *zeyshi* boy came into the room with a stack of bowls and put one in front of each of us. He looked old enough to be an early adolescent, with his hair all shaved off. Like the adults, he wore a grey *shayka* but his belt was plain, and his upper arms, protruding from the fabric, bore fresh, red-rimmed tattoos. When he came to our side of the table, Nicha said quietly, "The Delegate needs green-coded food and non-acidic water."

"Water?" someone said, the tone incredulous.

Some people laughed.

I was informed by a few people at the end of the table that *zeyshi* did not drink water. They drank zixas, and, according to Nicha, that was an acquired skill. It was served in tall glasses, each with no more than a thumb-width of vile blue fluid that breathed white vapour. I'd seen Coldi drink it in Barresh, where some bars served it. You had to let it stand for a bit and swirl it around. The vapour would crawl up the sides of the glass and ooze over the edge. The idea was to hold your breath and drink, because the smell would knock you flat. I had a fair guess that it would kill me in five minutes. The fact that it could not be served in anything other than glass was probably a fair warning.

Another boy came in, carrying a tray which he placed in front of me. It held two bowls: one with grain, the other with a fragrant sauce that made my mouth water.

"You're sure this is green-coded?" I asked Nicha, in Isla.

Thayu held her comm over it. The screen flashed. "Yeah, it is."

The water arrived on a separate tray, a single glass covered in condensation. I moved the scanner over it and it came up as marginally safe. While the others took their zixas and started the game of swirling and sloshing, I sipped carefully from the water. It tasted metallic and quite bitter. I was very thirsty but didn't dare drink all of it in one go.

The two boys went around the table serving everyone. Both of them took great care to serve Risha with bows and spoke with formal, polite pronouns.

The talk at the table was polite and confined to non-offensive subjects. Normally, Coldi custom was that you got straight to business, but never while sharing a meal.

That woman Nayu kept watching me. Occasionally, she consulted with the Aghyrian woman next to her, who had not been introduced to us.

Risha reminisced about some events in his youth that meant nothing to me. Everyone, young and old, listened with rapt faces. When I was very young and living in New Zealand, we had my great-grandmother come to a family dinner at our beach house once. To me —I must have been four or five—she looked ancient, with blotted, pigmented skin. She'd had a stroke and was very hard to understand. She was also deaf and didn't hear a word I said. I had received a scooter for Christmas and was most upset that my mother got angry with me for riding it down the hall. It was raining and I couldn't go outside. The adults were all sitting around the table, listening to this woman talk about the war or something, even if she kept repeating things.

That was how I felt about this gathering.

No one interrupted Risha, who was the great-grandmother at this gathering. If I hadn't known any better, I would have guessed that the *zeyshi* had agreed to work with the Inner Circle, yet there were so many layers of networks between the *zeyshi* and the Inner Circle that this was impossible. The whole situation was utterly, utterly strange.

During the meal, no one spoke of the events in the Inner Circle, and no one asked. I wanted to bring it up. I was burning for news. I'd been out for two days. What had happened in that time? But I sensed an unspoken code that the events should not be mentioned and that politics should not be discussed. Meanwhile, I was sharing a table with the Aghyrians who had probably made the claim on Asto. I needed to talk to them, desperately.

Thayu would sometimes look at me and shake her head and motion for me to stay quiet.

Just what was going on?

"Anyway," Risha said, while getting up from his seat. He met my eyes briefly. Everyone stopped talking. "I'm very tired so I'm going to leave you. You'll be safe here while you make all your plans."

I didn't want to make any plans. My frustration broke through. "We had planned to leave as soon as possible. I need to speak with the people who made the claim on Asto, and then we want to get back into the city to a place from where I can leave as soon as possible. So please, I ask to speak to someone representing the Aghyrians here. Please, I'm asking for your support."

Several people at the table took in sharp breaths.

Risha regarded me with a curious look. "Young man, you can discuss whatever you want with these people here after I'm gone."

So he wasn't going to support me. Moreover, he was just going to ignore this issue in a detached sort of way. *You youngsters can decide what to do.* And no one here pressed him about it. Wasn't he supposed to run the army? Wasn't he one of Ezhya's seconds?

He shuffled around the room, stopping at each person and putting a hand on a cheek here or touching a shoulder there.

People bowed, expressions of reverence on their faces.

As when he had arrived, he came to me last. "Come, I will show you something."

We followed him out the door. I was burning with frustration. There was something going on here that was beyond me.

In the foyer, Veyada and Sheydu were still waiting with Raanu. They had now been joined by Natanu and the rest of Ezhya's guard. They all stood in one corner of the room while the poor *zeyshi* guards held their ground in front of the door.

Risha ignored all of them, and shuffled to the far wall, where he ran his fingertips over the stone. In the smooth stone I could discern carved shapes, but they were too eroded to see what the figures depicted.

"This section of tunnels is part of the old city of Aghyr," he said. "You are now standing in the birthplace of all of the human species. When Asto was hit by the meteorite, Aghyr was buried under layers of dust. These corridors would have been part of buildings before they provided us with shelter and underground river beds. These people invented many things that allow us to live as we do today. Look at how many years have passed, and collective humanity has barely recovered from the great blow to that civilisation."

He walked a bit further. "These people were smart. Look at this. Here you can see a map of the city. A central area with roads leading out like spokes. Not much like we have today, with the circles. The Aghyrians used spokes, we use circles and barriers. Our society can't flow outwards. The pressure builds behind the walls, and builds and builds. Somewhere, some time something has got to give, don't you think?"

I opened my mouth—

"No, don't tell me, young man. Think on it in the days to come: which method do you think works better in society: spokes or circles?"

My frustration boiled to the surface. "I'm trying to arrange for Ezhya to stay in power and for you to maintain your position. We're quite in a hurry. I want to speak to the Aghyrian *zeyshi*. I'd like some help, if you can."

Much too direct.

He met my eyes. I had often suspected that the gold flecking in Coldi eyes became more prominent with age, and that seemed correct. His eyes were almost luminescent gold with it.

He touched my shoulder in a gesture of superiority. "Young man, you mean well, but you need to learn a lot."

And that was it, all the support I was going to get from him. I felt like screaming *I'm risking my life for you and this is the way you thank me?* but I couldn't do that. For some reason, he had no guards and a little voice of decency spoke inside me that it wouldn't be right to be rude to this gentle old man.

He bent down to Raanu. "You, little pebble, recite as many of your father's commands as possible. Try to remember them while you're on your way."

She nodded fervently, her eyes wide.

Risha spoke to Thayu. "You protect the young man. He's an outright fool, but he means well."

To Nicha, he raised his hand and touched his cheek. "Look after your mother."

Then he bowed to the guards and shuffled into a passage to the left.

20

I WANTED TO run after him, but Thayu held my arm.

"What the hell is going on?" I spread my hands, rolling my eyes at the ceiling.

"Shhh," Thayu said. "You'll get to talk to the *zeyshi* now."

"But it would have been so much better if Risha was also—"

"Shhh." Her expression was serious. She continued in a soft voice. "Listen, this is what we learned when we went with Asha: when the Exchange went down, Risha challenged."

I stared at her, then down the passage where the old man had just vanished.

"Risha?" That was ridiculous. But then . . . why was he here? I put the facts together. "He challenged, but he didn't win."

Thayu signalled *yes*.

And he somehow managed to escape being killed. But then *who* was in charge of his half of Asto's society?

"The inner hub went into lockdown and wouldn't let him through. His had been a quick plan and he didn't bring enough people or firepower to bash his way through."

Ah, I saw. That was Raanu's doing. That was also why Risha was still alive. He wouldn't have been had he been defeated by Taysha or another challenger. Was that why the *zeyshi* guards had stopped Raanu going into the dinner room? Risha had been kind to her on his way out, though.

What had he said? Something about remembering her father's commands?

Thayu continued, "After the challenge, Risha's own associations started breaking up. He was forced to dismiss his guards. That's why they were wandering around the building looking lost."

"What about your father?" I asked.

"He said that as soon as we went into the building, he felt the realignment of the associations. He was going to challenge."

"And I guess he didn't?" Shit, another break in the network.

She signalled *No*.

"Where is he?"

"He's safe."

That wasn't really an answer, and Nicha gave her a sharp glance and looked at the two *zeyshi* guards.

Thayu explained further in an even lower voice, "I was angry with him, because he'd promised you not to challenge. So I . . . locked him in the apartment's bunker."

I took a sharp breath. "No, Thayu." What did that action mean to her and the hierarchy?

"My loyalty is with you and Ezhya. I made it look like an accident. He doesn't know I was angry with him. He doesn't know I did it. That particular door is prone to falling shut without notice. People have been locked in before."

"Now he can't help us either." Nicha's tone was dark.

Thayu snapped at her brother, "Don't worry. He'll have found his way out by now."

"There was no need to do that."

"Yes, there was. I don't want him to be killed and I don't want to be the Chief Coordinator's daughter. He's got enough enemies not to last very long in that job either. I'd rather have him around."

Nicha was going to argue back, but I jumped in. "So that's why there was no diversion?"

"Yes," Nicha said.

"There never was going to be one." Thayu's eyes flashed.

"How do you know that?" Nicha shot back at his sister.

"I know him much better than you. I've lived with him most of my life."

I stared at her, horrified. Did she mean that her father had lied to me all that time? Had he only wanted to use my visit as a distraction for his own ambitions? "Tell me, why does your father hate me so?"

"He doesn't. He sees you as a rival."

"For what?" That was ridiculous. It was not as if I could do any of the things he did. Like lead the Asto air force.

"He says your presence disturbs *rimoyu.* He says he feels it."

"Do you feel that, too?"

She shrugged. "I'm not my father. He feels what he feels. I can't feel the same things."

There was a small sound behind me. The rebel leader Nayu had come to the doorway and stood watching us, leaning against the door frame, her tattooed arms crossed over her chest. It was probably not such a good idea to discuss all this in front of her.

She regarded me silently. Her eyes blinked. "I thought you were here to discuss the claim."

"I am." I tried to focus. I needed to talk to these Aghyrian *zeyshi* while I was here, but reasons to do so were falling apart around me. Hell, by the time the Aghyrian claim came up in the *gamra* assembly, everything I did now could be irrelevant.

And damn it, I was not going to let that happen if I could help it. I didn't know how, but I would support Ezhya while I still could.

We followed her back inside the room, where people were still eating. I sat down, but I was no longer hungry. The Aghyrian woman across the table glared at me. She had always known why I was here and now was the time for the business that Risha no longer wanted to be part of. Natanu and the other guards had also come into the room. There were no seats for them, and they took up position at the far end. Raanu stood amongst them, looking very serious. It would have been funny had the atmosphere not been so tense.

In the silence, Nayu asked, "So, visitor, you wanted to talk to us." Her voice was rough, as if she was old as the desert itself. The previous indifference had made place for careful hostility.

"I want to talk to the Aghyrians here." I met the Aghyrian woman's eyes. "Is that your ID on the claim? Are you Evala Sadet Arwan?"

She gave a low hiss, and I presumed this meant I was right.

"If you know this, you also know the conventions of using our names. You are no friend of mine, foreigner." Her voice was clearly female, unlike that of female Coldi.

"So what do I call you? I don't recall that we've been introduced."

"For you? Vanu."

All right, that made what she thought of me pretty clear.

"I've spent a lot of time recently talking to Aghyrian interest groups. I've asked for all interested parties to contact me to be included in the discussion of future ownership of land on Asto. Why didn't you come forward?"

Another low hiss. "Those people you call Aghyrians do not represent us. They have never suffered through the hardship. They have never suffered at the hands of your precious Chief Coordinator. They have never been hounded out of their houses, refused education and treatment at hospitals. They have never seen their families killed or sent off to work camps in mid-space or on other worlds."

"A lot of those things happened in the past. You are doing well enough today."

"No thanks to any of those so-called kinsfolk. Oh, they've been here. We could come and join them, they said. Just do this blood test. We only take the people with the best results, however they define those results. To us: no way. Aghyrian or *zeyshi*, they don't see that it's the same thing. These people . . ." She waved her hand at the others at the table. "Are my family. Would you leave your family because some fop says that I can take part in their great breeding program, but my family can't?"

She let a silence lapse.

"So, what? We hear that these rich boys over there in your plush capital are negotiating away our right to claim the land and world that is ours, so what do we do? We claim, before they take the right away."

Her eyes were like black holes boring into me. She stuck her chin into the air, as if defying me to argue.

I didn't.

From her point of view, this was absolutely the right decision to make and it voiced some of the unease I'd had about the Aghyrian group in Barresh. That group needed to be broken open, so that we could see what their interests were, or even just who their leaders were. These people had some very valid points and I needed them at the negotiating table in Barresh when the hearing started. I would need to employ extra legal advice and Ezhya—

Damn, Ezhya.

If he lost his position, I had no illusion that Taysha would continue to employ me. In any case, on the off-chance that he did, I didn't want to work for him. If this happened, the claim would go to the assembly unprepared and all smaller entities that wanted to see the power of Asto diminished would argue in favour. The Coldi would lose the claim and would be legally homeless. Asto belonged to the Coldi as much as it belonged to the Aghyrians. The Coldi were not going to give any concessions if forced upon them by the *gamra* assembly. Asto might boycott *gamra*. They might develop their own Exchange. There might be armed conflict. Heavens, they had the striking power, up there in that frightening orbiting station.

"So," she said. "What do you think, foreigner?"

"I think you have valuable points to add to the citizenship issue."

She looked at me in a puzzled, *Is that so?* kind of way.

Thanks to their claim, my job was a big mess and I would have to struggle to get as much as possible done before the sitting, but I wasn't going to tell her that. And I sure as hell wasn't going to tell her that I didn't trust Federza and that this was the main reason I wanted her at the table.

Then she said, "So, what do you want from us?"

"I need your help. I want you in Barresh when the claim comes up in the assembly. I want you to be well-prepared—"

"We are not making deals with those so-called representatives."

I bit down a snippy remark. "I'm not asking you to, until you've heard their arguments."

She gave me a suspicious look.

"But in order for you to even make it to Barresh, in order for me to do anything for you, we need to make sure that Ezhya remains in power."

"What do you think you are, playing kingmaker?" Nayu asked. "What is your interest in this affair? Are we under a foreign takeover scheme?"

"I do not wish to be involved in internal affairs of the Asto leadership."

Someone laughed.

The sound came from the other end of the room, and it was Natanu. Several people gasped with the rudeness of it.

Nicha gave me a sharp look. Thayu, too. It was a look of the kind that said, *Are you going to put up with that?*

I rose, and the weakness that I'd sustained when I collapsed chose that moment to return. My legs felt like they would give way under me. I held the back of the chair. It was one of those moments I was sailing solo. I didn't have the support of a handy instinct that told me what to do.

Natanu remained seated. That was a good sign, or was it?

My heart was pounding so much that it gave me a sudden headache.

"Maybe I am already too far involved not to have any influence, but whatever influence I have will be used to support Ezhya. I want all of you who decide to help me get back to either support my position or leave. Whatever is going on in the Inner Circle, we need to sort it out, get back in there and fix it. If the Exchange is coming back soon, Ezhya will be back soon, too. We want the situation to be stable. All of you depend on Ezhya's rule to survive, because if we leave it up to Taysha, he'd send his troops in here to solve the problem. Not peacefully."

I met Natanu's eyes. She said nothing.

Nayu said, "And if we helped you, what would that mean for us?"

I turned to her. "I'm going to be straight with you."

"Good. I like straight."

"If you're after money, I have none. If you're after favours from my home world, I can't give you any of those, either. If you're wanting to bargain with me for votes or a voice at *gamra,* you have the wrong person."

Her face was impassive, but she paused as if re-thinking her options. Had she expected me to ask for money?

She said, "We saved you and your party."

"Yes, and for that, I thank you. I don't think it should go unrewarded. I'm happy to listen to your concerns and raise them when the opportunity arises. I want there to be a solution that both Aghyrians and Coldi can be happy with."

More silence.

Then one of the *zeyshi* at the far end of the table said, "That bully has done us no good."

Someone else hissed, and Natanu rose. Her chair fell backwards. "He has allowed your children to attend Eighth Circle schools, hasn't he? He has allowed you to come into Eighth Circle to buy your supplies and sell your services, no matter that *some* of them are illegal—"

The original *zeyshi* speaker also rose.

I called out, "Stop it. If you want to fight, you can do that outside and after this meeting has finished."

To my surprise, Natanu sat back down. I nodded to her and hoped she would see it as a sign of appreciation. Whatever she felt towards me, I needed her support if she was still loyal to Ezhya.

Nayu said, "So then, what are you planning to do for us?"

"What I said: I am a diplomat for *gamra*. I will help you present your case. I will assist you with legal advice and make sure that the debate has the fairest possible outcome—"

The belligerent man at the end of the table said, "We can defend ourselves. No need for foreigners—"

Sadet snapped at him. "Shut up, Nera. These bureaucrats build labyrinths so complex you have no idea. I know what you all think of the group that claims to represent us in Barresh. Fops, soft rich boys with over-inflated heads. But. That takes away nothing from the fact that those fops know how to navigate the bureaucracy, and we don't. What worries me is why would this man, self-proclaimed delegate and peace maker, help us. We don't know who he is. He's not Coldi. He doesn't look Aghyrian."

"He does, a little bit," someone at the end of the table said in a low voice.

Sadet glared the man into silence.

"My world is a very early Aghyrian settlement. I don't know if that has any bearing on my plea. I'm here because *gamra* pays me to do this job." Funded primary by Ezhya, but that aside. "They wanted someone in the position who was neither Coldi nor Aghyrian. You, *zeyshi* and Aghyrians, do not want the Coldi to be hostile. You depend on them to help develop, make and buy your technology. Without them, you'd be nothing and none of the life you've made for yourself in here would be possible—"

"We built it all ourselves."

"Who made the materials? Who mined the ore, who made the sheets of metal, who formed the glass, who grew your food?"

Silence.

"You are too few to survive on your own, even if you could live at the surface. The Coldi have no particular interest in driving you away—"

Nayu said, her eyes burning, "What do you know about it?"

"Enough to have spoken to Ezhya about this. He does not want you to be driven away. He does not want conflict. His interest is in improving *gamra*'s view of Asto while keeping the peace."

"You believe him?"

"Yes, I do."

The silence around the table indicated that many here did not.

A strong voice came from the end of the table. "This delegate may be a stubborn idiot, but in this he speaks true."

Gee, thanks, Natanu.

"So this is your reason why you want our support in this crazy expedition?" Nayu now looked at me. "To keep Ezhya in power?"

"It is. Because we'll all be better off than under Taysha."

"And what do you get out of it?"

"Nothing, in your terms. No money or favours."

"That's stupid," Nayu said. "I don't believe that."

"Stupid as it sounds, it is also true." Natanu again.

Everyone stared at me, wide-eyed.

I said, "If it is any help in letting you understand, Ezhya pays for my job. Without him, I'd have—" *to return to my home world.* No, that would never fly as a reason. Returning was meant to be *good.* ". . . I'd have no work at all. Why my home world doesn't support me financially is another story, but they don't." I really didn't want to go into Earth politics and why *gamra* was seen as insignificant there.

Nayu snorted. "You got a clan?"

I shook my head.

Veyada said, "Domiri. Unconfirmed."

She nodded. "He's got the bluntness of one."

I cringed. This was going much faster than I anticipated. I didn't know if accepting clan designation would be a good thing. I was meant to be impartial. It might upset some of the very people I was set to speak for. Yet, if I didn't get out of here, nothing would make a difference. If a clan designation was going to help me, then I would have to accept that. Maintaining the status quo was not a neutral position.

I rose. "So, this is my plan, stupid as it may seem to you. I want to go back into the Inner Circle and do whatever I can to stop Taysha taking over. We can isolate a section of the building with the hub—"

"Without assuming control of it?" Nayu sounded incredulous.

"Yes, exactly. Taysha is a vindictive man who will not further the cause of Asto at *gamra* or anywhere else in the settled worlds. He is unreasonable and makes unreasonable demands on me and on his people. He is—"

"This will help." Veyada tossed a card into the middle of the table.

Damn. He'd somehow found time to write out the text of the damn writ that I—damn it—didn't want anything to do with.

Nayu picked it up, read it and handed it to Sadet. She read it and handed it to the person next to her, and so on until it reached Natanu.

She nodded and put it on the table. "Overdue," she said. "You speak true about Taysha. Kill him."

"Yeah," Nayu said and then met my eyes. "For someone claiming not to want to be involved in Coldi society, you know how get to the point of it."

I didn't know how this was meant. Not kindly, I think. And they still didn't get that I wanted no deaths.

"I am asking for help, because I cannot do this alone. I need a means of getting into the Inner Circle. I need—" *People with guns who can shoot well.* ". . . technical specialists." How was that for a euphemism?

"We're with you. You know that," Nicha said.

"And us," Sheydu said.

Natanu only said, "Yes." That agreement to help would cover her entire association, although I was unsure if Veyada and Sheydu were still part of that. The ground was shifting while I stood on it.

"It will be interesting," Nayu said, and I guessed that was her way of agreeing to take part. She chuckled. "Yeah, let's do that. Storm the hub, set up a perimeter and see who is strong enough to resist the temptation to take over."

Damn, the sarcasm oozed from her words.

I looked at Thayu, and couldn't gauge her thoughts from the expression on her face. I wanted my feeder. I'd fought against wearing the damn thing many times, but now I wanted it.

Nayu said, "Meanwhile, let us offer you a place to rest. We will need until tomorrow to organise appropriate people to come with us on this crazy scheme."

Now a flicker of annoyance hovered in Thayu's expression. She eyed Nicha. He frowned and did one of the brother-sister face twitches. I couldn't guess the meaning of this particular one.

21

───────

A COUPLE of *zeyshi* led us out of the room through a warren of worn and disused ancient passages until we came to a corridor where somebody had put a maroon runner across the uneven cobbles of the stone floor. Against the left wall stood the narrow table one normally found in an influential family's apartment. The arrangement on it consisted of a couple of rough rocks and a small fish-bowl-like glass vase with something inside. Arrangements usually included large vases with extravagant dried flowers or tree branches. This one was very modest in comparison. The small fish bowl contained the empty husk of a worm. These creatures lived in the underground streams and made cocoons spun together from grains of sand. They were delicate, tube-like structures, discarded by the creatures when their bodies outgrew the cocoon.

I couldn't begin to guess what the arrangement meant, but I had a vague memory that the worm husk had a significant meaning.

A couple of domestic staff—all demure and many quite old—stood alongside the carpet runner. It was all very weird, as if they had tried to recreate a small part of the Inner Circle down here.

Our guide stopped.

"This will be your room for however long you need it."

One of the servants opened the door to a dank room off the main passage. A waft of humid and musty air spilled out.

Inside the L-shaped room were several hard-looking bunks, a

threadbare carpet on the floor and a makeshift cupboard constructed of bent and warped shelves hidden by a piece of cloth.

Raanu climbed on top of the closest bunk to the right of the door and jumped around on the mattress, making the bunk shake.

"Can I sleep in this bed? Please, please?"

Thayu said, "You can have whatever bed you like, pebble. But please do remember that we're not here as friends, and you need to be quiet and respectful."

Raanu rolled around on the mattress, laughing.

Sheydu glared at her.

I quickly selected the bunk underneath Raanu, because we couldn't have any of the guards sleep there. They might lose their temper with her. Did they all dislike children so much?

Thayu and Nicha shared the bunk on the other side of the door and Veyada and Sheydu, Natanu and the others took the bunks at the far end of the room.

"Wow, great luxury," I said and turned to Thayu, remembering what she'd just said to Raanu. "Do you think we're in danger here?"

"Not immediately," Nicha said. "But I don't know about the *zeyshi*. I can't judge what their promises are worth. They may use our attempt to get into the Inner Circle as a way to further their own aims."

I spread my hands. "Further their own aims? That's what almost everyone else has been doing since I got here. Let them join the queue."

"I don't know these people. I don't sense what they want."

"My guess: money. Or power." Damn, I was feeling angry, irritated, blunt.

"I don't trust any of them either," Thayu said softly, coming to stand next to me. She glanced at the stone ceiling. There was no knowing if listening equipment was hidden up there, as there would be in all such apartments in Barresh.

I made an Indrahui hand signal I'd learned from Evi and Telaris: *Don't trust anyone.*

She nodded, casting a glance at the other end of the room, where the guards were stretching out on their beds. Veyada and Sheydu sat next to each other on a bottom bunk, looking at a screen.

Damn, the way they sat there reminded me of Evi and Telaris.

How I longed for my comfortable home. The fear that I would never see them again clawed at me.

We decided that it was unlikely that anything would happen for a few hours, until "certain people" could be notified. Whoever these people were, none of us liked it much.

Natanu mentioned some names, to which Thayu retorted that half of those people were known to be dead and that she should stop perpetuating rumours and talking people into legends who were just common criminals.

"And you know so much about these people," Natanu sneered.

"As a matter of fact, I do."

"Is that why you dragged us into this fucking warren? Are any of them your bed-mates?"

I rose from the bed and crossed the room in a few steps. "Will you stop talking to my *wife* like that?"

Lying on her back on the top bunk, Natanu regarded me with an emotionless look over the top of her legs, crossed at the ankles.

"Cory," Nicha said behind me, his tone full of warning.

"No, Nicha, I'll not have this sniping in our group. I understand that there are difficulties with associations—"

"Denaryi," Natanu said. Total chaos.

She met my eyes in an intense look.

I spread my hands, out of my depth. "At least *try* to get along."

That remark was only greeted with deep silence. Sheydu and Veyada didn't meet anyone's eyes. Raanu lay on her stomach on the top bunk, watching with wide eyes. No doubt she understood what was going on much more than I did. And I should shut up before someone killed me.

Oh, for fuck's sake.

I returned to my bunk, hot, frustrated, smelly.

And I still couldn't talk freely to Thayu and Nicha. I asked if there was an opportunity to have a bath. Nicha went out. He said apparently there was a bathroom across the hall, but it was occupied.

I had lost all track of time, but Nicha said it was late afternoon, and we should probably get some rest.

I didn't feel like resting. My mind was racing. I wanted to get out of here. In any case, I didn't feel tiredness of the kind that makes you sleep. My bones and muscles ached and that meal I'd eaten sat like a stone in my stomach.

While all this was going on, Raanu had fallen asleep, with one arm hanging down from the top bunk. I lay on my back, watching her hand twitch. Thayu got up and covered her with a blanket. I don't know if she thought that I was asleep, but I caught her giving Raanu a smile that made me choke up inside. There was no doubt about it: she wanted a child, and she would be an excellent mother. Thayu hid her desires well, but every now and then she would lift a little veil of how much it hurt her to have left her son in the care of Taysha's brother.

An image came to my mind of Thayu at our wedding party in Auckland, playing cricket on the beach with a bunch of my young cousins. Her laughter as she hit the ball into the ocean and one of the dogs jumped in to fetch it.

I imagined Thayu in a hospital bed in Barresh with a newborn baby at her breast.

While we lay in our bunks and dozed, a man brought a plate of refreshments. "If you want to bathe, there is a bathroom across the passage, but it will be in use for some time. I'll let you know when it is free."

We had noticed that.

Thayu nodded and took the tray from him.

He bowed and left. It was all very official and solemn. I didn't understand what these domestic workers were doing here, since they were not *zeyshi,* and couldn't imagine Risha as a frail old man hurrying through the underground tunnels with a train of domestic workers in tow.

The domestic staff had evidently been instructed about my eating requirements, because one plate came with a green-coded label. While the others ate mushrooms and drank piss-coloured juice whose red-coded acidity I could smell across the room, I ate some kind of cooked grains and drank water that tasted metallic.

Thayu really enjoyed that acidic juice and took three glasses of it.

I'd never seen her radiate health as much as she did here. The odd wrinkling of the skin that made it velvety made her look incredibly healthy. Sexy.

If ever we got out of here, maybe I should have a room in the apartment brought up to a temperature comfortable to her. Maybe I should ask Eirani to buy some red-coded food for her and Nicha. They both insisted that they didn't need it, but clearly they did.

Natanu and the other guards stretched out on the ground, playing a game. I was glad that at least the tension had defused somewhat, even if Sheydu and Veyada still didn't take part in the game.

I was watching their game when Natanu suddenly tensed. Not a moment later someone entered the room.

A domestic servant came in telling us that the bath was free now, did we want to use it?

"Maybe it is time for a bath," Thayu said.

I was dying for a bath, but after the adventure of my collapse—I had truly believed that I was safe in the tunnels—I was less sure of taking off my protective suit. Temperature in the room had been going up again despite being under the ground.

I suspected that some of the ceiling outlets belched hot air, because most of the inhabitants would find it chilly down here.

Some *zeyshi* might be Aghyrian, but they clearly still had a higher temperature tolerance than I did.

Despite my reservations, Thayu dragged me across that dark hall to the bathroom.

It was not very large, a square room with moisture-stained walls. In the centre was a shallow hollowed-out basin in which water bubbled from an outlet in the centre. Dry as Asto was, this had to be recirculated water, rather than the fresh supply of hot water we had in Barresh. I tested the temperature with my hand. Ouch. Definitely too hot to sit in.

Thayu was taking off her clothes in the corner. The skin on the normally-hidden parts of her body was just as velvety as on her arms. She noticed that I was watching and smiled.

I closed her in my arms. "You look gorgeous. Much more alive than in Barresh."

Her skin felt warm through my suit. I felt sweaty, pathetic and smelly compared to her.

She cupped my cheek with a warm-skinned hand. "You are very brave."

"Or stupid. I can't get over the feeling that everyone is playing games with me."

She chuckled. "Maybe they are, but you're good at playing back."

I blew out a breath. The situation stressed me out so much and made me feel so inadequate.

"Let's just wind down for a bit," she said.

I pulled her close for a kiss. She pressed herself against me, running her hands over my sides and back. That was nice. Very nice. I pushed down the top of my suit and wrestled my arms out of the narrow sleeves. Then did the same for the bottom part, before the suit became too tight in certain—um—places.

Thayu's skin did not just look rough, it *felt* rough, like a cat's tongue. Very sexy. The heat of her body against my skin made me certain: I would not take very long at all.

She whispered, her voice hoarse, "Here or in the water?"

At home, I liked the water very much, but I shook my head. "The water will have to wait until we get home. It's too hot for me."

I sat on the bench. She swung a leg over mine and was about to settle on my lap when the door opened and Nicha came in, holding Raanu's hand. She was chattering away about what she knew about the tunnels and the history. Damn. So much for *this* particular type of relaxation.

Nicha crossed to the bench while unfastening the front of his suit, then frowned at us standing there awkwardly. "Did I interrupt something? Never mind us. Carry on."

Well, *that* was a part of Coldi custom I had never gotten used to. I could do public nudity. I could do *nethana,* but share the most intimate moments between lovers in public? No way. Not with a child watching. Not even with Nicha watching.

Damn it. We'd have to find some other time.

Thayu slipped into the water and Nicha followed a bit later. Raanu took off her clothes and splashed into the water before settling next to Thayu.

She eyed me, frowning, and said with childish innocence, "You look funny."

Well, fancy that. I not only *looked* funny, but I *felt* funny. Thayu met my eyes. To her credit, she did not laugh. But damn, I might die tomorrow. Would that be without having made love to my *wife* one last time?

I sat at the edge of the bath, cooling down certain parts of me and dangling my feet into the water until they, in turn, got too hot. There was a pile of cloths next to the bath and I used one to dunk into the water and wash myself. The cloth was white and came away with pink smears of dust.

Then Thayu said, "The main reason I suggested a bath was not for bonding or relaxation. I wanted to get us away from the guards."

That's what I'd gathered. "What's going on in that association? Have Sheydu and Veyada been cast out?"

Nicha frowned at me, and then his expression cleared. "You *might* have a point there."

Thayu said, "Natanu is very angry that I led the group into the aquifers. Once the mess in the Inner Circle became apparent, she's only had one aim."

Didn't we all know what that was.

"Natanu is nice," Raanu said.

Well, that wasn't exactly the way I'd put it. I would call Natanu a fire-breathing dragon sitting atop a mound of treasure. Just her swipe or breath would be enough to kill. But with every little tidbit that revealed itself about life in the Inner Circle, my suspicion grew that Natanu was Ezhya's long-time lover and might well be Raanu's mother.

And we might well have killed any chance she had to take the Chief Coordinator's job. If there was going to be a change, she would be better than all of the alternatives. Being Ezhya's lover meant that she would at least leave him alive.

I hoped.

I asked Thayu, "Did you want to talk to us here because you got any further information about what's going on in the Inner Circle?"

"I don't think there is anything new coming out of the Inner Circle. Ezhya's routines are apparently still holding and Taysha has not yet broken out or managed to defeat Asha."

That was her father she was talking about, and *defeat* was short-hand for *kill*.

"No," she continued, "I wanted to talk about us. We're going to have to move, and we may have to do it without Natanu and any of the others."

"But everyone agreed to come along and help. We *need* the help."

"Cory, regardless of what they promise you, everyone going into that hub room will be doing it for themselves. This is one of the strongest instincts we have. I can feel it, even if I have no hope of ever assuming the position of Chief Coordinator. Nayu pretends to be all calm about it, but she wants power, too. They say that *zeyshi* don't have the *sheya* instinct, but some of them do, especially those who were born as *zeyshi*. Nayu was born in the tunnels of the desert. She came to Eighth Circle briefly when she was young and did very well, but she grew lazy and fell in with a violent crowd. She probably realised she could do better with the *zeyshi* so she returned. She is cold and calculating. She will pretend to have no associations, but I think she does. I suspect she is part of Risha's informal association. Immediately after the Exchange went out, *zeyshi* went into the city and looted warehouses, which is pretty much standard for when there is a crisis, but she put a stop to that. She couldn't have done that if those looting people did not have associations, because they wouldn't listen to her. So yeah, *zeyshi* like to present themselves as lawless bandits, but as you can see here they're not. They can be as structured as the rest of society. So of course Nayu wants to get into the hub."

Because she wanted to try a shot at the top job as well. Was this a never-ending list of contenders?

What the hell had Thayu done in her previous work? "So you suggest sneaking away from the others and going in by ourselves? Do you know the way through all these tunnels?"

Thayu lowered her voice. "I do. There is a direct route. It's . . . interesting."

Not sure I wanted to know about *interesting*.

Considering my experience as a kid at Midway Space station, I guessed it involved crawling through ducts, or something else that in this heat would be utterly foul. Or would put us in the path of man-eating robots that misunderstood my accent. Interesting indeed.

But Thayu was obviously not going to be more specific. She took the washcloth from my hands and gestured for me to lie on my stomach. She dipped the cloth in the water and squeezed it out above my head. The feeling of warm water trickling down my hair was relaxing.

I closed my eyes, resting my head on my arms. The stone floor underneath me was relatively cool. Her hands massaged my back in a very relaxed, very suggestive way. I pushed away that feeling of desire. I wanted her so badly that a simple touch was enough to send shivers of desire through me, and that would never do in the presence of a child. But I'd have to do something about it soon.

I tried to force my mind on other matters. "What should I do about this writ? Veyada is keen for me to act on it. Do you want me to send it?"

"It's about what you want."

"Yes, but I'd like some advice. It affects you as well." *Stop being subservient.*

"He has offended you badly, probably on purpose. What did you do with his writ?"

"I handed it back to him. I can't accept anything like that."

"Well, in that case, acting on it is your only option."

I said, "Veyada said that I could claim membership of the Domiri clan. I don't know what all this means and I don't know what to do about it. What would you do?"

Nicha met my eyes. "Both clan acceptance and writs are serious business, Cory. If you start getting involved with clans and our law, I don't know where that's going to end."

It wouldn't end well, it was clear that he thought so.

Thayu looked at me in an odd way. "Did Veyada say that? You could apply for membership of the Domiri clan?"

Her expression was so intense that it chilled me.

"I have no idea where he got the information and how much it's worth—"

Nicha said, "If Veyada says it, a lot. You do know that he's a formal lawkeeper? His word on these matters is final."

Thayu said softly, "I'd love you to be part of my clan." Her eyes went misty.

Nicha still didn't like it.

22

———————

BY THE TIME we returned to the room, the guards had gone to bed. I lifted Raanu to the top bunk and tucked her in. She put her head down, her eyes already half shut. I could only imagine how exhausted she must be.

Then I went to Thayu. In the alcove under Nicha's bed above, I lay down with her for a long kiss. Natanu in the top bunk against the far wall was unlikely to be asleep, so I didn't dare speak, but there was so much I wanted to ask. My body told me that I should go to sleep, but I wanted her so badly. I held her and kissed her. She kissed me back, pulling me on top of her. Her skin felt even hotter than normal. She was about to go into that delightful state of flush. How easy would it be to take off the suit and have a quickie right here.

A soft snore indicated that Nicha had gone to sleep. The guards were breathing softly, asleep as they would ever be. I didn't care much if they knew what we were doing. But I couldn't be sure about Raanu.

I whispered, "How about we go back into the bathroom?"

"Now?"

"Why not? Everyone is asleep."

She grinned. Her cheeks were already red.

I pushed myself off the bed, took her hand and led her out of the bedroom. The passage outside seemed darker than it had been before. Maybe it was my imagination, maybe one of the lights had run out of charge.

Holding Thayu's hand, I pushed the door into the bathroom. But the sound of voices drifted out.

"Damn, someone in there."

I faced Thayu in the darkness of the corridor. My breaths were heavy. Her eyes glittered with the effect of the sexual flush.

She said, "We'll find somewhere else."

I didn't *want* to run around this maze trying to find a private spot, risking running into someone else who wanted to talk to me, annoy me or fight me. By that time, her flush would have passed.

There was no one here. The door to our room was set in a small alcove where it was very dark.

What the heck. I closed my arms around her and pushed her back against the wall while kissing her deeply.

She gave a kind of surprised squeak. "What? Here?"

"No one will mind. No one is here. I'm not going to take very long." I breathed the scent of her skin. "I don't want to wake up anyone in our room. I don't want Raanu to see us."

"Nich' is right. You *are* becoming more Coldi."

I stifled her words with kisses. Slid my hands between the two sides of her jacket, feeling her hot skin and the softness of her breasts. She pushed my shirt off my shoulders, running her lips along the nape of my neck. Licking the salt off my skin.

"You taste Coldi," she whispered.

The humid breeze through the passage stroked my naked skin. I pushed her jacket off. Her breasts were soft under my hands.

She fumbled with the fastening of my trousers. "Should have worn a *shayka*."

She laughed, but the rumour went that proper *shaykas* were worn the way they were—open at the front for men and at the back for women—precisely for this reason. *Zeyshi* warrens had been small, cramped places. Sparse private moments had to be capitalised on quickly.

She wriggled herself out of the bottom half of her suit. Her skin was pale in the semidarkness. I lifted her up so that she rested with her elbows on my shoulders. She wrapped her legs around me. I leaned her back against the wall and let her slide down. I went deep inside her. She was so hot that it almost made me come but I managed to hold it off.

Calm down. We didn't have much time, but we had more than a few seconds.

Supporting herself by leaning on my shoulders, she rocked against me. She leaned her head back against the wall, breathing deeply. Her flush was about to peak, I could smell it.

I moved with increased urgency, breaking out in sweat all over. Thayu's hands kept sliding off my shoulders.

Almost there. Thayu arched her back, moaning.

There was a small sound behind me. If that was Nicha, I didn't care. If it was someone else, I didn't care either.

Almost.

Oh, damn. Oh damn, I was going to blow. The wave of release washed over me. I clung onto her, burying my head in the hollow under her chin, trying to stifle my breathing. Maybe whoever had come into the corridor would walk past and not notice us and I could do it again.

A breath of cooler air went over my skin. I vaguely registered that the door to our room had opened before something hit me very hard on the back of my head. I saw spots and stumbled.

Thayu yelled out, "Cory!"

I stumbled, fell on to my knees and almost blacked out.

People rushed in and the passage exploded in voices. Natanu, Veyada, Nicha, Sheydu. Raanu as well.

Nicha said in a stern voice, "Give that to me before you hurt someone else with it. Why did you hit him?"

Raanu replied, dead serious, "He was attacking her!"

Then Natanu started laughing. Sexual jokes were a perfect excuse for Coldi to laugh and the guards laughed now. Thayu laughed, too. It was a rare enough sound that it made the embarrassment sting less. I fumbled to pull up the bottom of my suit.

Raanu's eyes were wide with indignation. "Why are you all laughing? It's not funny. Thayu is nice. I don't want anyone to attack her."

Thayu put a hand on her shoulder. "Let's go inside, before anyone from the *zeyshi* comes."

Sheydu yelled into the room to the other guards, "No need to get dressed. It's all fine. Just a misunderstanding."

Funny sort of misunderstanding. I brought my hand to the back of my head where a swelling lump grew.

I heaved myself to my feet, wrestling my arms back into my suit and stumbled into the room, where Veyada came around the corner, hopping on one foot while trying to get dressed.

Natanu slapped me on the back. "This restores some of my faith in you. I almost doubted that you could even do it."

Was that what they had thought because of my need for privacy? Taysha had called me impotent. Damn it, did they really need a demonstration to the contrary?

Raanu said, "What's going on? Why do you all think it's funny?" She glared at me past Nicha. "He *was* attacking her, I saw it."

The guards avoided that question by skittering back to their beds.

"Let's go back to sleep," I said, gnashing my teeth.

She climbed to her bed and crossed her arms over her chest. "I'm not going to sleep. I'm going to sit here and watch you."

"Raanu, please—"

"No. I don't like you anymore."

I sighed.

Thayu held out her arms. "Come and sit with me for a bit."

She lifted Raanu off the bed and sat her down on her own bed, in the shade of Nicha's bunk. Nicha pretended to be asleep, but his shoulders were shaking with laughter.

Very quietly, Thayu explained to Raanu that there was this thing men and women did when they liked each other very much.

Raanu listened, her eyes wide, and occasionally glanced at me. Suspicious.

I wondered what Ezhya would think of this impromptu education of his daughter. I understood that Coldi started mentoring at thirteen. How do you give a birds-and-bees talk in an alien culture?

We went back to sleep—each in our own beds—and for a long time, I heard Raanu rustle the blankets, and imagined her peeking over the edge of the bed to see if she could catch another glimpse of this mysterious adult activity.

Poor girl.

Why had Ezhya never said anything to me about her?

The Coldi attitude to children baffled me deeply.

～

I WOKE up in the pitch darkness with someone holding a mask over my face.

"Hmmm!"

I tried to push away the hands that held it, but they were too strong.

Panic surged through me.

"Shhh, calm down, it's all right." It was Thayu's voice.

I raised my head. The hands holding the mask were hers. By the faint light of a comm, I saw that she was wearing one as well.

Nicha was rummaging around in the room. I could hear the rustling of a protection suit.

I began, "Why—" My voice sounded muffled in the mask.

"Sleeping gas. Come, let me do up the strap. We need to go."

I let her tighten the mask over my face, trying to process what had happened. Had she really set off a sleeping gas bomb in the room? I swung my feet out of the bed and fumbled for my clothes.

Something creaked in the far corner, probably one of the guards turning in bed.

"Shhh."

I checked my timer, squinting against the glare from the screen. It was very early in the morning, Athyl time. Seeing that on the screen as local default gave me a little thrill.

I was here, it was happening, and I guessed it was time for some duct-crawling action or whatever else was going to take us back to the Inner Circle.

I pulled on my suit layers, clipped the tank in the vest, heaved it onto my shoulders while trying not to get tangled up in the hoses, and put on my helmet. The latter wasn't necessary yet, but the less I needed to carry, the better.

Nicha came down from the top bunk, strapped his armour over the top of his clothes and clicked on the bracket with the gun.

Thayu opened the door a crack.

"What about Raanu?" I asked.

"Getting to that." Nicha climbed up on the bunk and lifted her out of bed. She moaned and mumbled.

"Shhhh."

Thayu opened the door wider. The faint eerie glow from a bulb a bit further down the passage fell over the floor and edged the beds in silver.

I followed her into the corridor.

Nicha came out, carrying Raanu over his shoulder. She stirred, but her eyes remained closed. One of her hands hung relaxed over his back.

Thayu shut the door behind us and pushed the mask off her face. Nicha did the same.

"Are we going to be able to move while carrying her?" I asked.

"She'll wake up soon." She unlooped the mask from around her neck and stuffed it in a pocket on her jacket.

She turned in the direction opposite to where we had entered the section last night.

There was a fair bit of activity at that end of the corridor. Domestic servants walking in and out of a room where the door stood open, flooding the corridor with light.

"Someone gets up early," I said. "Is that Risha's room?"

Thayu gave me an uneasy look. That strange feeling I'd had during dinner came back, the feeling that I was missing some vital clues.

"Is everything all right?" I asked Thayu. "Should we check on him?"

She raised her finger to her lips. Her eyes met mine squarely and then she gestured for Nicha to stop. "I know you well enough that you're not going to stop asking until you know what's going on, so I'll show you this. I hope you'll understand. Take off the helmet."

"Thayu?" But I did as she said, and also pulled off my mask and turned off the coolant supply from the tank. I didn't need it yet.

She gestured me towards the door. Two servants came out and some sign language passed between them and Thayu that I didn't understand. The two moved into the corridor, giving me a view of the interior of the room.

On a table in the middle lay a pale body. Risha's white hair was free of the ponytail, flowing over the table like an aura. Someone had placed coloured gemstones around his head.

He wore his long white robe, his feet sticking out from underneath, the skin waxy and white. His hands were folded over his chest, holding the fish-bowl with the husk that had been sitting on the small table in the corridor last night.

With a sick feeling, I remembered how I'd heard of it before. It was a funeral relic.

I stared at Thayu. "What? Did he. . . ?"

"High-ranking people from the Inner Circle often come here for their last respect to the city."

"You mean he killed himself."

"There was no choice. He challenged. He lost. There was nowhere for him to go."

As I met her eyes, a gulf of understanding opened up for me. Last night, he'd spoken of *rimoyu* and how the *zeyshi* balanced the Inner Circle and they were part of the same society. To be reunited with the other half was their idea of inner peace, the last thing to do before stepping out of the rain of life.

My mentor Amarru in Athens had said how most high-ranking Coldi did not die a natural death. I had assumed that most were murdered.

Stupid me.

The signs of what was to come had been everywhere. That he had taken no guards, the way the *zeyshi* treated him. The dinner, the speeches, the way he went around the group giving everyone a message.

Last night, the domestic worker—one of the few who had come with Risha—had told us that people would be using the bath.

First, Risha had bathed, and gone to bed, then he had taken poison. When it had done its work, people had washed his body again and dressed him in this robe.

All this had been going on while I had been stupid, selfish and acted like a hormonal teenager. And I had been blind to it, a stupid, selfish boor—

I felt like hitting my head against the wall.

Thayu met my eyes, her expression intense.

And then another thought.

When I first woke up in the hospital, Thayu had said that this was the only place where I could be if I was still alive.

I saw the truth in her eyes. She had feared that I was dead. She had fought Natanu to come here and won. Even Natanu was still smarting about that.

"Thayu?"

"We should get moving." Her voice was soft and unsteady.

I took her hand and cast one last look at Risha lying peacefully on the table. Damn, I owed him . . . I don't know what. To do my best and not make any more stupid blunders. To fight for Ezhya and try to resolve the situation with the Aghyrian claim peacefully.

But damn it, I was a fucking idiot.

23

———————

THAYU SET a cracking pace along the passages, following a map on her reader. I jammed the helmet back on my head and ran after her. Nicha followed me, with Raanu slung over his shoulder.

We went down long dry passages, rough and narrow corridors with puddles where I banged my helmet against the roof, up ancient stairs with slippery and worn treads and across an open space that might have been a train platform in a previous life, at least a few thousand years ago.

Some passages were natural, others were ancient and still others much more modern. We crossed a train line with rails caked with dust and grime, into another passage, until we came to a cave through which flowed an underground river. A light in the very highest point of the ceiling cast an orange glow over the water. The surface churned with upwellings and eddies. Pretty decent current.

Our path ended on a small beach surrounded by huge boulders. On the sand lay a flat-bottomed boat, anchored to a hook in one of the rocks.

"Ah, I was wondering where you were leading us," Nicha said. He set Raanu down and massaged his shoulder. She managed to keep standing, but her eyes remained unfocused and her expression slack. A track of drool ran down the side of her face.

Thayu untied the rope and dragged the boat into the water and held onto the bow. "Come on, get in."

I stepped in from the beach, but not without getting wet feet. I hoped the water was safe.

The boat wobbled with my weight.

"Sit down, grab a poncho."

On one of the boat's benches lay a pile of cloths such as those worn by mushroom harvesters. The cloth looked fresh, as if it had been left there less than a day ago. Some connection of hers had left these here for us?

How much had Thayu been involved with the *zeyshi* before coming to Barresh?

I unfolded the fabric. There was a hole in the middle where I poked my head through.

Nicha passed me Raanu. I sat her on the bench next to me, arranging another poncho over her. It was too big so I tucked the ends under my leg. Her head lolled onto my shoulder.

Thayu was fiddling with the engine, some sort of jet-powered structure with a massive fan.

Nicha pushed off hard and climbed in. The current tugged at the boat, dragging it into a dark passage.

Thayu started the engine with a huge roar. A blast of wind tore over my head, almost sucking up Nicha's poncho which he had just thrown over his head but hadn't pulled down yet.

He wobbled. "Whoa."

"Sit down." Thayu grabbed hold of the rudder and turned us sharply upstream. The boat shot over the water back to the cavern with the beach and into the tunnel at the other end. The engine blasted air and noise and a fine spray of water. The fast-moving air blew in my face. Sheer walls and mushroom racks whizzed past, not an arm's length from the boat. How could she even see enough not to crash into the walls? Coldi had notoriously poor night vision.

We screeched around tight corners, through large caves with still water, down shallow rapids. Water sprayed in my face. I could smell the acid tang of it. For all I knew, it was eating into my suit, but it was too dark to see and I needed my hands to hang onto Raanu and the bench underneath me.

Finally, Thayu cut the engine and we drifted into a large cavern filled with deep and mirror-like water. A soft beam of pre-dawn slanted into the underground lake. A flock of sliver-winged insects took off from the surface, their wings glittering.

The entire left-hand wall of the cavern was covered in plants with leathery leaves and bell-like purple flowers. I had seen these plants often enough on pictures, and some people in Barresh kept sorry-looking specimens in hothouses. They did not have roots, but had sucker pads which they could pull loose and place somewhere else. Their leaves would angle themselves to the best flow of air and light. They weren't sentient, because the process was entirely mechanical, governed by expansion and flow of fluids driven by chemical reactions under the influence of sunlight. But one could be forgiven for believing that these plants were thinking creatures. The entire cavern wall *moved* and rustled with the constant shifting of leaves and stems.

Although the air was hot here, it was also quite humid. The water surface reflected the mass of moving plants like a mirror, disturbed only by the faint ripple the boat made as it gently drifted across the cave. Underneath the boat, the water's blackness revealed none of its depth.

"Wow." I took off my helmet and wiped sweat off my forehead.

The boat glided across the deep water to a jetty on the other side of the cavern. It sat in the shade of a rock shelf. There was more plant life on the overhanging rocks: mosses with leaf-like fronds, mushrooms and other structures that didn't neatly fit into our plant descriptions.

An Earth scientist by the name of Richard Morton had drawn a lot of attention on both Earth and Asto by tracing back shared ancestry between some Earth plant families and plants of both Barresh and Asto. Barresh's megon trees reminded me a lot of the Christmas bushes that grew on the shore near my father's house in New Zealand, not only because they looked related; they *were* related.

I was standing not only in the birthplace of all of humanity, but of a significant part of all life. I could only imagine the beauty of this place before that meteorite had done its damage.

That was the driving force for the Aghyrian claim. For Asto to be beautiful and green once more. And why shouldn't it? And why shouldn't it be the home of both Aghyrians and Coldi?

Nicha leaned over the side to stop the boat colliding with the pylons of the jetty. When we had stopped moving, I became aware of a low roaring sound. To the right of the jetty, water fell over an artificial edge into a slit of darkness. I shivered, probably about to find out what *interesting* route we were going to take.

Thayu climbed up on the jetty while Nicha tied up the boat. I handed Raanu to her. She was looking around confused, but more awake than before. Thayu peeled off her own and Raanu's poncho. I left mine next to Nicha's in the bottom of the boat.

A narrow rock ledge led away from the jetty. There was a door at the end, which Thayu opened by tapping a code into a modern-looking panel on the wall next to it.

We plunged down a couple of flights of stairs into the darkness. Our footsteps echoed dull as if we were in a concrete bunker. The sound of a lot of falling water roared somewhere close.

Nicha clicked on a light. We were in what looked like a pump house. One wall was made out of glass, next to which a few control panels were mounted on the wall. On the other side of the glass, water entered through an inlet at ground level. A huge screw-like device sloshed water up into a basin at the level of the room's ceiling from where it fell back into the basin below. Through the gap that let in water from outside, I saw the fast-turning blades of a watermill, presumably to drive the screw.

"What's the point of this? The water is just going around in circles."

"Aeration," Thayu said. "Purification and de-acidification. This whole area is a water purification area. It's a reserve. You're not really supposed to come here."

Everything about her said that she was more than familiar with this area. That would also account for the ridiculous speed with which she had taken us through the aquifer network.

From the pump house, a narrow circular staircase led down into the earth. Thayu went first, I followed her by the glow of the small light from her comm. It grew a lot hotter the further down we went. I even had to put my helmet back on.

We ended up in a narrow tunnel. Nicha was still carrying Raanu and had to be careful so as not to bump her into the walls.

From somewhere nearby came a steady hum, probably the pumping station.

My pack was starting to get heavy with the shoulder straps cutting into my shoulders.

Thayu walked ahead with the comm, stopping to check something every now and then.

Raanu mumbled, "Daddy?"

"Shhh, we're going to see Daddy," Nicha said. He put her down, wiping his face.

"Where are we going?" she asked, her tongue thick with sleep.

"Hmm, the guards will have woken up by now, too," Thayu said.

She had been using Raanu's alertness as guide, because Raanu was the only one exposed to the sleeping gas.

"The chase is on," Nicha said.

"You're ready?" Thayu asked, looking at me.

For what? "Do I have a choice?"

"In theory, yes. But this is the point where it gets interesting."

So roaring through an illegal part of the aquifer network in a boat at speeds that made my toes curl was not interesting? "One day I must ask you what you did before you came to Barresh."

To the right of the passage, a ladder led up to a hatch in the ceiling. Thayu grabbed the bottom rung, climbed up the first step and stopped. She turned to me. "Trust me, if I end up telling you, it means that something bad has happened. Although I suppose you can figure most of it out."

All right, she had worked as an agent for Ezhya, I already suspected that, but had she been part of a task force spying on the *zeyshi?*

She climbed further up the ladder until she reached the hatch in the ceiling. The handle creaked when she turned it. With a soft *pop,* the hatch opened. The humming grew louder, now accompanied by soft beeps and hisses.

Thayu stopped at the top of the ladder to detach the gun from its bracket and then climbed out of the hole. She vanished from sight. Through the gap, I could see small lights in a bluish glow.

"You can come up," she called.

As I climbed up, the air became colder and drier.

At the top of the ladder, I came out into a large hall lit by a blue glow. To one side, there were pipes and banks of machinery and control screens, to the other . . .

I recognised the gleaming shapes of drones, dark and lifeless, neatly parked in a grid pattern.

I stiffened. "No, not those things again."

As I said that, one of the nearby machines blinked into life. It whirled around, showing me the red window.

I yanked my gun from its arm bracket.

Thayu shouted a command. The thing turned to her, approaching slowly. The lights on its head blinked. The blue beam scanned her. It stood blinking for a while and then it scanned her again.

I said, "You have to give it a number." What was it again? I rummaged for my comm. Dratted helmet. I couldn't see my pockets.

The drone jerked aside, facing me once more.

"Shhh," Thayu said. She stretched out her hands and the drone concentrated on her again. It came even closer and used one of its pincer claws to taste her skin. The light flashed yellow.

"All right, this one is mine. Who's next? Cory?"

"I would prefer not to go anywhere near those things."

"You have experience?"

"When I went into the hub with Sheydu and Veyada. They told me the code, but the drone wouldn't recognise my voice and it was going to shoot me, so I shot it. Then Veyada and Sheydu had to shoot a couple more."

Thayu cursed. "Damn, these things have collective memories. You'll be in there somewhere."

"I can't remember the code." I found my comm, but my gloved hands were too clumsy to operate it.

"You don't need it. These are not the same type of drone that crawls over the walls at the Inner Circle. These are much smarter than that."

"Great." Why did I have the feeling that was not a good thing?

"We're not going to tame them. We're going to ride them."

What?

"Don't look like that. You use a feeder."

"But there is no Exchange capability."

"Not under the ground, no, because the rock layer prevents reception and *zeyshi* jam the frequency wherever they can, but aboveground, we can use it. That function returned a while back."

That was good news at least. I wondered how far they were away from restoring off-world capability.

Thayu dug in the pocket of her suit and handed me a black spindly thing. A feeder.

"I got these from Veyada." Her expression was serious.

I thought I knew why. "These are Ezhya's feeders, aren't they?" Capable of tapping straight into the command hub.

"They are."

Damn. "Are you trying to kill me?"

"You are the only one who is safe from the network backlash."

I thought of the flood of images that had overwhelmed me at the hub. That was only a fraction of full functionality.

"Come on, it's your turn to pick a drone."

I hesitated. Did I want to know this much about Ezhya's private life?

Nothing for it. I lifted the feeder. It climbed into my hair, found the skin at the base of the skull and settled down. A strong burst of power went through me. I gasped.

In my mind, coloured images flew past at too great a speed for me to follow.

"Stop!" I brought my hands to my head.

The images vanished. I stood there, panting.

"You all right?" Nicha said. He'd been doing something on his comm.

"He sees the stream," Raanu said.

Nicha and Thayu frowned at each other.

Something *connected* in my mind.

An orange desert.

A glass and metal building.

Brilliant blue sky.

One sun.

"He's at Kedras," I said.

"What?" Nicha frowned at me.

"Ezhya. At Kedras." Margarethe's face drifted into vision. She sat in the front seat of an aircraft. "I think they just restored the Exchange."

"Daddy?" Raanu said.

"He's coming." I only needed to defend the hub until he came back. As long as we got there in time, that shouldn't be too hard.

"Really? Is Daddy coming?"

"Shhh." Nicha drew her close to him, shielding her from any attention from the drones.

Thayu went on, "Cory, cut the external feed. Use it as a regular feeder to the local network. You need to connect to the machine so that you can control it." She pulled my arm.

"Huh?" I shook my head, trying to dispel the images.

"Keep your mind on the job. Please."

Yes, sure. Let myself be killed by one of those monster machines. After having a chat with one of them. Awesome.

But I managed to close the channel so that my thoughts were mine again.

"Stand here. Attract its attention." Thayu pushed me towards the parked inactive drones and retreated a few steps.

One of the drones lit up. It lifted itself off the ground, exposing its wheels. These machines were much bigger than the wall-crawling ones. Their bodies consisted of a cylinder-shaped piece of metal with oddly curved plates. They had far fewer feelers and bristles than the other ones, and looked much more sleek and modern, but the sleek exterior gave away nothing about the machine's function. For all I knew it was a rocket, with its smooth shape.

It crept towards me. The dull red window lit up. My legs told me to run, but that would be silly because it would only shoot me more quickly.

The thing ambled over to me. I didn't dare breathe.

"Let it touch you," Thayu said.

I held out my hands, trying and failing to stop them trembling. The pincer came closer. It blew a puff of air over my skin without touching me.

That was all?

"Relax," Thayu said.

"That's easy for you to say. The last one of these machines I came face to face with tried to kill me."

The blue beam tracked over my body. I held my breath, watching that red window. Next thing it would ask me for the code that I didn't have, or if I found it in time, it wouldn't understand when I read it out.

The window remained empty, emitting a dull red glow. Then two yellow lights started blinking.

"You've done it," Thayu said.

Done what? I lifted my hand to my head. I'd done nothing. I couldn't feel any way of controlling the drone.

"Doesn't work?" Thayu asked.

"I'm not feeling how I could control this thing."

"Hmmm." She dug in her pocket, taking out another feeder. "Maybe try this one."

The drone shifted position, now focusing on the feeder dangling from Thayu's fingers.

Yes, that looked more promising.

I took it from her and the moment it contacted my skin, I could feel the command channel.

This was also one of the feeders Veyada had collected and with it came another damned string of Ezhya's image feeds, mostly of people in corridors and offices. Taysha, Risha, Raanu. Natanu wearing *what?* Damn, I really didn't want to see this. I pushed the stream away, stubborn as it was, almost lost contact with the drone. *No, Natanu, that dress reveals way too much skin. No, don't do that.*

Damn it, *stop!*

"Cory?" Thayu frowned at me.

"Just having a little difficulty separating useful feeds from . . ." *personal raunchy videos* ". . . less useful ones."

Behind her, Nicha faced a different drone, while Raanu stood further back covering her face with her hands. The blue beams scanned Nicha's suit. The light blinked yellow.

Thayu walked backwards, and her drone followed her like a little doggie.

"Come, Raanu."

"But they will kill us." Raanu's eyes were so wide that the whites showed on all sides. Living in the Inner Circle, she would know how dangerous these things could be. Maybe she would have grown up fearing these drones as Earth children feared monsters under the bed.

Thayu held out a hand. "It's safe now. Come quickly, we're going to see your Daddy."

Raanu ran across the hall and slammed into Thayu's back, out of view of the drone.

Thayu almost fell. "There's no reason to be so afraid. We'll use them to get back to the Inner Circle."

The drone had stopped an arm's length from her. She untangled herself from Raanu's grip. She jammed the tip of her boot in one of the gaps between the drone's body plates and heaved herself up onto the silver back.

Raanu gasped.

Thayu held out her hands.

"Noooo." Raanu ran to me.

A string of images assaulted me. Raanu sat up in a bed with yellow sheets, her hair mussed up. Her huge black eyes looked at me. I flooded with feelings of warmth for her and held her in my arms, except my arms weren't my real arms, but Ezhya's arms.

In reality, I lifted Raanu and handed her to Thayu. I had expected her to struggle, but it was as if she felt that I was using her father's feeder. It occurred to me that no one had checked her hair to see if she had any more feeders apart from the ones that Veyada had taken off her.

Thayu met my eyes. "Come on, get on yours, quickly. Use the belt of your suit to keep yourself in place. Anchor it behind this plate and around here." She pointed to a couple of protuberances on the drone's back.

I went back to my drone and climbed onto the metallic surface which was very smooth and cool under my hands. I loosened my belt until it, like Thayu's, hooked behind a protuberance on the drone's back.

"Lift your feet up, like this." She showed a ridge on the drone's side. "You can use your knees to hang on."

Like a horse. How did she know I was crap at horse riding?

This thing was slippery but did offer a rail over the back that was perfect for holding on.

The drone's feed projected a *ready and wait* status to me.

Thayu steered her drone out of the hall, and told us to follow. Looking at the back of her drone, I started worrying about the "interesting" part of the trip again. If her definition of "interesting" was not that boat ride, then I wasn't sure if I wanted to do this. The drones *did* have a kind of rocket shape, and as far as I understood, we *were* fairly far away from the Inner Circle.

Where were we going?

We rolled through a corridor devoid of all furnishings except for some markings on the ground in orange paint. This seemed some sort of service tunnel to wherever—

Was I imagining it or were these things speeding up?

No, I wasn't. I could feel the flow of air between my suit and helmet. Thayu's drone blocked my view of whatever was at the end of this passage.

No, I could see past her, and it ended in a solid metal door. We were heading for it at full speed. Did Thayu know how to open that door—

Hey! It slid aside in front of Thayu, giving me a view of a desert landscape with, in the distance, the buildings of Athyl, a wide vista spreading in front of me—

—without anything in front.

Thayu's drone dropped over the edge. A squeal from Raanu faded from hearing.

I twisted around to look at Nicha, but I couldn't see him anymore. My drone had reached the end of the corridor and plunged off the edge.

We were falling, tumbling through the blue pre-dawn sky.

I screamed, but the sound reflected back at me inside the helmet. I grabbed onto the railing on the drone's back.

But I was hanging upside down and fast losing the grip on the thing with my knees. My hands were slipping, too, with sweat.

Blackness returned to the corners of my vision.

There was a sharp click in the drone's back. Something unfolded from the sides under my feet. The surface under me vibrated with the hum of an engine. The drone righted itself and pulled up.

We glided over the desert landscape on huge metallic wings. And I wasn't going to fall because the metal surface had become rough and kind of *sticky*.

What the hell?

24

MY TERROR turned to amazement. Hanging on with one hand, I pushed up the visor of the helmet. Warm air streamed over my face.

"Steer it with your feeder!" Nicha called behind me. His drone had already caught up with mine, the early morning light reflecting off the surface of the wings.

I concentrated on the feeder input, which showed me the basic drone commands. It also showed me the position of Nicha and Thayu's drones. She was ahead of us, flying over the edges of the city, silhouetted against the lightening sky on the horizon.

Damn, I loved her.

I know, she said.

You're crazy. Now I'm even more curious what you did before you came to Barresh.

Because she knew all these things, she had done this before, right?

She laughed. *You have no idea.*

The drones soared over the outer edges of the city. Nicha's and mine followed Thayu and Raanu. In the distance, light glinted off the roof of the Inner Circle. The flower-like structure of the airport rose from the surrounding buildings.

Several of the platforms were lit and a shuttle was approaching one of them.

Ezhya?

I opened the stream from my first feeder a sliver. My head exploded with voices, all talking in business-like manner. Someone said *This one has top priority.*

Thayu reminded me, *Cory, concentrate.*

My drone had veered away from both hers and Nicha's.

But Ezhya is on his way back.

How long did it take to get from Kedras to here? I couldn't allow Taysha to win at the very last minute.

We were closer to the Inner Circle now, giving us a magnificent view over all the complex's domes and towers. Daylight was much stronger now and growing brighter quickly.

The first of the suns crested the horizon not much later. The entire sky turned baby-pink with a tinge of rust brown on the western horizon. The dust that always hung over the city reflected the light with a soft orange glow which cast the buildings in sepia tones. Arched walkways, elaborate towers, sleek metal and glass designs, the cacophony of intricate Athyl architecture woke up with the same pink and orange tones. Overhead, wisps of clouds were edged with yellow and orange. The sky itself turned orange-purple. The colour of the sky on Asto had been deepening over the last couple of years, I had read, because the more frequent rain settled the dust.

I'd seen the wonders of Earth, of Damarq and Kedras, but I had never seen anything like this.

Thayu had told me that there were hills and rooftops in Athyl where people gathered every sunrise and sunset to watch this spectacle. The most beautiful sunrises and sunsets in all of the settled worlds. I'd seen pictures, but those were not a blip on the real thing. A serene feeling of calmness came over me. If I died here, at least I would have seen this.

Thayu commented, *Hang on, you're not going to die.*

I hope not, but it's amazing.

Told you.

People wondered why Coldi lived on Asto. It was a scarred, dusty, hot and harsh world, but it was theirs, and the climate was starting to turn a softer cheek. But most of all, Asto was incredibly beautiful.

Sunrise also didn't last very long and we needed to be inside when the heat came.

Thayu steered her drone to the highest dome in the building. I was glad she knew the way, because I would not have recognised the tower that held the hub. The complex was massive.

If I wasn't mistaken, down there was the bridge where I'd run in the rain with Veyada and Sheydu.

We flew around a corner and up again. Oh yes, this was the wall with the ledge where I'd shot the drone. There was still a black mark on the roof.

Nicha flew past me and turned to the window where we had climbed in with Sheydu and Veyada. My drone kept flying straight ahead. I told it to follow Nicha, but it remained unresponsive.

Hang on, stupid thing. I searched the feeder inputs. I swear there had been an option to manually control the steering other than *follow the others,* but I couldn't find it anymore.

The damn thing wasn't going to bail out on me right now, was it?

What are you doing? Thayu wanted to know. She was too far behind me to see.

I have no idea.

I tried to activate the commands. Shouted at it. "Come on, stupid thing!" As if that would help. *It's frozen. Won't respond to anything I do.*

The drone's engine was also slowing and as a result, I was rapidly losing height.

Do these things run out of fuel?

I was already way past the main gate of the Inner Circle. If this continued, I'd crash somewhere in the streets of the First Circle complex and I would have no way of getting back to Thayu and Nicha, and I had Ezhya's feeders, which they needed if they had any hope of defending the hub.

Hang on! I caught a glimpse of Nicha turning his drone. He was coming after me. What for and what he thought to do, I didn't know. I held on tight, bracing for the inevitable crash into the street or roof or some such.

Damn, where had Nicha gone?

"Cory! Up here!"

I looked up.

Nicha had turned his drone upside down and hung from his seat, arms hanging down to me. I reached up and managed to grab one of his hands. His grip was warm and strong. I let go of my falling drone and dangled in the air below him, with the hot exhaust from his drone's engine buffeting my legs. He righted the drone, causing me to half-fall, half-fly in an arc. Sky and city spun around me. I landed roughly on the seat in front of him. Thank the heavens for strong Coldi arms.

I looked down for signs of a crash, but instead of crashing in the streets, my drone had come back to life. It soared over the roofs, turned and came straight for us.

"Nicha, that drone is coming for us." The drones had collective memories, right? And this infernal piece of equipment had worked out that I had been one of the people who had destroyed some of their fellows. Ah, we'd flown over the spot where it had happened and I'd thought about it. While wearing the feeder that linked into its memory.

Stupid.

Nicha glanced aside. "I see it. Does it have the side flaps folded out?"

I peered into the light. "I think so."

A sharp crack pierced the rush of air that buffeted me.

"Shit. It's shooting at us. Hang on." Nicha made the drone swerve sharply to evade fire. Up, then down again, and sideways. Charges crackled through the air like bolts of lightning. We soared around the building with the damn thing at our tail. I wrestled my gun from its bracket and made a few attempts at firing at it, all of which missed.

You know in movies, where the hero shoots the bad guys from the back of a speeding motorbike? Well, reality is not like that. When you're in a speeding vehicle and have the typical weapons skills of a diplomat, you can't hit anything for shit.

In passing in front of the building, I caught a glimpse of Thayu and Raanu at the window in the corridor next to the hub. Since I had come through it with Veyada and Sheydu, someone had repaired the security grille, and Thayu was taking it out again. Nicha steered around, ever faster. The other drone was still gaining on us.

Thayu helped Raanu climb into the window.

Nicha steered around again and out towards First Circle. What was he doing?

A sharp turn back to the front of the building. Nicha made straight for the window. I closed my eyes and hung on. Right now, I knew I had to trust him, but it looked awfully like we were going to crash. I held my breath.

The drone slowed down suddenly. I opened my eyes just as it flew in through the open window. It clipped the frame with its wings and toppled. Nicha jumped off, dragging me with him. We landed unceremoniously on the floor. The drone flipped on its back and skidded down the corridor before coming to rest against the wall.

Also in movies, it would explode. It didn't, and sat there looking crumpled. Was it now inactive? Was it going to turn back and shoot at us?

For a few seconds, everything was quiet.

From outside came the pops and crackles of a fire. Black smoke rose past the window. Evidently, the other drone had crashed onto the roof.

Phew.

Neat skid marks, by the way.

I took off my helmet and breathing mask. The breeze through the corridor chilled my face. My sleeve came away black when I wiped my face.

"What did you do to your drone?" Nicha asked.

"I think when we flew over the spot where we shot the others, it picked up my memories and recognised me as enemy."

Nicha's eyes widened. "I've always wondered if that was a myth or the truth—shit."

The fallen drone hummed to life.

Nicha grabbed his gun.

"Don't!" Thayu pushed the barrel aside. "Don't be stupid."

"What? It will turn against us."

"Maybe, but if we can stop thinking about what just happened, it can still be useful to us. If you shoot it, we'll have to deal with all the wall-crawlers. The window doesn't shut anymore."

The drone righted itself and folded up its wings. One of them had bent and didn't fit properly in the recess anymore. The panel that was supposed to cover it hung halfway down the side.

"Let's go," Thayu said. She grabbed Raanu's hand.

We had gone not more than a few steps when there was the sound of people running from elsewhere in the building. It sounded close, perhaps around the corner. I'd been here before and remembered that the corridor at the t-intersection ahead ran to the lifts.

Thayu ducked against the wall, pushing Raanu behind her. Nicha and I followed. Nicha clicked the gun out of its bracket.

Thayu cursed. "What are they doing in here? The guards should have stopped them getting into the lift."

"We didn't use the lift."

She gave me a blank stare. Right. One didn't make jokes with security in action. I should have learned that by now. Silly Delegate. I took my gun out of its bracket. "I'm almost out of charge."

Without taking her eyes off the t-intersection, Thayu handed me one of her spares, a weapon much heavier than I was used to or happy with.

I turned on the gun and waited until the charge light showed yellow. It had a few capabilities that my own simple gun didn't: infrared scan, metal-cutting mode, auto-variable intensity. Whoa, this was a serious weapon.

Nicha gestured me to show it to him. He turned the beam strength setting up as far as it would go. The look in his eyes was penetrating.

We're on my territory now. I know you like to save lives, but this is no game and we take no prisoners.

I nodded, feeling sick, determined to fire over people's heads unless there was no other option.

He held my arm. "Please, Cory. Don't be stubborn about this. Anyone you don't kill is likely to kill us. Promise me you will play by our rules."

Coldi rules. Kill your opponents before they can kill you.

I nodded. Sweat was pouring down my face. Outside, both suns had cleared the horizon and the light was no longer filtered by the low-hanging haze. A piercing beam of light shone into the window.

"Can you hear anything?" Nicha asked.

"I'm not getting a feed," Thayu said. "Something is blocking the local network feed."

"Taysha," Nicha said, his expression grim.

"Probably."

"I still got infra red," Nicha said. He was looking at his comm. "Whoa, someone coming."

There were footsteps and someone peeked around the corner.

Like a finely-tuned bundle of nerves, Thayu fired. A sizzling beam of light shot through the corridor and made contact. The figure exploded in a ball of flame, and fell down, still burning.

Raanu squeaked and sheltered her head with her arms.

I pulled her against me, so that she didn't have to look at the burning body on the ground.

Smoke drifted into our section of the corridor. I wanted to avoid breathing the sickening air, but I had to preserve my coolant for when I really needed it.

Shit.

How did she even know that this person was hostile? It could have been one of the domestic staff.

"We're going to have to make a move," Thayu said. "We're too exposed."

"What if he was alone?"

"He wasn't." She showed me the screen of her infrared visor, with a couple of light spots in the lift foyer. Coldi rarely were alone in any case.

There were also a bunch of spots in front of the hub door.

"Who are those?"

"Guards loyal to Ezhya."

There were at least ten of them.

"I've got control of the drone again. It's finished repairing," Nicha said.

"Have you got a visual feed?" Thayu asked.

"I do. Not a very good one, but possibly informative."

"Check out these guys." Thayu showed him the screen.

Nicha sent the drone ahead into the corridor. It trundled off quietly, lights blinking. It disappeared from view.

For long moments, nothing happened. Thayu kept her gun trained at the t-intersection. Raanu clung onto my suit. I watched Nicha, his expression one of concentration.

The light outside grew brighter.

Something moved at the window. A thin metal rod rose over the wrecked remains of the security grille.

"Nich'." I jerked my head at the window.

He glanced over his shoulder.

The rod grew longer and was joined by another one, this one bent with a camera attached to the end. Then came the edge of a metal plate and a dull red window.

It was one of the wall-crawling drones. I should have known that it would come, and we couldn't even close the window since Thayu had done an even more impressive job demolishing it than Sheydu had.

"Stand still," Nicha said.

Raanu gave a small squeak and jammed herself between the wall and my back.

The thing crested the windowsill and crawled down to the floor. The wheels whirred. The arms at the front probed and tasted. Slowly, it made its way towards us.

Shit. Now we were under siege from both sides.

Unless . . .

Veyada had given me the code. Could it be controlled through the feeder?

I checked my comm for the number that Veyada had sent me, and pushed off from the wall. The drone stopped. A few lights blinked on its "head" and along the legs. I held the gun in my hand in case things went wrong.

The blue beam tracked over me. Then the dull red window said *Input code.*

Slowly and clearly, I read out the numbers. "Six, nine, four, twelve, two, seven."

I waited.

It blinked. The red window pulsed with light while it digested my reply.

Then: a yellow light.

Phew.

Maybe it made a difference that I wasn't wearing a helmet.

Thayu had been watching me, and lowered the gun she'd held pointed at the drone.

"Watch out," she said, jerking her head.

The other drone had come back around the corner. It turned slowly. Lights blinked on the side facing us—

—and it stayed there, blinking, not doing anything.

"What the hell is it doing?" Thayu asked.

"It didn't find anyone live, although there are a bunch of bodies in the foyer," Nicha said. He brought his hand to his temple. "It wants to know what to do next."

Thayu frowned at us. "Bodies? The people we just saw?"

"I don't know. Seems unlikely, or they would have shown up on the infra red."

While they were still warm. I shuddered.

"Then where did those people go?"

Nicha shrugged.

"Damn it. What the hell is going on?"

"Looks like we've walked into a stand-off in progress."

"What do we do now?"

"I'd like to go into the hub," Thayu said.

I said, "Why don't we send this drone ahead as decoy? It can spring any traps that the disappearing guards have set."

"The hub is only around the corner. I'll be much happier to send it from there."

"Our task is to defend it. Not necessarily to get in. Will the guards let us in? As far as I know, Ezhya's command key is still in control."

Thayu spread her hands in an *Are you trying to do my job?* way.

"He's right," Nicha said.

Thayu rolled her eyes at the ceiling. "I want to get into the hub, because the hub is defensible, because it has only one door. This corridor is as defensible as fuck."

I said, "You're right about that, too, but those people we saw will be waiting for us to do something stupid."

"No, they're waiting for—"

"Thay', have a look at this." Nicha handed her his comm. She glanced at the screen.

"Shit."

"What?" I looked over her shoulder. The screen on the comm showed an infrared scan of a huge group of people coming up a set of stairs somewhere else in the building, walking in the classic association formation.

"That's our father on his way up here. He must have heard that Taysha's people got past the guards."

And no doubt Asha Domiri wasn't coming up here to defend Ezhya's position. This was a grab for power from both men.

"Do you know where Taysha is?" I asked.

"I guess we'll find out soon. There will be a lot of fireworks."

Up until now I had thought that neither Thayu nor Nicha were terribly emotionally attached to their father. But Thayu's wide-eyed expression sent a chill through me.

"We can . . . help him, if you think—"

"He would never accept that." Too curt, too snappy.

"But we . . ." I let it rest. She was right, he would never accept offered help and moreover, it would make me look like a foreign idiot.

Then what was the best thing for us to do?

Hope that we could get past the guards and shelter from the coming firefight until the victor came into the hub? Try to convince that person that supporting Ezhya would be best?

Like that would ever work.

It might also mean we'd have to confront Asha Domiri if he managed to get past Taysha. And neither Thayu nor Nicha would have the strength to do that.

Damn.

If I tried to stop him, would he kill me?

Or his children?

I didn't *think* so, or at least I *hoped* not, but that was just wishful thinking, because I had no idea if the Coldi instinct to occupy a vacant higher position was stronger than family ties.

He certainly wouldn't have any hesitation about me.

Was I meant to come out of this alive?

My very human instincts screamed at me to get out of here. We shouldn't have come. There was only so much a non-Coldi person could meddle in Coldi hierarchy. I endangered not only Thayu and Nicha, but Raanu as well.

Thayu's instinct clearly told her to find a safe place and bunker down, because the upcoming showdown was going to roll on like a freight train and our presence would not make one iota of difference. She was right, this corridor was *as exposed as fuck.*

But it was too late to withdraw.

We waited.

Nerves made me shiver.

Thayu stood against the wall, holding her gun raised at the t-intersection. The drone still sat in the middle of the intersection, lights blinking as if waiting for some sort of input.

I guess the tumble into the window had done more damage than at first apparent.

The smaller wall-crawling drone had come to a halt next to me. I could send it out into the lift foyer so that I could see what was happening, if anything started happening.

I sent a command through my feeder and it jumped backwards, banging into the wall.

Crap.

"Shh," Thayu said.

I wiped my face, slick with sweat. "I want to make use of this thing."

"You'll need better control."

Probably, but I could also do something else with it. A seed of an idea was forming. These people liked fireworks, huh? I'd give them fireworks.

I closed the drone's connection via one feeder and tried the other feeder. It returned a more detailed control menu. Clearly one of the feeders was more suited to this task. I had never been aware that there were different types of feeders. Any I'd used had always been the same.

I sent the drone moving slowly towards me. Raanu whimpered, hiding behind my back.

In my pocket, I found the explosive pad that Sheydu had given to me. I unwrapped the cover, crawled to my knees and stuck the pad on the underside of the drone's belly. It was soft and squishy, fluid in a clear membrane. I ripped open the bag with the detonator, pulled off the backing and stuck it onto the squishy membrane. The outer cover of the wires was sticky, and I pulled them along the drone's belly so that the antenna stuck out from underneath.

There.

I sat back. Nicha nodded.

His feeder probably picked up my intentions, never mind that my feeder input was all messed up. It would probably be better if I removed one of the feeders, but I didn't dare to because I needed to keep in contact with the drone. And Ezhya, if he arrived in the building.

I'm going to send it in there. I pointed to the t-intersection.

Neither Nicha nor Thayu objected.

While the drone trundled through the corridor, I worked out how to get a visual link from it.

It turned the corner, past the burnt body and went towards the lift foyer, which was, as Nicha had established, deserted except for a couple of blackened bodies that weren't going anywhere.

I focused on the closest one. This guard lay facing away from the drone. The top half of the body was blackened—but the temperature suit still intact. The remains of a red sash lay on the floor behind the guard's back.

One of Ezhya's guards.

It seemed Nicha was correct about these bodies having been here for a while.

I made the drone turn on the spot.

The foyer was a circular domed structure with about six or seven doors leading into it. According to the map, Ezhya's private quarters were behind the doors to the left—on the same side of the building as the hub.

All the doors were closed. Not just that, but my display marked them as locked, protected by DNA scan locks.

So where did those other people go, the ones that had shown up briefly on Nicha's infrared scan and were probably Taysha's?

"See anything?" Thayu asked.

I shook my head.

The drone turned around again. Where could they have gone?

"We should try to get to the hub anyway," Thayu said. "We'll be safer there." Once we got past the guards, but she was probably in contact with them, and they were probably quite happy for us to join them. Or at least they would be if they were human and realising that their lives were pretty much forfeit.

Shit.

I still didn't like it, but had run out of arguments to stop her.

Nicha's comm emitted a small squeak. He glanced at the screen. "Ezhya's back in orbit."

Thank the heavens. "How long before he can be here?"

Nicha gestured *I don't know*. There might be trouble at the airport. On second thoughts, Ezhya would probably land on the roof of the building.

Maybe people were waiting for him there.

Maybe—

The lift door opened in the foyer. I swivelled the drone so that I had a better view. A couple of silver-clad guards ran out. One of the doors in the foyer burst open. The people who came out of this door wore dark civilian clothing.

Army. Asha Domiri's people. I couldn't see him yet.

Someone fired from elsewhere in the hall outside my field of vision. One dark-clad person went down, the others dropped flat on the ground.

Thayu and Nicha had reached the corner to the intersection and pressed themselves against the wall. The flying drone still stood there flashing. I followed, clutching my gun, and shielding Raanu with my body.

The fight in the foyer broke out in all seriousness. There were flashes of discharging weapons, shouts, people running. There was so much smoke in the foyer that the poor quality visual input from the drone became too grainy to show important details such as who was fighting.

Thayu was closest to the corner, but not even she dared stick her head around.

I sensed movement to our right. "Thay', watch out—"

It was the guards in front of the hub—the last ones loyal to Ezhya. They held their positions, but were looking wide-eyed, white-faced into the foyer, knowing that when the fight there was over, it would be their turn. Thayu gestured one of them over and spoke with a female guard who looked like a Natanu-clone. Their voices were inaudible to me because of the noise of discharges.

Someone knocked the drone in the foyer and I almost lost contact with it.

The lift door opened, disgorging more people into the hall. They came under fire as soon as they stepped out of the lift. Several of them went down. A sizzling beam crossed the drone's field of vision. It came from *above*.

I directed the drone's eye up. Through the smoke and graininess, I could make out Taysha's guards, hanging from ropes inside the dome's roof. That's where they'd gone, out of reach of the scanners.

The guards on the ground ran to whatever shelter they could find.

The lift door opened again and I recognised a single tall figure amongst a few more guards: Asha.

Damn, he was going to be dead as soon as he stepped out of the lift.

A barrage of fire went off inside the foyer.

Thayu gave a squeak. She stepped out from behind the wall, her face a mask of horror. She shot a few times in rapid succession at the ceiling.

Nicha yelled, "No!"

"I've got to help him!"

Raanu screamed and almost knocked me over.

The vision from the drone showed part of the floor. Someone had knocked it over. There was no time to right it. There was only one thing left to do.

I grabbed Raanu's hand.

"When I say run, you run."

She nodded, her face pale.

Three of Ezhya's guards ran past into the foyer. One of them was yelling into his comm. Ezhya was in the building?

I sent the command *Detonate*.

"Run!"

Raanu and I ran around the corner.

25

———

THE REMAINING GUARDS at the door gave us a startled look, but I ran straight past.

"Find shelter!"

I hoped Thayu and Nicha were following, because—

An explosion rocked the ground. I yanked Raanu to me and sheltered her against the wall just inside the hub room. The shockwave tore through the corridor, bringing clouds of dust. Plaster rained down from the ceiling.

Holy shit. What sort of stuff was it that Sheydu had given me?

The noise outside calmed down, fading to the crackle of flames. Thick smoke drifted into the door. I peered, but couldn't see Thayu and Nicha, or anyone else for that matter.

A chill took hold of me. They *were* all right, weren't they?

I had to believe they were. There was nothing I could do.

The hub showed little sign of activity.

The walls were mostly dark, with a few routines scrolling along the bottom. Wow, Ezhya's chain of commands had died out fast.

"We need to help your daddy," I said. "Can you show me how to start this up?"

Raanu nodded, solemn.

Slowly, I sat at the stool in the middle, at the controls and the receivers. The Asto command hub, the one that Ezhya used three feeders to control. I had two feeders. All of Asto lay at my fingertips, presuming I knew how to use this thing. Press one of these coded buttons and someone would do something. One word. Some people would kill to be in this position.

The command key still sat in the slot where I had inserted it.

As I pulled it out, my feeder stream burst into life. The images in my mind flowed too fast for me to make sense of it all.

Raanu had climbed on my lap. She raked her hand through her hair and produced another feeder. I stared at it.

"You had this with you all the time?"

She nodded. "You need it. It doesn't work with only two."

I took the feeder from her. Using it like Ezhya did could kill me, but if I did nothing, Taysha's guards out there would overwhelm Nicha and Thayu and whoever else had turned up. Natanu was in the building, too. I could see her ID displayed in my vision.

I slowly raised the feeder to my head. It clung onto my hair almost as if it was keen to join its fellows. It settled on the skin between the other two.

A burst of heat. Contact.

The stream of images that flowed through my head almost bowled me flat. I could see . . . everything. People walking in streets. Guards standing at the airport. A shuttle was landing there. Ezhya was a bright spot inside the cabin. Two drones were about to come into the building through the window. I sent them to check for Taysha's guards. Wait—the lift was full of Taysha's guards. I sent a command that it was not to proceed above the second floor.

I was half aware that a small and warm hand was guiding my fingers to certain places. I could feel the touch of buttons under my fingertips, but my vision was entirely taken up by the feeder input.

A brief flash of panic. What if the feed took over my vital processes?

A bright blue map sprang into being around me: a representation of the building showing the locations of all the people in it and their IDs.

We'd start securing our position from the centre out. There was a breach in the Inner Circle defences that needed extra personnel and a few streets were flooded where people needed assistance. In the First Circle, the hospital needed power. A few major thoroughfares were blocked. There was a train in the station but no driver.

Too much. It was too much.

I shut off all non-urgent requests. The stream slowed but not enough so I limited the scope to only the Inner Circle.

Security of the hub. Guards were asleep in their dorms. I woke them and sent them up here. The south tower gate was open. I shut it. An army of drones was on its way to the broken window. I told them to stop.

As I did those things, the flow of images slowed down to a more comfortable pace. They organised themselves into priorities: security first, then communication. The Exchange stream was a bright path in my vision.

Ezhya, if you hear me come down here as soon as possible.

There was a shout from somewhere outside that stream. "Cory!"

What was real, those images or the voice, or the feel of the seat under me or the acrid scent of smoke?

I managed to draw myself back from the stream into an atmosphere of noise and chaos. Flashes tore across the door opening. From where I sat, I could see Natanu shooting. Veyada was also there. There was no sign of Nicha or Thayu. The walls of the room had come to life with images of things happening elsewhere in the city.

"What's going on?" My tongue felt thick. My eyes were still hazy.

Raanu looked at me, her eyes wide. "Is Daddy still coming?"

I hoped so. I thought so. I didn't know. What was going on?

I pushed myself off the seat and walked to the door, my knees weak.

A thick layer of smoke hung in the corridor. The burned-out shell of the flying drone lay on its side. Veyada was taking cover behind it. People ran in from around the corner. There was shouting and screaming but it was too smoky to see what was going on. I couldn't see Thayu and Nicha. Flashes went off everywhere. I had no idea where my guards were, or the other drone or Sheydu. Or Natanu, Asha or Taysha.

Or Ezhya.

Veyada yelled, "Anyone who can help, we need you now!"

I took the gun back out of the bracket. Turned it on. My hand hovered over the strength setting, but I heard Nicha's words, and left it on the most narrow-beam, lethal, destructive setting.

The lift door on the other side of the foyer opened. A couple of flashes went off and people shouted.

Someone replied, but I couldn't hear either the words or who it was. A sound of metal grinding on metal came from somewhere else in the building.

I clutched the gun trying to peer through thick smoke. There was not going to be much point shooting unless I could see what I was aiming at.

A single person came out of the smoke. He walked in large paces in my direction. I recognised that distinctive jerky walk. Taysha. Coming for the hub.

I raised the gun and aimed.

I glanced aside, panic clenching a fist around my heart. Veyada had gone from his previous position, shooting at two people who ran in the other direction, both of them with red belts.

Damn, Taysha's people.

His eyes met mine. He stopped and it was as if the world stopped with him. The expression on his face told me that he knew that I would shoot. He did not run or try to defend himself.

And I knew I had no choice.

I'd promised Nicha.

Veyada had issued a writ.

I'd promised Thayu and Nicha that they would not have to act on it.

The blood roared in my ears. My hands acted of their own accord. I pressed the release.

The charge flashed across the space between us. He was close enough that it was impossible to miss him, even for a hopeless shot like me. The flash engulfed him. His eyes widened, his face took on a surprised expression, then he took what felt like an eternity to topple forward. He fell flat on his face and did not move again.

For a moment all was quiet except the crazy thudding of my heart. Blackness encroached on my vision. I had actually done it.

Then someone came from behind the burnt-out shell of the drone. Natanu.

She crossed to Taysha's body, knelt next to it and raked her hand through his hair. Two feeders attached themselves to her fingers. She deposited them in her own hair and walked away without a word and without looking at me.

Next thing someone came running from the direction of the lifts. I recognised the shape of him and the bounce in his steps.

Ezhya.

He stopped, looking wide-eyed from me to Taysha. I still had the gun in my hands, so there was no need to explain. While he watched, I returned it to the bracket. His expression was the most intense I'd ever seen.

That would have been my job.

The input from the feeder was clear.

I did it for you.

I trembled all over. I had no idea if this state of affairs was going to be acceptable to him. This would be the *sheya* instinct talking and the past had shown how much—or rather how little—I understood of that.

Ezhya came up to me, walking in slow steps. His eyes held an intense expression that chilled me. Damn, he wasn't going to fight me, was he?

I raised my hands, wanting to say so much and not knowing how to say it. My tongue had taken on the consistency of rubber.

Ezhya took my hands in both of his. I couldn't believe that the feel of his skin was cold.

He met my eyes for a few long moments.

"You are an odd case," he said after an intense silence.

"I'm sorry if any of what I've done upsets you."

"I'm all right." He used *denaryi,* that he was physically all right, but the associations were not. It *did* upset him, I could feel that through the feeder. Damn, what should I have done? Let Taysha take over?

"I acted in defence of my own position. If you lose your position, I lose mine, too." I used more formal pronouns than I normally did with him. Then I bent my head and held my arms, palms facing back, to my sides in the classic subservient position. My feeder stream exploded with contradictory messages.

I should teach him a lesson.

He's not Coldi. He won't understand, and there is no point.

I can't allow him to hold any influence over me.

He is weak. I can easily defeat him.

That doesn't mean that I should.

He will think less of our relationship if I fight him. That's how those people work.

But everyone in the Inner Circle will see this as a weakness.

No, they won't, because he's not Coldi—

His internal argument flowed backwards and forwards, bring up new arguments all the time, weaving them into the current stream, speeding up. I tried to cut off the feed, but it was so strong that it simply crashed through my block.

I raked my hand through my hair and two of the feeders attached themselves to it. Then I plucked out the third one. The stream of confused thoughts stopped as if someone had thrown a switch.

I held out my hand with the feeders dangling from my fingers. "I believe that these belong to you."

He held out his hand. In his presence, the feeders seemed glad to let go of my alien, cold fingers.

"Thank you," he said. There was a strangely solemn tone to his voice.

Then he gave the tiniest of chuckles. "Well, let's say that you've been quite capable of creating a stir. I guess that should not be a surprise to me."

He deposited the feeders on his neck, where all three settled in his hair. Then he made his way to the centre of the hub and sat down in the chair. With the touch of his hand, the entire panel came to life. All the screens flashed up with fast-scrolling images, mere flashes of colour passing too quickly for me to discern. Image streams inter-twined and split off. Voices talked to him, at least four or five at the same time. The sound waves squiggled over the wall projection. Threads of green wove through all those projections, making each vanish as it touched them. New streams popped up at the bottom of the walls; they were new queries, new things for him to look after. Many of them were extinguished before they had progressed halfway up the wall. Above that level, processes bloomed into full images, showing projections of parts of the city where people were doing things on Ezhya's orders. The green threads wove through and bounced between streams.

I watched him in awe, knowing that this was something few people ever got to see. Knowing that it was something I could never do. People on Earth would sometimes ask me how could one person be in charge of billions? Well, this was how.

It was said that he used three feeders to keep up, but I'd *given* him three. He must have had at least one already in his hair. I was certain: this much external input would freeze the brain of a normal person. I could never withstand this amount of input without it encroaching on my body's vital functions.

I sensed movement next to me. Thayu and Nicha had turned up. Nicha sported a cut on his forehead and Thayu's suit had dark splatters of something undetermined that I had no wish to identify. I hugged each of them wordlessly. Both of them glanced at Taysha's body on the floor, but neither of them said anything about it.

A little hand touched my leg. "Daddy's back."

"He sure is."

"That means everything is going to be all right."

I loved the simplicity of a child's thoughts.

I put my hand on Raanu's shoulder.

The four of us continued watching Ezhya at work.

Eventually, Ezhya judged the situation stable and left the chair. The screens kept flashing, people kept talking. He did all this while walking through the room, while facing me, while picking up Raanu and lifting her to his arm.

"Thank you," he said.

"I didn't know that the political situation was this fragile." I said. "You should have mentioned it, then someone might have done something earlier."

"You could not have done anything. The situation at the top is always fragile. When something happens, people try to take advantage. That's the way things are."

He met my eyes and I was reminded of how, at one time, I had feared him. Something changed, when he looked at me, seeing Taysha dead on the floor.

That expression was one of pain. It had been my writ I had acted on. Had I been Coldi, his position would have been mine. He knew that, I knew that. He was indebted to me, and that was not a situation that Asto's Chief Coordinator could be in, ever.

I touched his forearm in a *let's forget about this* way. "What about Margarethe?"

"She is at your apartment." Was that a smile?

"I would like to speak with her before she returns home. Unless you still need me."

I left that hanging, with no idea what was going to happen next.

"You can go," he said. "I'll see to it that you get transport."

"Maybe Asha—"

"*Not* with the armed forces."

All right that was a line not to cross in the future. Damn, was that part of his discomfort: that we'd been to the orbiting base?

"While this is being arranged, do me a pleasure and take some refreshments in my private quarters."

26

FROM THE HUB, we walked through the corridor that led to the lifts. We had to pick our way between the remnants of the fight. I counted two burnt-out drones and twenty-three bodies. There were likely to be a good number more than that.

It was Coldi habit to commit suicide rather than to submit to being ruled by a rival.

Ezhya walked ahead holding Raanu's hand. He made no attempt to shield her from the sights of blood and burnt flesh. My urge to cover her eyes had to be a human response. I had a hard time believing that Coldi wouldn't be affected by this carnage. By all accounts, they *were* affected, but just in a *different* way that I hadn't even begun to understand.

"The more I learn, the less I know." Who was it who said that?

It was a game and I was in far too deep.

Ezhya's private rooms were behind a door off the lift foyer.

A couple of domestic workers already busied themselves cleaning. Three bodies lay unceremoniously stacked on a trolley. A male worker was scrubbing the floor.

As Ezhya entered the foyer, all workers, and there were five, snapped into subservient positions.

A door off the foyer led to a rectangular hall with a door directly opposite the entrance and a corridor going to the right. The setup reminded me of my apartment in Barresh.

Next to the door to the living room stood the customary table with an arrangement of a flat tray filled with pebbles on which stood two glass containers like fish bowls. At first sight, they appeared of equal size, but one of them was ever so slightly bigger than the other. I glanced at Thayu for the meaning of the arrangement, but at that moment there was a commotion in the lift foyer behind us.

One of the voices sounded very familiar.

Ezhya turned around, handed Raanu to me and walked straight back into the foyer.

A couple of people had come in: Asha, dressed in a uniform more elaborate than he'd worn at the orbiting base. Natanu, looking like she'd jumped through a mince machine and missed most of the cutting blades, if not the sprays of blood.

Ezhya crossed the hall, past the remaining bodies, buckets, mops and brooms. The domestic staff scurried to the sides.

Asha and Natanu stopped in the middle of the foyer, side by side. Both took up the subservient position. A beam of filtered natural light fell in through an opening in the ceiling. It cast a hazy patch of light that hit the top of Natanu's head. Despite her filthy state, her hair glittered like a peacock's feathers.

She was strong, healthy and formidable.

Ezhya faced both of them. He reached out both hands and placed one on each of their shoulders. So they remained standing for a reflective, solemn minute or so.

One person at the top. Two on the next level, four on the level below that. I imagined Natanu and Asha facing the other way around, each with one hand on the shoulder of their subordinates. Then there would be a third level and a fourth, each increasing in exponentials of two.

That was Coldi society.

Ezhya lifted his hands and brought the fingertips of both hands to Asha and Natanu's chins. He pushed their heads up until both looked into his eyes.

No one spoke, no made a sound. The domestic staff watched from the perimeter of the hall. Sheydu and Veyada had joined them, standing in the entrance to the corridor. A good portion of hair had escaped from Sheydu's ponytail and Veyada's suit had acquired a large rip from the left shoulder across his chest. When Natanu stepped back from Ezhya, I expected them to approach her, but they didn't.

Even when she turned in their direction, they ignored her. She walked past them without looking at them. The two looked at Thayu, who made a gesture at them. *Stay.*

Veyada's arm twitched.

Thayu made another gesture, one I didn't know.

Veyada ran forward. Thayu sprang like a tensed-up predator.

I yelled, "Hey!" I hadn't seen that coming.

The two crashed into each other with a bone-jarring thud. Thayu grabbed hold of Veyada's belt and tipped him upside-down over her shoulder. He landed hard on his back. She rolled and sat on top of him, pinning down his arms with her hands. The whole thing took no more than a few seconds.

They regarded each other, panting.

"You win," Veyada said.

Thayu let go of his arms and clambered to her feet. Veyada rose more clumsily. He was holding his arm against his body in a funny way that made me think he'd hurt something.

Sheydu joined him and both did a *sheya* greeting. Thayu put her hands on both their shoulders as Ezhya had done.

So, he and Sheydu now belonged under Thayu. That meant Nicha needed two assistants, and we would be a complete association again. And to think that I'd thought my apartment in Barresh was too big.

The two guards had made a huge tumble in status, from being just below the top to working with someone who didn't even rank.

I met Thayu's eyes. She radiated health and happiness.

I said to her in a low voice, "Do make sure he sees a doctor, right?"

She glanced sideways at Veyada, whose face had gone pale. "Yeah, all right."

Ezhya sent the four of them in search of the bath and led me into his private apartment. His hand still rested on Raanu's shoulder.

I felt it was necessary to say something about my poaching the two guards. "I'm very sorry about what happened to your guards."

"They were a complete association. I did not stand at the top of them. Natanu did. I thought it would be safe, but it seems I misjudged. Take the two."

"But I can't possibly—" Did he have any guards left?

"Take them," Ezhya said, his voice definite. "I have no use for people whose loyalty to me has broken. You could use a lawyer. My guards need to be sorted out anyway. Natanu has moved up as my second. That whole association is broken. I'm thinking of employing a group of ex-Hedron guards."

"Why?" I wondered how that would be interpreted in the Inner Circle.

"They'll do their jobs without attempting to stab me in the back."

"What? Did Natanu . . ." The words *attack you* died on my tongue. It wasn't appropriate to discuss this kind of thing.

"Not her," he said. "She'll be up here tonight to have dinner with us, won't she, pebble?" He ruffled Raanu's hair.

An elderly servant with a kind face came to bring a tray of dishes with all kind of snacks, which he placed on the table.

"All green-coded," he said and bowed to me.

Ezhya waited to speak until the man had left.

"The problem is partially solved. The Inner Circle is stable again, but the Aghyrian claim stands. *Gamra* has no option but to discuss it. It is clever to link the claim with the treatment of the *zeyshi*."

"According to these people, Aghyrians and *zeyshi* are linked. They say it's not something that can be determined by taking a blood test."

"Aghyrian genes can easily be determined by taking a blood test. But I accept their point. Many threads are going where the blood cannot."

"Misha Palayi, Chief Coordinator of Asto." And for the first time, I understood that proverb, *really* understood it. "Still, what I saw of the *zeyshi* are not people suffering the effects of poor treatment. These *zeyshi* are quite rich."

"Gambling money and proceeds from crime."

"Not exclusively, I think."

He raised an eyebrow. I told him of the well-appointed hospital and all the patients visiting, many of them from within the city's Circles. Strangely enough something Risha had said came to my memory.

Circles or spokes. What do you think is better?

"This is what worries me," Ezhya said. "Aghyrian medicine is very good. They can do things to bodies that we cannot. I shudder to think of all the knowledge buried in those underground passages waiting to be discovered."

"Then you should talk to them. I believe this is a group whose first interest is Asto. I'm afraid I cannot say the same of the Aghyrian enclave in Barresh."

"Federza is an idiot."

That was not how I would put it. "If he's an idiot, he's a smart one, and a rich one."

We spoke of how we would deal with the claim, the details and fine points. Ezhya agreed that I should try to plead to Chief Delegate Akhtari to take it to mediation instead of letting it be heard by the full assembly. He added, "Mind you, being Aghyrian, I'd say she'd have a vested interest in this claim."

"Maybe, but I think we can discount my suspicion that they are behind this group. It's not a bad thing. I think we can work with these people." *Spokes, not circles.* Spokes reaching out from the centre to those on the outside. "I don't think they're interested in conflict, and they're definitely not interested in *gamra* politics." And the latter could only be a bonus.

He met my eyes in one of those chillingly sincere expressions. "I can only assume we will see more of you, then. That's not a bad thing either."

"Thank you." I made those two words as sincere as I could.

He grabbed and squeezed my shoulder, his eyes closed and lips pressed together. It was an embarrassing thing to see so much emotion in his face. I looked aside, meeting Raanu's keen eyes.

"Next time when you come, don't leave her alone."

He snorted. "What's this, advice from someone who doesn't have children?"

"There will be some, soon enough." Amazing how quickly that decision had taken root in my mind.

He patted my shoulder, when he stiffened and listened. I was afraid something bad had happened, but he said only, "The staff tells me your craft is ready."

It was with regret that I got up from the couch. From the time since I'd started working for him, this was by far the most informative and amicable talk we'd shared. I said goodbye to Raanu, poor little lonely girl, growing up too fast in a sea of adults.

In the foyer, the domestic staff had removed all the bodies and cleaned the floor. If it wasn't for missing chunks of plaster on some of the pillars, you could never tell what had happened there that morning.

A woman in a dark blue uniform approached, her head bowed. In her outstretched hand she held a parcel, a rectangular box wrapped in foil. "I've been asked to deliver this."

Ezhya reached to take it, but he retracted his hand. "It's for you."

For me?

I took the parcel from her. The handwriting on the label was vaguely familiar, but I couldn't place it. The box didn't weigh much. I turned it over. A label on the side said, *Asha, clan leader of the Domiri clan.*

Well, what the. . . ?

I wasn't sure if I should open it, and judged it probably better to wait. I followed Ezhya into the lift. On the roof of the building, the lift opened into a covered, security-glass-sided room. Thayu, Nicha, Veyada and Sheydu were waiting on chairs around the perimeter, oblivious to the heat. Veyada held his arm in a sling.

Ezhya's craft stood outside the structure. A member of the Inner Circle staff was cleaning the windows.

Holy crap! How hot was it in this glasshouse?

Ezhya pressed a button and a door slid open, letting a blissful breeze into the room. He patted my arm.

"I won't keep you long. I know that this weather distresses you."

"Thank you. It does."

I climbed up the ramp into the positively arctic cabin.

Most Hedron-made craft came with an interior an eye-blinding shade of orange. This one's interior was—you guessed it—maroon. I could only begin to guess what the Coldi saw in the colour, which came up as purple-black when you discounted red hue, which Coldi eyes didn't see.

Thayu, Nicha and I settled in the benches closest behind the pilot. Veyada and Sheydu looked a bit lost. I told them to have a rest, and they vanished in the back cabin.

The craft lifted off and flew low over the buildings of Athyl before rising sharply. Nicha grabbed a couple of drinks from the dispenser.

For a while, we sat in silence. It was good to be together with them again. I could turn my thoughts to other things, such as preparing for the discussion about the claim and finding a suitable father for our child. It had to be someone from Hedron, I decided. This *sheya* instinct was too hard to deal with.

I finally broke the silence. "Well, what did you make of that?"

"He's still very confused," Thayu said.

Nicha nodded. "What actually happened in that hub room? That seemed to be the cause of it."

"I killed Taysha."

Nicha took in a sharp breath.

"You didn't get to deliver the writ?"

"No."

"Damn, that is confusing."

"He has trouble placing you. I think you better lie low for a while, and let things settle."

"That arrangement in his hallway worried me," Nicha said.

"Yes, me, too. I'd never seen those slightly unequal bowls before. What do you think it meant?"

"Confusion. Wondering where you belong."

Thayu frowned. "You know what I think?"

Both Nicha and I looked at her. "I think that for the time being, he has decided to treat you as equal."

"But he's already been treating me—" No, he hadn't. Also, she didn't really *mean* equal, because Ezhya had treated me as diplomatic equal for some time. What she meant to say, but didn't, was *zhayma*. And Chief Coordinators didn't have *zhaymas* because that implied someone else stood above them. Shit, this mess was becoming more tangled all the time. Because it didn't matter whether or not *I* wanted to join Domiri clan. It mattered that *they* thought that I had the right to do so.

Two thoughts came to me at the same time: *If that's how they see it, then I should probably do it* and *I'm not going to survive this tangling with Coldi instincts.* Thayu and Nicha didn't need to say anything for me to know that they thought exactly the same things.

Well, that was sobering.

Then I remembered I hadn't opened Asha's parcel yet. I ripped the foil and peeled it off. A small card was inserted in the wrapping. I folded it open, half-afraid it was going to contain some kind of threat or ultimatum, but it said only, *Glad to have you with us.*

Inside the box lay a pair of earrings. The delicate rose-gold filigree held a blood-red stone, the colour of the Domiri clan.

Nicha's eyes widened.

"Put them in," Thayu said. Her single earring—because I wore the other one—dangled against the skin of her neck.

I unhooked my own earring with a white opal from my right ear. It lay looking forlorn in my hand. Eirani had bought these somewhere at the markets in Barresh. The white symbolised peace, but in some *gamra* worlds white was the colour of death.

These earrings had served me well, but it was time to move on.

I met Nicha's eyes. Being un-partnered, he still had both the earrings his parents had given him. Emerald green ones, because he'd taken the Palayi clan from his mother.

I dropped the white-stone earring in the box and hooked the new one into my ear. I gave the other one to Thayu and she did the same.

It was a very solemn occasion.

There would be no going back.

IT WAS early evening when we landed in Barresh. Walking down from the ramp, carrying the tank and both temperature retaining suits, I couldn't believe how I'd once thought Barresh was hot. The air was soft and humid. The breeze full of earthy scents.

The craft kept its engines running. Ours was a quick set-down and departure. The pilot was very keen to leave again. Most likely she was hoping to get back before the spots in Ezhya's new guard were decided. It also occurred to me that Ezhya had not been overly concerned that he had no protection.

Now that the tension was gone, fatigue washed over me.

I almost fell asleep in the train to the *gamra* island. Thayu and Nicha sat talking over my head. Veyada and Sheydu looked decidedly out of sorts. They'd be ill with adaptation for the next few days. I could think of which rooms I was going to use for them. If they took my second-best guest room, I'd have to move Margarethe to another room. If she wanted to stay, which seemed unlikely; she probably should go home as soon as possible.

Melissa—damn, I'd forgotten about her.

Nicha had to jolt me awake when the train started slowing down. Sleeping in public would never do.

The train came to a halt in the underground station. Nicha, Thayu, Veyada and Sheydu followed me out.

It was so good to be back. I looked at all the buildings and the rampant vegetation with renewed appreciation.

I felt incredibly light, and the humidity made me breathe easier. The sight of Evi and Telaris at the door almost made me cry.

As soon as we entered the hall to my apartment, Eirani came rushing from the living room where, as was to be expected, she had been setting up a meal.

"Oh, Muri, I am so glad to have you back."

"I'm glad to be back, too, Eirani."

She frowned at Veyada and Sheydu. "You've taken them back with you?"

"They're part of my association now. They'll live here from now on."

"But Muri . . ."

"We have enough space, do we not?"

"Yes, we do."

"Then find them a room. They'll be quite uncomfortable while they go through adaptation. I think the second guest room would do perfectly. It has a nice view."

"Certainly, I shall inform the staff."

Devlin had come to the door of the hub.

"Everything working again?"

"Perfectly."

I wondered about the nature of the outage. Maybe it wouldn't be such a bad idea to set up a backup system. We might need to talk to the Aghyrians about that.

The mirror in the hall showed me my peeling face and sun-streaked hair. I looked like I'd been working on an ocean-going sailing boat for months.

There was tea in the living room, where I also found Margarethe and Melissa, deep in discussion. They seemed friendly. Both stopped talking and looked at the door when I came in.

"Cory! You made it back." Margarethe looked healthy and relaxed.

"Yes, I'm still alive, surprisingly."

I let myself fall unceremoniously on the couch. All the stress had left me. I felt like I could sleep for days. And sit in a bath that was not too hot, that I didn't have to share with children, or Nicha, or with anyone else except Thayu. And sleep, eat and simply sit still without sweating.

My eyes met Melissa's. "I'm sorry that you got stuck here. I guess your employers have been making a fuss." There was something different about her, about the way that she wore a local shirt from the markets and her hair was loose, tucked behind one ear.

"I quit Flash. I've been writing down a lot of notes Margarethe made about Ezhya's attitude to *gamra* and Earth in particular. She's asked me to write a series of articles about it." She sounded different too. More gentle, less angry.

Well, there was at least one positive outcome of this whole debacle. "What about you?" I asked Margarethe. There was one question I wanted to ask but couldn't.

She smiled. "It's going to sound ungrateful, but I've had a most wonderful holiday. We went to see something else every day. I've spoken extensively with the people at the Trader Guild and our own Traders."

"Let me guess, they want to sell more coffee, right?"

She chuckled. "There isn't enough coffee in the world to satisfy demands."

"Black gold indeed."

"The talks were very useful. We also visited some outlying communities and development projects. Beautiful country."

I nodded. I'd been to Kedras a few times. Kedras was a small world, with its economy mainly running on the Trader Guild headquarters, but they did produce some high quality products, both tangible and virtual. And the countryside around the Trader Guild headquarters was something to behold. Vivid orange rock, sheer canyons, blindingly green oases, blue sky. It was a fairly cool world, ancient and rich in certain resources. And then the Trader Guild headquarters were a wonder by themselves. A magnificent complex in its modern elegance.

"So you thought it was useful and enjoyed yourself?"

"Yes, I'm sorry, but I did. He's an entertaining host."

Oops, what the hell did *that* mean? Her face showed no kind of emotion.

What did that mean for *nethana?*

He hadn't tried it.

He had tried it but she had politely refused and nothing more had been said about it?

Or, heaven forbid, he had tried it and she had thought why the heck not—I knew she wasn't married—and had liked it, and attached wrong, human conclusions to the feeling.

Shit.

There was my imagination running away with me again. Of course she was smart enough to do no such thing.

"Whatever was happening at the Exchange, I didn't feel threatened at any time. We were assured that technicians were working on fixing the outage. I never felt that we were in any kind of danger."

Ezhya was notoriously good at hiding his distress. He must have done a stellar job.

And being part of the Ratanga cluster of the Exchange, Kedras was not likely to succumb to panic and hysteria.

"Have you spoken to Nations of Earth?"

"I have. I guess a good side of Earth not being an official member of *gamra* means that no one gets overly upset if something like this happens."

"They must have noticed."

"Sure, they did, but the Exchange staff in Athens did a very good job at keeping tempers calm."

Well, that was at least one lesson that had been learned from the panic that had ensued after Sirkonen's death.

"I assume you'll be returning soon."

"Tomorrow."

"I'm glad it's been useful, and not too distressing."

"Enjoyable."

Margarethe smiled at me and the twinkle of light in her eyes made a chill clamp around my heart. Damn, she hadn't, had she? Surely she wouldn't have been so stupid?

I had to bite my tongue to stop myself screaming *What did you do with him in your room at night?* But if that question didn't piss her off, she would remind me that she was a big enough girl to take her own decisions and that it was none of my business. Which she was right, it wasn't.

One day, I would have to talk to Ezhya about *nethana;* then again, being him, it would be unlikely that he would listen. I must talk to her about it, too.

One day.

We enjoyed a light meal together, served by Eirani with all her bustle and gossip. She joked with Melissa, who seemed to have used some of the time I'd been away to learn keihu—if ever there was a language that was less useful to learn.

Nicha was preoccupied with something on his reader, but he didn't seem distressed about it, and I didn't get the chance to ask.

Before following Thayu into the bathroom, I went into the hub to check messages with Devlin.

He sat by himself in the semidarkness dealing with my unsent correspondence. The controls worked, projections flashed through the air. Even though he was alone in the hub, the room exuded an air of activity.

"Anything important come in that absolutely has to be dealt with today?"

Devlin flicked through the backed-up messages, not as many as I'd predicted, but he said he'd already shifted anything non-urgent to a low priority queue, so no doubt an avalanche would still arrive within the coming days.

Already, there were a few requests for reports on my Asto visit, but little that needed to be dealt with straight away. I was glad for my staff and their understanding of our relationships. At least they weren't liable to stab me in the back if I went away for a longer period.

The Exchange manager Yetaris Damaru wanted to see me, but that could wait. Everything was working again now. I needed a bath and needed to take care of those annoying regrown hairs on my chin. I'd have to visit the clinic for another treatment.

Amazing how quickly life again became so disturbingly normal.

27

THE EVENING turned very pleasant. After filing the necessary notes and reports, Thayu and I enjoyed a drink on our lovers' seat on the veranda overlooking the silver marshland. A couple of punts heavily laden with lily bulbs came in from the fields. The bridge builders had gone home for the day, and the newest unfinished struts for the bridge stood uselessly in the middle of the water, awaiting the construction of the horizontal beam.

I thought of the relentless dry air at Asto, already much less dry than I'd even had the displeasure to experience.

"This place is beautiful," I said.

"Asto is beautiful," Thayu said, with a playful challenge in her tone.

"In a harsh kind of way. I don't know how you live in a place where the oceans are toxic and the only natural water is under the ground."

Thayu smiled. "I don't know how you live in a place where you get wet each time you leave shelter."

I grinned. It had rained a lot when I took her to the town in New Zealand's Bay of Islands where I had grown up.

We went back inside and found that certain things are much more pleasurable when you're not sweating and having everything stick to you. Also much more comfortable than when a precocious child has decided you're attacking the other person. I'd probably have to hear that one for the rest of my life.

I could still hear Natanu's voice saying, "I didn't think you were capable."

Well, wasn't that great? I was now officially part of a clan where people were comforted by the thought that I could "service" my legal partner.

Good grief.

We sat in the bath in the relaxing afterglow of making love when Telaris came in. "Excuse me, Delegate, but the Exchange owner Yetaris Damaru wants to see you."

"I've already replied to him that I will see him first thing tomorrow morning."

"Yes, Delegate, but he and Chief Delegate Akhtari are most insistent on seeing you right now."

I frowned at Thayu. Whatever could that be? No less than Chief Delegate Akhtari? "All right. We'll be there soon."

So much for a relaxing night.

❧

A BIT LATER, Thayu and I walked into the reception area of the Exchange, where it was deserted at this time of the day, and where the only evidence of the upheaval was Asha's guards' cobbled-together radio, which stood ready to be packed up or disposed of in the corner.

That, and at the top of the stairs, a couple of armed guards whom I had never seen, in a place where guards were not usually posted.

That didn't make me feel any better.

In his office, Yetaris Damaru sat at the couch in the corner. Facing him on the other couch, back held ramrod straight, was Joyelin Akhtari.

Ah, that explained the guards. So, this was serious business, huh?

I sat down on the couch next to Yetaris.

There was a reader on the table, and when Thayu had also sat, Yetaris touched the corner to activate the holo-display and placed the apparatus in the middle of the table.

The projection sprang into the air. "This is a compilation of recordings we made from a number of different nodes at the time of the outage. It pretty much speaks for itself."

The Exchange logo hovered in the air briefly before the projection coalesced into a web woven of strands of light. This image I recognised from the Exchange nodes. It represented the currently-active network. A line of text underneath indicated that this was recorded from Damarq. As the construction of light shimmered and meandered in its usual way, a single, blindingly white thread reached from outside, and immediately the network vanished.

This was followed by another recording, this one from Barresh. Same thing.

Miran. Same thing.

Kedras. Same thing, same time.

The projection finished, and it was silent in the room.

"What . . . what is that thread?" I asked.

"Well, that . . ." He hesitated. ". . . is a very good question, but we've ruled out any network malfunction. To the best of our knowledge, naturally occurring strains are not as powerful as generated ones."

I nodded. I knew about that, all right. Earth's sole access through the network was through one of those natural strands, one of the few they'd located that was strong enough to carry ships.

Yetaris continued, "That strand you saw there was more than a thousand times stronger than anything we're able to generate. With anpar lines, the stronger the concentration, the further the distance spanned."

Which was why Hedron required many jumps. The number was currently sitting at fifteen, but had been much higher in the past. In the future, it might go lower. Not much, not any time soon, people in the know said. Generating anpar strands cost an insane amount of energy.

"So . . . what are you saying?"

Yetaris met my eyes. "This strand comes from a long way off. Like, outside the galaxy."

"But . . ." None of the anpar strands left the galaxy. Too much energy was needed to sustain them.

He nodded. "Meaning that this is probably not natural. Anpar lines have a wake, especially the stronger ones. If you have an Exchange node set up to capture the wake, you can siphon off quite a bit of information. The Hedron Exchange has that, because they're suspicious buggers, and because Hedron built our core, we have it, too. We've analysed the data and cross-referenced with Hedron to cull any artefacts of the process." He touched the corner of the screen again. A block of text sprang into being.

"It's Aghyrian, the old dialect."

"But how. . . ?" An old resonation from way back?

Delegate Akhtari said, "This is the conclusion we've reached while you have been away: many, many years ago, when the Aghyrians of Asto were almost exterminated because of the meteorite strike, three ships managed to flee the planet. One, containing mainly clerics and philosophers and teachers, came to Barresh. One, containing government people, came to Miran. We never found the third ship and it was presumed lost. It was a research vessel, a generation ship with more than ten thousand on board, fully equipped for long journeys. The Aghyrians had used the ship to seed populations on many worlds that are still inhabited by people today.

"There are accounts of history that state that when the seriousness of the situation with the meteorite became obvious, the captain had disagreements with the government about forcefully carrying many more passengers than it was designed to carry for a long distance. There are long dissertations in the old texts about how the captain of the ship, a man named Kando Luzcon, was an arrogant, selfish, authoritarian man. This here . . ." She pointed a long and slender finger at a bit of the text. "Says Kando Luzcon."

I stared at the curly characters. For all I knew, she could be telling me anything. Then again, she probably wasn't. I still didn't trust her—how close was she involved with Federza?—but she probably spoke the truth.

"So now you know where the third ship went." It was a belligerent, accusatory kind of *you* that I used.

She nodded. "Or, not really. We can guess, but we're not sure who they are, who they're with and what they want. We don't know where they've come from."

"Outside the galaxy," Yetaris Damaru said. "They didn't just tap into the Exchange network, they sent in a super-charged strand and destroyed it."

"We don't know if it was intentional," I said. "It might be a ghost ship with no one left alive on board."

"Could be," Yetaris said. "But I wouldn't want to bet on it. This beam is highly targeted and I'd have trouble believing that could be a coincidence. There are millions and millions of coordinates that the beam could have hit if it was a random occurrence. This not only hit the Exchange network, but it pinpointed the very centre of it."

Delegate Akhtari nodded.

A chill went over me. "Could they possibly have been listening into the Exchange for a long period?"

Yetaris said, "Possibly? Most likely. Most likely, this is the cause of all the temporary hiccups we've had recently."

Hiccups and unexplained flashes.

I looked accusingly at Delegate Akhtari. "Did you know about any of this?"

"You may not believe me, but I wouldn't be sitting here if we did." It was also the first time I heard her refer to Aghyrians as *we*. She sounded defensive.

"Any guesses as to what they want?"

Thayu said, her voice dark, "Likely, they're not here to come to a family party. Anyone who can travel outside the galaxy and who can make strands that are strong enough to bring down the Exchange network will have the technology to know that Asto's climate is changing. They're here to re-claim Asto."

A cold feeling went over me. Did the Aghyrians on Asto know about this?

Damn, and here I was thinking we'd solved the problem. "How long do we have before they're here?"

Yetaris shrugged. "They could be here any time they choose. They'll have advanced one-way slings. I'm guessing that they're keen for contact with local Aghyrians. Maybe they sent out a communication and accidentally made the strand too strong. They'll probably turn up here soon."

Thayu met my eyes, and I could see what she was thinking.

Oh hell, the Aghyrian claim.

～

THANK you for reading Ambassador 2: Raising Hell. In the next book, Ambassador 3: Changing Fate, the Aghyrian ship arrives in inhabited space. What do they want and where have they come from?

Be a champ and buy Ambassador 3 direct from the author in ebook, print or audio.

ABOUT THE AUTHOR

Patty Jansen lives in Sydney, Australia, where she spends most of her time writing Science Fiction and Fantasy.

Her story *This Peaceful State of War* placed first in the second quarter of the Writers of the Future contest and was published in their 27th anthology. She has also sold fiction to genre magazines such as Analog Science Fiction and Fact, Redstone SF and Aurealis.

Patty has written over thirty novels in both Science Fiction and Fantasy, including the *Icefire Trilogy* and the *Ambassador* series.

pattyjansen.com

BOOKS BY PATTY JANSEN

For a complete list of books, scan the image below with your phone.

www.ingramcontent.com/pod-product-compliance
Lightning Source LLC
Chambersburg PA
CBHW060915190726
48286CB00002B/511